They Who Bring the Light
Ghost Flower Verse Two
Jessica Conwell

For Mya. This was lonely without you.

Behold

The Forsaken

Come and see.

The ruins of Rook Lake were still smoldering, and the life I'd spent my whole existence wishing for lay shattered in the wreckage. Family. Friends. Home. I'd had them all for one sacred moment.

And then they were gone, lost in the night.

The first rays of the morning sun were beginning to peek over the eastern hills, and in a handful of hours the citizens of the sepulchral town would begin stirring, awakening to the bleak new world they had spent the night creating. There would be excuses and justifications, misattributed blame and bald-faced lies. But that would come later. As they emerged from their fitful slumbers, one by one they would be forced to reckon—if only for their own sacred moments—with what they had become. They would never again be able to know themselves as the people they'd known the morning before, as people who had never taken up arms against their neighbors, joined a blood-crazed mob, or hunted two young women like animals for no reason other than someone they'd vested with authority had told them to. The excuses and lies would have their time, but in quiet moments they would not sustain. The good citizens of Rook Lake would spend the rest of their lives running from what they'd let themselves become.

And so would I.

But for now, I walked.

We'd won, and this is what winning looked like. Cennend was once again bound in the darkness. The Juniper Society was dead in every meaning of the word, as was the blight that was the town of Rook Lake. But so were the children of Cennend's cult, and Elodie's adopted mother, and Ezri's sister, whom she had just met.

And, in a way, Ezri herself.

She curled up against me as I carried her, holding her like the Pieta. She stirred in my arms, but had yet to awaken. Though anima gave me a strength that made lifting Ezri no physical burden, carrying her was hindering my ability to move with any swiftness, which I feared would soon become a problem. I'd so far managed to avoid being seen by any passing vehicles or wayward hikers, but the sun was climbing higher, and being caught moving an unconscious and heavily battered young woman through the woods was probably not going to lead to any kind of ideal situation for me. What worried me more, however, was that while the sleep Elodie had put her best friend under had held so far, it wasn't going to last forever, and if I didn't reach a safe place to leave her soon I would find myself with a distinctly not *unconscious young woman who'd have a lot of questions that I would have no idea how to address. Elodie had taken all of Ezri's memories of their time together. Had that meant she had taken the memories of me, too? If Ezri woke, would she even know me, or would she find herself in the arms of a stranger?*

Lost in my own thoughts, I stepped down hard on a dry twig that cracked like a gunshot through the forest. I froze, anticipating that any second Ezri's eyes would pop open. Would she start screaming? Would she start thrashing and kicking against me? Maybe I was worse than a stranger to her now. Maybe I was part of her trauma, another monster that came out of the dark and took her hope, her joy, her love.

But instead of waking, she shifted again in my arms, her face nuzzling against my chest as if seeking shelter. It didn't matter what she thought of me, or if she knew who I was; I knew who she *was. She was Ezri Quinn, love of my sister's life. Together, they had stood hand-in-hand to face down the most powerful entity in existence.*

They'd won, and all it had cost was each other.

This is what winning looked like.

Above me, an osprey soared over the trees. I watched it glide on the air currents, remembering how it had felt to be so high above the Earth. If I could soar as I had in those last days when Elodie, Ezri, and I were dismantling Cennend's plan for freedom, I could cover more ground at a faster pace. For at least the tenth time, I inhaled and focused on the vessel Elodie and I had crafted together, the body I loved because, in its substance, I could still feel my sister's love for me. I remembered how creation had felt, what it was like to craft from raw anima. I guided my life-force with the same delicate precision my sister had taught me, and from the left side of my back burst forth a single wing of ebony feathers, the new limb extending into the air, pristine, glossy, and beautiful.

On the right side, however, was a ragged, bloody stump of bone and shredded feather, the persistent wound inflicted by my parent in the husk of Deputy Aiden Moser, who had, with supernatural strength, torn my wing from my body like ripping a weed from the ground. I tried again and again to heal the damage, to rebuild my wing from the wreckage Cennend had left the same way I had closed my other wounds. The battle with Cennend had shattered bones and torn ligaments throughout my body, and I had healed each of those with little effort before leaving with Ezri. This was something else. It wasn't just an injury. It felt as if when my parent tore away my wing they had left something in its place, like a splinter holding open a wound.

"God fucking dammit!" I hissed, borrowing a favorite phrase from the girl I was carrying. I knew stopping was the last thing I should be doing, but my legs were tired, and now so was the rest of me, pain pulsing all the way through to my anima. I sat down with my back against the trunk of a pine, Ezri still in my arms, my single black wing wrapping around both of us.

In her sleep, she mumbled a series of incoherent noises that were, quite frankly, adorable.

"I'm...I'm so sorry," I whispered to her. "I'm sorry I'm all you have now."

In a small, dark, warded chamber of my mind, I held all of Ezri's memories of Elodie. I'd asked for them because I hadn't wanted my sister to have to carry that burden, but was there more to it than that? She'd taken them from the woman she loved without consulting her, me, or anyone else. She'd just made the choice, and now Ezri would have to pay for it, even if she never knew the cost. Maybe I asked for them because I didn't think Elodie deserved them.

But neither did I.

I could have given them back, could have done it right then and there. Just poured them back into her vessel before she even knew they were gone. But then she would have done exactly what Elodie feared and rushed right back to the Heartwood to live out the rest of her days in a dead town filled with her demons and pain. And maybe she and Elodie would be happy there, living alone together among the wreckage. Or maybe she wouldn't, and maybe Elodie seeing the woman she loved wasting away in misery would finally accomplish what Cennend had spent so many years failing to do: Convince her to give up on the universe. What was all of reality compared to the happiness of the woman you loved?

As if reading my thoughts, Ezri reached out in her sleep, the palm of her hand pressing against the center of my chest, right over my heart.

What was all of reality compared to Ezri Quinn?

"I don't know if you can hear me," I whispered, holding her tighter. "I don't know if you'd know who I am even if you could. I'm sorry we had such little time together. I'm sorry for...everything, really. I'm going to take you somewhere where you can have a chance to be happy, to live a life away from my family and all of the pain we've caused you. It's what Elodie wanted, and she loves *you. Even if you don't remember that, even if you don't remember her...I just want you to know that you were loved so, so fiercely. By her and—"*

I looked down at her and saw a tear running from the corner of her right eye.

"Anyway," I said, tears falling from my eyes, too. "Anyway. I need to get you out of this forest. So, one more time...."

I inhaled again and directed all of my anima toward my ruined wing. I could feel the blockage, the thing left by Cennend in their rage. Except, it wasn't a blockage, not really. I couldn't tell where I ended and it began, it was just a section of me that I couldn't craft. Pain lanced through me every time my anima touched it. It was like Cennend had corrupted my vessel itself, had caused it to grow wrong, *to become—*

Cancerous.

It was me, but it was not me.

Gently, I lowered Ezri from my arms and rested her on a soft patch of ground.

This was going to hurt. A lot.

I had spent most of my existence without matter, living as free-floating anima. I'd become very, very knowledgeable about the strengths of having no form, and the ways I could use them to conceal, to infiltrate, and to attack. It was how I'd defeated the shard of Cennend that had been given a home in Aiden Moser's body. But now it wasn't Cennend I would be attacking.

Gathering up all of my anima, I focused myself into a spear-point and in a hard thrust gouged into the corrupted part of my own vessel. Pain shrieked through me, my limbs contorting and my whole body convulsing. The corruption lashed back in defense as I burned it away, searing agony tearing through me as Cennend's curse tried to find a new foothold. My anima plunged in again and again like a white-hot knife, rending it away from me just for it to reattach before the next thrust. I crashed to the ground next to Ezri, who was still blissfully asleep as I battled my own body, the bond between it and my anima weakening with every assault. I wanted desperately to stop, to give up, to rest, but I couldn't. Attacking this cancerous thing had awoken it, and if I stopped I knew—with complete certainty—that it would spread like wildfire to the rest of me. It was death itself. It was destruction....

In her sleep, Ezri's hand flopped outward and landed on my forearm, her touch so warm and comforting that, for a moment, all the pain stopped.

The thing inside me was destruction.

So I would be creation.

I took one last strike at it, severing it away from me just long enough to regroup my anima before it could sink its tendrils back into me. My life-force surged past the cancer I had cut away, stitching together bone fibers, sinews, tendons and muscles. I felt the corruption try to sink in again only to get wrapped up in the force of my creation as layer after layer of feathers formed on my new wing. The last touches finished, I let go, my anima flowing back through the entirety of my vessel, silencing the screams of my nerve endings, healing the damage I'd caused myself.

It was then that I looked over at my new wing and my heart sank into my stomach.

It was white. Pure white. The kind of white that is so free from blemish that it starts becoming hideous to your eyes. This was not a natural wing. This was not a wing made by one such as me. Each feather was perfect to the point of being offensive, so unnaturally exact that your mind hates looking at it for reasons that could not be articulated.

I pulsed my anima through it again and again, trying to change its form. I could dissipate it and rebuild it, but every time it was still as repulsively pristine as the last.

This was the wing of a perfect being. This was the wing of one who craved order above all else.

This was Cennend's wing.

I probed into it again, looking for shreds of the corruption, but I found none. It was gone. The slow, horrible realization crept upon me. I hadn't built around the pestilence at all.

I'd built with it.

Cennend, whatever trace of themself they'd poisoned me with, was now a part of me. Forever and ever, amen.

My talons grew at the ends of my fingers without me even concentrating. I wouldn't let my parent win! I wouldn't let them be part of me, I wouldn't let them infect the beautiful gift my sister had given me! I could cut this abomination from my body, slash through the grotesque perfection, through the feathers, through the bone. I could leave it here to rot on the forest floor, and—

Ezri's hand shifted against my arm. I needed to get her to safety. That's all that mattered.

My talons disappeared and I closed my eyes, more tears escaping.

It didn't matter; they'd been a part of me all along, really.

I moved Ezri's hand away, letting my fingers linger against hers for one breath longer than I needed. Scooping her back into my arms, I beat my wings—one perfect, one beautiful—and ascended up through the trees.

I

Hymn of Unconditional Love

"All growing up, all I ever heard was 'you might give up on God, but God won't give up on you," Sage said, looking down at zir feet as the rest of the circle's eyes focused on zem. "Well, that's a bunch of bull—a bunch of garbage."

"It's okay, Sage," Pastor Ben said from his seat at the top of the circle, leaning in toward the newest resident of Agape's Rainbow. "I understand that sometimes big feelings require less than polite language. I think everyone around this circle has dropped at least a few 'bullshits' in their time here, right?"

The other residents responded with a smattering of affirmative noises and light chuckling.

"Okay, well, it's a bunch of bullshit, then," Sage shrugged.

"Why do you feel that way?" Pastor Ben asked, unfazed. "I'm not saying you're wrong, and you're not the first to say it, I just want to hear your reasoning. If you are willing."

"Uh, sure," Sage said. "Well, it's bullshit because...because I never gave up on God! I was a good little church kid. I did Sunday School, sang in the kid's choir, helped out at the family carnivals. Hell, I was getting ready to go on a damn mission trip when my parents found my secret social media accounts. And like...I knew they'd hit the damn roof. The damn roof *and* the damn me. I knew we were done the second my dad turned around his iPad and my chats with my Discord friends were on the screen. And of course their first move was to contact all of my offline friends' parents to ask them if they knew about this and if their kids were involved blah blah blah, which of course meant I lost a bunch of them, but fuck it, what queer isn't used to losing friends, right? But the church...I thought that would be the one that held on. Like, I knew we weren't, you know, affirming or shit, but Pastor Watson never preached about, like, gay people going to hell. I thought I could go there and they'd understand."

"But they didn't?" Pastor Ben asked. I watched from the kitchenette that connected to the fellowship hall, trying unsuccessfully to stay focused on my task of preparing post-meeting refreshments without eavesdropping.

"Hell no," Sage said, zir voice quivering underneath zir anger. "The pastor and the youth minister—who I thought was chill—both dragged me into an office and started talking about how they supported my parent's decision, and how the church had taught me better than to 'do the things I'm doing.' It was a goddamn hour and a half of them dragging me for being gay, telling me how I'd let everyone down, how I'd failed God. In the end, they told me I wasn't welcome back until I was ready to repent and make amends for the harm I'd caused."

"What did you say when they told you that?" Pastor Ben asked, as I stopped just short of pouring fruit punch over my own hand.

"I put up two middle fingers and walked backwards out the front door," Sage smiled, with everything except zir eyes.

"That's a completely reasonable response," Pastor Ben said, and then with a slight smile added, "I may have been tempted to do just the same. I'm so sorry for what they put you through, Sage, and I know that after all that you're probably not eager to hear any more yakking from a pastor, but I just wanted to set the record straight: You didn't fail God. And, in our creator's defense, he didn't fail you, either. The church did, however, and your pastor did, and your family did."

"Well, like I said, my family failing me was nothing new," Sage shrugged. "But the church—"

"The church should not cast out her children, no matter what," Pastor Ben interjected. "Especially the ones who are hurting, confused, vulnerable, and looking for love and guidance."

"Yeah," Sage said, sitting up straighter. "Yeah, like, that's it, isn't it? Like, that's all I wanted. I wanted them to tell me God still loved me and I was still part of the, you know, body of Christ. Because the shitty thing is, even after all that, I still believe. I just don't know if God is happy about that anymore."

"He is," Pastor Ben assured Sage. "And while I can't heal all the wounds your church gave you, I promise you he still loves you, and that's what they should have told you the moment you came to them in crisis. You deserved support then, and you deserve it now. I'm glad you found your way here."

Abby, the pink-haired girl seated next to Sage on zir left, opened her arms and, waiting for the nod from zem, embraced her new friend.

"I...I appreciate it," Sage said, forcing back tears as the hug released. "And I appreciate the place to stay. But I've got to be honest, I'm just...."

"We're kinda sus, aren't we?" Pastor Ben laughed as several of the other residents groaned and rolled their eyes. "I know, I know...I'm way too old to say 'sus,' and you all probably don't even say 'sus' anymore. But we seem a bit too good to be true, right?"

"I mean, yeah," Sage shrugged. "Like, I know Seattle is this big progressive city, but even here shelters still sort you by genital type. And even the ones that don't put you through that bullshit still treat you like a freak. So, yeah, sorry, this place does seem too good."

"Don't apologize!" Pastor Ben insisted, leaning forward again in his chair, toward Sage's spot in the circle. "Show of hands, how many people here thought the exact same thing when they first showed up at our doors?"

One by one, six hands extended around the circle, Abby being the last to timidly put hers up. A sheepish smile spread on Sage's face as ze looked back down at zir feet.

"Y'all are just trying to make me feel better," ze laughed, tears still in zir eyes.

"Nope," Pastor Ben shook his head. "One of our cardinal values here at Agape's Rainbow is honesty. Everyone around this circle knows that I would rather eat another cup of Lenora's spicy ramen than have them lie for me."

Lenora, her legs drawn up into her chair, smiled as much of a smile as a goth ever smiled.

"Your white tastebuds are not my ramen's fault," she said.

"That's fair, that's fair!" Pastor Ben laughed. "But seriously, Sage, I don't expect you to believe us just because we said you should believe us. Frankly, you don't have to believe us at all, ever. You came in of your own free will, and you can leave at any time. And then you can come back as often as you want, as long as you're not disruptive and we still have beds available."

Sage looked around the circle at all of the other residents, and then shot a quick glance over a me, reminding me that I should be preparing pizza rolls.

"I guess it's just like I said," Sage shrugged again. "I liked my church. I believed they were all good people. And before I was outed, they liked me, too. I'm...I'm not used to churches being affirming, I guess."

"I get it," Pastor Ben nodded. "Churches have failed a lot of people, including several of those around this circle. To be honest, that's why I opened Agape's Rainbow. We're a safe space, Sage. A safe space for youth like you to figure themselves out. There's a lot of pressure out there, in all sorts of directions. Pressure to be one way or another. It can lead to a lot of confusion and self-hatred, and that's the last thing I want for anyone."

"So," Sage asked, shifting in zir chair, "not to be nosy or anything, but are you...?"

"No," Ben shook his head. "I am not a member of the LGBTQIA2S community. Which I know makes it even harder to trust me. Like, 'Great, this middle-aged cis heterosexual white man is going to teach us about being queer,' right? But I'm not going to do that. I'm not here to tell you how to be you. I'm here to facilitate, to give you a space to figure things out. I get it, though. If it helps make you feel more comfortable here, while I am—as several of your new friends around the circle call me—boringly straight, many of our staff are members of the community. Including Lyra back there. Lyra, is it okay if I put you on the spot?"

"I believe you already have," I called across the fellowship hall, getting a laugh from Abby. "But yes, I don't mind attesting that I am, in fact, a member of the queer community."

"Lyra, huh?" Sage said, tilting zir head toward me. "Okay, good, I was wondering about the mysterious figure hovering around back there in the kitchen."

Pastor Ben led a smattering of laughter from around the circle.

"Hey Lyra!" Saeed called back to me, "the new person thought you were a ghost!"

"I didn't say 'ghost'!" Sage objected, laughing. "Just mysterious!"

"Oh, the only thing mysterious about Lyra is how they manage to put up with me and my—if you'll excuse me—bullshit," Pastor Ben laughed. "Lyra's a resident here, but they're also my right hand. Their official title is administrative assistant, but really they may as well run the place. Lyra, would you mind sharing a bit about yourself for our new friend?"

"Well," I said, feeling my face flush as I became keenly aware everyone was staring at me. "I'm Lyra Morne, they/them pronouns. I've worked here about three months after being a resident for about two. I do all the office and miscellaneous tasks."

"All the stuff I'm too stupid to do, is what they're trying to say," Pastor Ben laughed.

"Okay, cool," Sage nodded, zir dark brown eyes studying me. "Of course, if he's writing your checks, can I really trust you to give your honest opinion of this place?"

More laughter from the circle.

"Although I am not actually paid, I don't know that I would extend that trust in your position, no," I said, honestly.

"Heh, right answer," Sage smiled. "Okay, so what brought you here? If I may ask."

"You may," I said, feeling a slight sinking in my stomach as I carefully started my story. "I originally came to Agape's Rainbow shortly after I arrived in Seattle. I had come here to help a friend, but my friend didn't end up needing as much help as I thought she would. I am embarrassed to admit that I had not thought to secure employment or housing before moving to the city, and, well..."

"This place ain't cheap, huh?" Sage nodded.

"No, it is not," I agreed. "After some unpleasant experiences—the kind you referenced having gone through yourself in the shelters—I came here. That, in a nutshell, is what brought me here."

"So, homelessness and rejection," Sage nodded. "Seems familiar. Okay, but what keeps you here?"

"Purpose," I said, my heart tingling as I spoke. "I believe that I am here for a purpose. I cannot define it more than that. I came to Seattle to help a friend but discovered she needed me less than I thought she would. I am *here* because here is where I found I could help. I am one person, but what I do here is bigger than just me. What I can do here will reach outward and touch more lives than I can count. This is how I can make the gifts given to me matter."

"And you've been a gift to all of us since the day you got here, Lyra," Pastor Ben said. "I truly don't know what we ever did without you. Everyone here is a gift to everyone else. By coming here, by sitting in this circle, by being honest and raw and real with one another, you give of yourself and you help each other. If I can share a little of my story, I was inspired to create this shelter by a woman I used to know, a woman who was very dear to me. I know that, for some of you, you've known who you are and who you love from the day you were born, but a lot of you have gone through a questioning period, and that can be a confusing time. A time when you need the people who love you more than ever, but a time when those same people can turn away from you. That's what happened to this woman I knew, and I am ashamed to admit that I was one of those people. I turned away when she was questioning, when she needed help figuring herself out. So she ended up turning elsewhere, to people who didn't have her best interests at heart. They led her down a bad road, used her, abused her, and called it love."

"What...what happened to her?" Sage asked.

Pastor Ben looked down for a long minute, his face tear-streaked when he looked back up.

"She is no longer with us. She's why I made this place, to atone for my sins. Agape's Rainbow represents the love that every person deserves, regardless of sexuality or gender identity. It represents the love I failed to show her."

Saeed and Ren, on either side of their pastor, each put a hand on his back as he wiped away his tears.

"I'm sorry," Sage said. "And I'm sorry for, like, the interrogation. I've been done dirty before. But this place...you all seem okay. And I really like that it's a church, to be honest. I didn't want to leave God behind."

"And you never have to," Pastor Ben said. "And he will never leave you behind, either."

Sage opened zir mouth to say something, but nothing came out but a warbled cry as tears began pouring from zir eyes. Pastor Ben opened his arms the same way Abby had, receiving a frantic nod from Sage.

"I'm sorry," Sage said into Pastor Ben's shoulder. "I'm just...."

"It's okay," Pastor Ben said, nodding to the rest of the circle. "You're safe here."

I watched as the other residents stood and placed hands on either Sage or Pastor Ben as they cried together, an act I had come to learn was a lending of strength.

"Lyra," Pastor Ben said, gesturing with his chin for me to come join the ritual. I walked over and placed my palm on his back, right between his shoulder blades. To the youth who came to Agape's Rainbow, Pastor Ben was almost as much of a savior as the Lord he worshiped. He was warm, and welcoming, and kind to people who no one else saw fit to be any of those things for. He was, by the world's metric, a good man.

By the end of that week, if all went according to plan, everything he spent his life building would lay in ashes at his feet, and, if I had my way, he would lay dead at mine.

Come and see.

The trees formed a canopy over us as Ezri stood before me, naked and illuminated by the soft blue glow of ascended ghost flowers. She bit her lip and rushed toward me, her skin softer than I could have imagined as we collapsed into each other's arms, falling in a gentle frenzy to the ground, our hands frantically dancing over each other's bodies.

"Holy shit," she gasped as our lips met and parted again and again. "Holy shit, this is real; this is actually happening!"

"This is real," I said in the moments between kisses, through the haze of her electrifying caresses. "I love you, Ezri."

Her lips left mine and she pushed back enough for me to be looking into her beautifully deep, dark eyes. She bit her lip again and smiled the most radiant smile I had ever seen.

"I love you, too, Elodie."

I blurted out some combination of profanity and raw sound as I spasmed awake, the verdant canopy being replaced by the dark, grimy underside of the bridge I'd sought shelter under for the night. Sitting myself up against the cold concrete wall, I retreated into my own mind and redirected more anima to the walls I'd used to cordon off Ezri's memories. They were leaking again.

I'd left Ezri at a hospital in a town called Klathmath Falls. The men who had met me at the emergency room entrance had many questions, but I'd borrowed a dirty trick from my sister and removed all traces of myself from their minds as I absconded back into the shadows, leaving part of my anima behind to make sure Ezri was well taken care of. She woke up about fifteen minutes after I had, for all intents and purposes, departed. Whether that was luck or part of the way Elodie had designed the sleep she'd put her under is something I'll probably never know. Either way, she woke up scared, confused, and in a raw panic. The first words of her new life were a wailing, terrified, "I can't remember!"

I hated my sister, almost as much as I loved her.

The nurses sedated Ezri again when she couldn't be calmed. When she woke up for the second time, all she could do was cry loud, bleating wails that she tried frantically to stop but were pouring out of her in a torrent. I knew if she continued the nurses would return with more sedative, so I joined my anima to hers, her cries stopping dead the second we were linked.

"Is...Is someone there?" she whispered, her voice raw and hoarse. I wanted to answer, but I knew that would only make things worse. She didn't know who I was, or even what anima was. I held all of those memories, along with the knowledge of the only woman she'd ever loved. I could give them back, but then what would this all have been for? I could give them back, but....

But what if Elodie was right?

I hated myself, too, and I had no love to act as a counterbalance.

I could have given them back, made her whole again, but instead I let just enough of a feeling slide through from me to her, and her whole being filled with the sensation of holding my sister's hand.

And for Ezri Quinn, all was well again.

It was several days before Ezri was released from the hospital, mainly due to the administration having to sort out what to do with her. By that point, the incident at Rook Lake was making national news, though the truth of it had been obscured behind a story about the lake releasing a spontaneous burst of carbon dioxide that had been responsible for the deaths of the Juniper Society and their children. Whether that was an intentional bit of obtuseness or an attempt by human minds to comprehend something well beyond their accepted reality, I wasn't sure. But either way, Ezri's life became complicated in a new direction when it was discovered she was a survivor of the incident. Journalists, TV hosts, and even podcasters were clamoring for her story, and the hospital staff was not always the best about keeping them at bay.

But Aunt Shelby was.

Shelby Hernandez was everything that her sister Maria—Ezri's mother in title only—had never been. She was warm, kind, and loving, with a wicked sense of humor and a contagious laugh that could fill a room twice. But she was also, despite standing just under five-four, one of the most intimidating human beings I had ever encountered. A Seattle civil rights lawyer, she entered every room like a deity ascending to her seat of power, poised, immaculately groomed, radiating power and, more than anything else, love for her niece. She was there immediately for Ezri, giving her a shoulder to cry on, a fierce defender, and something she'd never truly had before: A home.

And so the newly formed family of Ezri and her aunt departed Klamath Falls, headed for Seattle and a new life, both unaware that they were being followed by an eight-eyed osprey and the sibling of the girl Ezri didn't even know she missed.

I could lie and say I didn't know why I followed them to Seattle. Ezri was safe and protected, I could have journeyed back to Rook Lake and been with my sister, or ventured out into the world on my own to write my own story. She didn't need me, and I knew that well before the Emerald City's skyline appeared on my horizon. And yet I followed.

But Seattle was, as Sage would later point out, not cheap, and I—with no paperwork or traceable past—was not technically a person in the eyes of potential employers, even if I'd had any desirable skills. Ezri had a new home in one of the city's wealthier neighborhoods, while I had public parks, homeless shelters, and soup kitchens. And at every one I would eventually be told I was too odd to trust, too quiet to know what to do with, too weird to make anyone comfortable with me around.

And so that's how I ended up under a bridge, alone save for Athena, who was perched on top of a nearby streetlight. She had been my constant companion since leaving Rook Lake, a good and loyal friend that I probably didn't deserve but was happy to have. Feeling a new kind of loneliness as the tremors of Ezri's memory I'd seen as a dream left me, I called Athena down to my side and an odd thought occurred to me that I couldn't shake.

If it was Ezri's memory, shouldn't I have seen it from Ezri's perspective?

"Hello, friend," I whispered to Athena as she landed beside me.

Was it Ezri's memory?

Athena lowered her head and bumped it against my hand, which was my cue to gently stroke the plumage just above her neck. The city had been a jarring change for both of us. We'd both spent our lives—mine much longer than hers—in a forest or, at most, a tiny tourist village. Now we were in one of America's largest, busiest, and, I had to assume, loudest cities. The noise was what got to both of us, the constant cacophony of vehicles, voices, construction, and the deafening hum of electricity that most people had gotten so used to that they no longer even heard. I hated it, living in such an overwhelming maelstrom of sounds, sights, and sensations, and yet in the moments like that one, under the bridge beside Athena, when the world was comparatively quiet, I almost yearned for it.

Noise kept the thoughts at bay, but in the silence I could think and wonder. Wonder why I was seeing Ezri's memories from Elodie's perspective. Had I taken some of her memories, too? She didn't seem to have any difficulty remembering Ezri, so that seemed unlikely. But Ezri's memories had lived, ever briefly, in Elodie's mind before she transferred them to me....

And I remembered my new wing, and my heart sunk.

Anima doesn't stay where you put it. Cennend left fragments of themself in me, and now, like shrapnel, they were a part of me.

I had walls around Ezri's memories, but they were failing.

Anima doesn't stay where you put it.

It moves.

It grows.

It melds.

It becomes.

I wasn't seeing Ezri's memories, or Elodie's either.

Because something new was being birthed behind those inadequate walls in my mind, something—

"Hey!" a man's voice barked, jerking me out of my thoughts, its owner hidden behind the bright white corona of his flashlight beam. "You can't be here. Get your things and go. You—oh holy fuck!"

Athena lowered herself and prepared to swoop at the man's face. I frantically linked with her and ordered her calm, directing her to leave through the other side of the bridge. With more than a little reluctance, she obeyed as the police officer fumbled for his gun.

"For fuck sake, where did that thing come from?" he muttered in amazement, deadly weapon hanging limp in his hand, as Athena soared away from us. His distraction only lasted a moment.

"Anyway, I said leave," he barked again. Of all the new experiences the city had brought to me, this was not one of them. I knew cops. This man had the same tone as Sheriff Wexton, as all of his deputies, as generations of lawmen, slave owners, soldiers, and warlords. The tone that said you were less than he was. The tone that said how fucking dare you.

"Yes, sir," I muttered, gathering my things and shoving them back into the backpack I'd found in a church charity bin.

"Oops," he said, giving it a hard kick, sending the bag flying and my meager possessions spilling out. "Pick that up, girlie."

"I'm not a girl," I mumbled, as a reflex more than anything.

"I truly could not give less of a shit which letter of the alphabet you call yourself," the man grunted. I looked back at him as he strode toward me while I was bent over hastily shoving my things back into the backpack. The aura of his flashlight was hiding his features from me, but he was tall and had a shaved head vaguely the shape of a trapezoid.

"You got a seriously nice ass for 'not a girl,'" he chuckled as he approached, driving his boot once again into my bag. "Oops again. Are you going to pick that up?"

I started to reach for my bag again, but something in me—maybe something that had once belonged to Ezri—stopped me, and instead I stood.

"Oh?" the officer said, tilting his head. "Are we going to have a problem?"

"Well," I said, straightening my shoulders, feeling the weight of everything that had brought me to this place, this disgusting, loud, hateful place, lift off of me. "I'm not."

Through the light, I saw his smile falter.

Mine, however, did not.

"Did you see the new one?" Matthew, Agape's day shift team leader, asked.

"The black kid with the weird hair?" Jason responded.

"They all have weird hair," Matthew laughed.

"Yeah, but, this one's black, right?" Jason said. "I think it's a boy?"

"Sure as hell had better be. Would make a fugly girl."

"Excuse me," I said, stepping in from the hall, both men freezing as if I had just pulled a gun on them. "Sage is genderqueer and uses ze/zir/zem pronouns."

"Oh, ah, sorry," Jason mumbled. Though short for a man (and very defensive about it), he had one of those faces that I knew certain people found very attractive, and based on his general attitude, that was something that he also knew. He was not used to dealing with someone who did not find him charming, and I believe I made him feel unsafe.

Too bad.

"Okay, okay," Matthew, who looked something like a tall, brown-haired ostrich, said, putting his palms up. "We're just talking here, it's just us Lyra. And, like, even you have to admit some of this is weird."

"Some of what is weird?" I asked, tilting my head and feeling bile rising in my stomach.

"Like, okay, so...look," Matthew said, his face flushing and betraying the cool, logical vibe he was trying to project, "I'm gay. It's not like I'm the bad kind of Bible-thumper who thinks all of us are going to hell. I'm gay, and some of my best friends are lesbians, and I can be okay with the transsexuals. And okay, I'll be honest with you, Ly, it took me awhile to get used to the idea of nonbinary, no offense intended."

"I'm not nonbinary, I'm agender."

"Okay, whatever. It took me a minute! But, like, at least they and them are actual words."

"Yeah, like, what the hell does ze zir zem bleep bloop blop even mean?" Jason laughed right up until the point where his eyes met mine and he realized that the concept of a courtesy laugh was fully alien to me.

"Jason..." Matthew groaned. "But, he's right, though. What the hell is that?"

"Words, Matthew," I said, now tasting the bile at the back of my throat. "New words. Two and three letters long. They seem well within the capabilities of two adult men to learn and use. Because they're words that Sage uses for zemself, and part of why we're here is to show respect and care for our residents."

The mirth fell from Matthew's face as he took a step toward me.

"I think you need to watch your tone, Lyra," he said, his voice low and stern. "Because last time I checked, you may play secretary, but you're also still just one of the residents, and you don't get to go around setting policy here, much less lecturing me on it."

"It's not my policy," I said, unflinching as his eyes bored into mine. "It's Pastor Ben's."

"Matt, careful," Jason mumbled behind his friend.

"Careful? What's she going to do?"

"They," I said, taking a step toward him.

"I said what I said," Matthew shrugged. "But go ahead and go tell Big Daddy on us. If your mouth's not too full."

"Jesus, Matt," Jason hissed. "You trying to get fired?"

"Don't think we don't know what goes on in those little private meetings you and the good pastor have, Lyra," Matthew said, leaning close enough for me to smell the lunch meat on his breath. "Don't think we *all* don't know. You think you're the first? Heh, Jesus, Jason, I think she thinks she's the first!"

"Matt, you need to leave me out of this," Jason said, putting his palms up and looking away.

A broad, slimy sneer spread on Matthew's thin face, and every fiber of my being itched to manifest my talons and remove it.

"See, the thing you seem to forget, Lyra, is that you might sit at the big fancy desk and get to be daddy's favorite right now, but you're just another resident. Your little dorm room is right down that hall! But the pastor and I? We go way back. *Way* back. See, I'm his special case. He pulled me up out of the gutter and showed me the way and the truth and the light, praise Jesus!"

The theatrical cackle that burst from his mouth rattled through my teeth.

"So, who is he going to side with?" Matthew asked, scowling down at me as I scowled right back up. "His titless little flavor of the week, or his first big success story?"

He had no idea. Good.

"Call Sage the words ze wants to be called," I said, trying not to let my voice shake. "Or yes, Pastor Ben and I will be having a talk about it."

"Out there, sure," he said, with a chuckle. "I'm a good little house faggot, I'll do my duty. But back here? Back here is grown-up time and we're not going to use made-up words. Now let us finish our lunch in peace, or we will go and let Pastor Ben know that you've been harassing us while we're trying to rest, and we'll see who's the favorite."

It would be me. But I couldn't afford the distraction.

"We understand each other?" Matthew smirked. It would be so easy. Just a flick of the wrist across the throat.

"Yes," I said through my teeth.

"Good," he said, stepping back and smiling like a crocodile. "Now go do some 'filing,' secretary."

Jason stifled a laugh as Matthew made an obscene gesture that involved putting his fist up to the side of his mouth and inflating his opposite cheek.

I turned on my heels and stormed back down the corridor, toward the entryway, my skin crawling and a torrent of rage bubbling inside me that threatened to erupt over the next person who looked at me the wrong way.

As I passed, the main entrance popped open and, fortunately for both of our sakes, the last person I'd ever consider blowing up at walked through.

"Lyra!" Abby gasped, rushing over to me and throwing her arms around me in the most balm-like embrace I'd ever received.

"Hello, Abby," I said, the anger I had been filled with suddenly dissipating like morning fog.

"Hey," Abby smiled, releasing me and studying my face. "You okay?"

"I...am having a challenging day," I sighed, forcing a smile.

"Oh, I'm so sorry," Abby said, grabbing my hand with both of hers. "Do you want me to make a new pot of coffee and we can talk about it? Lenora showed me how to use the machine...."

"That is very kind of you, but I'm okay," I said, smiling for real, which was hard not to do around Abby. Abby had arrived at Agape's Rainbow on my second day serving as Pastor Ben's administrative assistant. When she showed up at the door, she was scared, shivering, and utterly, abjectly alone. As I processed her intake, I learned that she had been kicked out of her home by her parents after they discovered an unsent love-letter to her female best friend while nosing around her room.

The moment I met her, I could tell that Abby was one of those people who was born aching to become the person she was meant to be, and all she'd needed was a group of supportive friends who would let her. For her first two weeks, I was the only person at Agape, including Pastor Ben, whom she'd speak a complete sentence to. But little by little, she started coming out of her shell. First it was letting Saeed paint her nails a bright neon pink, which she whispered her parents never would have approved of. A few days later she and Toby, who had arrived just a week before she had, bonded over a cartoon they'd both loved as kids. That weekend, Ren and Nova took her to their favorite boba tea place in the city, and she came back talking so non-stop that Pastor Ben had to ask for the floor when discussion circle started. A month later, she celebrated her nineteenth birthday with us by taking Lenora up on her offer to dye her hair its now-trademark bubblegum pink. The journey to self-actualization is one you can't sprint through, but with every step, even ones as small as hair-dyeing and nail-painting, Abby was becoming more, well...Abby.

"You don't lie well," Abby winked, releasing my hands. "I won't pry, but...."

"People have been...difficult today," I said, with a long sigh.

"They do that, don't they?" Abby nodded. "Okay, so, not coffee, but how can I make your day better? If you want help with that. I don't want to be another difficult person."

You couldn't help but smile at Abby. Or at least I couldn't.

"Honestly, I'd like to not think about it for a moment," I said. "If you could tell me about your day...."

"I can!" Abby beamed. "Actually, it's pretty exciting, and...and I'm really glad you're the first one I get to tell. You were there at the beginning, and you've always been so sweet to me and you're just...you're an amazing person, and I just wanted to say that. When I came here, I was so scared and didn't know anyone, and you were so kind and made me feel so at home, and you just...you have this way about you, Lyra, and every time I see you I just feel safer, and oh my God that sounds weird when I say it out loud, but it's true and—"

"Abby," I said, putting a hand on her shoulder. "What's going on? Why does it sound like you're saying goodbye? Did...did you find somewhere else to live?"

My heart sank at the prospect. Abby had quickly become one of my favorite humans and, if I was honest, in a lot of ways I felt safer when I was around her, too, or at least more at peace. I knew what was true: That Agape was a temporary shelter, and that moving on would be what was best for Abby on a lot of levels. But the whole place would be gloomier, and the small, selfish part of me was sadder for me than the rest of me was happy for her.

"Even better," Abby said, lightly bouncing up and down. "I got accepted!"

"Accepted to—?" I started to ask, and then realized what she was saying.

My heart sank deeper.

"To the SafeHaus program!" Abby beamed. "I'm so excited! I didn't want to tell anyone because I was afraid of jinxing it, but I had my interview today—not with Mr. Hausman, oh my God, can you imagine?—but with his assistant. She said I got in before I even left, which was surprising because I thought I was totally blowing it because she is *super* pretty but, like, in a terrifying way, and I think that was making me ramble, and...."

I tried to mirror her exuberance with what I fear was little success as she continued to tell me about the interview and her time on the Safe Haus Enterprises campus. Mr. Hausman was Russell Hausman, the billionaire CEO of SafeHaus, a company which had started in security technologies but now had their fingers in a remarkable number of industries. He had been a long-time partner of and a major donor to Agape's Rainbow, paying for everything from the facility and our computer system to the snack food in the break room where Matthew and Jason were most likely still chortling over their own transphobia. Part of SafeHaus' partnership was what was called the Rainbow Crossing program, a series of internships available to qualified Agape residents which would give them an entryway into the lucrative technology sector and, potentially, lead to employment with the mega-corporation. It was, on its surface, an amazing opportunity that the youth who stayed with us would never have had access to otherwise.

But two things worried me about Russell Hausman and his lovely promises. One, while I didn't know much about the man, I knew he was obscenely wealthy and influential, and obscenely wealthy, influential men never do anything that isn't primarily in their best interest. Two, I had met him before, albeit briefly, what seemed like a lifetime ago in the office of Mayor Edith Prine. Still formless anima, I witnessed the two of them spar with words like gladiators would with spears, arguing back and forth about Hausman's new resort, which had been under construction at the far end of the lake before what was now called "The Rook Lake Incident." There was no love lost between the two, but even that tenuous connection to Edith Prine, the Juniper Society, and Cennend was enough to make the hairs on the back of my neck stand up.

"...and it's just so freaking exciting!" Abby said, finally taking a breath. "Not that I don't love it here! This place has been amazing, and the people have been so nice, and...and I just want to say thank you, Lyra. You've always been so sweet to me. Thank you. Thank you for the times you sat with me and let me cry on your shoulder, or watched *Bridgerton* with me and let me ramble at you about my fan theories all night, and I know I'm still rambling now but...."

She threw herself into me again, her face resting on my shoulder, tears soaking into my sleeve.

"Thank you," she whispered. "For everything."

"Of course," I said, putting a hand on her back and holding my own tears at bay.

"I'll text all the time, I promise," Abby said into my shoulder. "And I'll stop by, and we can still have our Saturday coffee together. And I'll have money, so I can buy the hazelnut lattes for us now! I won't be like the others who left and got 'too busy' to message or visit. No matter what. I promise."

She didn't need to promise: If Abby said it, she meant it.

"So...so when do you have to go?" I asked as we parted, two tears slipping by.

"Next Monday," she said. "Which I guess means we'll do my going away party on Sunday. You'll be there, right?"

"Of course," I nodded.

Next Monday.

Seven days.

My timetable had just moved up.

The officer's hand was already resting on the hilt of his nightstick as we stared each other down, and I could feel the anger pulsing through his anima, thrumming like a guitar string, joined by disgust, bravado, and hate, but absent the one emotion he should have been feeling.

Fear.

"If you're not going to leave, I'm going to have to arrest you," he said, through his teeth. "And I don't know what wing of the jail you'll get put in once we get

the pants off you and check, but I don't think you're going to fare very well in either, understand me?"

"I understand you better than you understand yourself," I said, the tips of my fingers itching to extend their talons. He was a big man, both tall and muscular. On his person he had mace, a Tazer, a nightstick, and—the chosen accessory of all men who are small on the inside—a gun. More than that, he had the backing of a violent system that had given him the authority to deal with street trash like me in any way he pleased. He'd let this all convince him that he was more than just powerful. He believed himself invincible.

He was nothing.

He was vermin.

He was a virus.

He was—

My blood froze.

Those weren't my words.

I burst through the haze that had overcome me like coming up out of dark, cold water, scattering the cloud of intrusive thoughts that had occluded my thinking and becoming very aware that there was a large, potentially violent man currently staring daggers at me.

"Okay," I said, putting my palms up. "I'll...I'll go."

"Actually," he said, as a profane smile visible even in the dark spread across his face, "no, you won't."

Before I could react, his hand grabbed my wrist and twisted it behind me, spinning me around and bending me at the waist.

A map of the arteries and organs of the human body flashed before my eyes. A quick spin on my heels and I could be wrist-deep in at least five different sections of his grotesque body—

I shook the fog away again.

That wasn't me.

"Let go!" I grunted, trying to pull away only to be yanked backwards, his groin slamming against my hips.

"Not yet," he sneered. "You're going to learn some respect...."

His free hand began running up my side, slipping up the edge of my shirt.

But maybe it could be me.

My talons sprang into existence and I was one breath away from shearing through his throat when a woman's voice called out.

"Excuse me, Officer Nelson," she called from the opposite end of the tunnel, her face concealed in the darkness. "There a problem here?"

"Shit," the officer hissed. "Police business, please stay back and do not interfere or you will be subject to arrest."

"Oh, is that what's happening here, Officer Nelson?" the woman asked, taking slow, deliberate steps toward us. "It is Officer Nelson, right? Peter Nelson? Currently two incidents of excessive force and three accusations of sexual misconduct on your records? All found baseless, of course. Wink wink."

"Back off, Jayla!" Officer Nelson barked. "This doesn't concern you."

"Actually, Nelly, I find it very concerning," the woman named Jayla said, taking another step toward us. "And so do the folks watching at home."

She reached over to the chest pocket of her patch-covered denim vest and tapped the cellphone peeking out.

"Smile for the camera," she said, sweetly.

Now I could feel his fear.

"C-Camping in public parks is prohibited under Seattle municipal code—"

"Yeah yeah yeah, eighteen dot twelve dot two-oh-five," Jayla said, waving her hand in a little circle. "But who's camping? This is my friend Lapis. They were just waiting here for me to get back from using the bathroom, and then we were on our way home. And according to eighteen dot twelve dot two-forty-five, we have another fifteen minutes to legally be in this beautiful park that our tax dollars pay for."

Officer Nelson's hand loosened on my wrist, and for a moment I thought he was going to let me go. Which he did, but in the form of flinging me to the ground.

"I told you to back off!" he yelled, storming toward Jayla, his face beet red and his heart pounding. "I—"

In that moment, I made a choice, but not the one that part of me wanted to make.

The officer's anima entered me as I inhaled, and just as quickly I released it, snapping his life force back into his body faster than his nervous system could process. He dropped to the ground like a stone two feet from Jayla, alive but unconscious.

"Oh, fuck!" she gasped. "I—I did not do that!"

"No," I said, standing. "I did. But he'll wake up soon. We need to leave."

"Yeah, no shit," Jayla said, still looking at him. "How the hell did you do that?"

"We need to leave!" I responded, dodging the question.

"Okay, okay okay okay," Jayla said, holding her palms up. "I got a place; come with me."

'A place' was more than I had, and this woman had risked her own safety for my sake, so I snatched my bag off the ground and followed after her as she ran through the park and out onto the street.

"This way!" she yelled. I stayed on her heels as she took a hard left down an alleyway that smelled like a mixture of stagnant rainwater and garlic wafting from the Italian restaurant in the building on the left side.

"Fuck, fuck fuck fuck!" she said with half a laugh in her voice. "Well that is not how I thought my night would go. Hell, that's not how I thought that would go. I thought he'd just bust out a hard-R and storm off like last time. Also, in case you couldn't tell, I was lying about recording. Phone died like an hour ago. I'm Jayla, by the way, just in case you didn't catch it."

Catching my breath as we stood under the glow of a floodlight, I was finally able to get a good look at the woman who had saved me from murdering Officer Nelson. She was tall, not Elodie-tall, but taller than me by at least two inches. She had dark skin and a mane of hair in locs that started jet black and then faded to a blood red by the ends, which came just past her shoulders. Her eyes were a dark, rich brown and full of the intriguing mixture of warmth, kindness, and what Ezri would have referred to as "fresh out of fucks to give," which was reinforced by the many patches sewn to her denim battle-jacket which stated a variety of social opinions in the most profane ways possible. She was, to be more frank than I usually am but less frank than Ezri would have been, the most striking, fascinating human being I'd met since leaving Rook Lake.

"You okay?" Jayla asked, tilting her head at me and making me realize I had been staring in silence for far longer than was typically considered socially acceptable. "You kinda checked out there for a sec."

"Oh! Oh, yes, I'm sorry. Yes, I am okay," I stammered, feeling a profound lack of control over my own pitch and volume.

"No worries," Jayla laughed. "You're cute, too. But typically you would have told me your name by now. Unless I guessed right with Lapis."

"You...did not," I said, though for a brief moment I considered changing my name to please her, which I realized wasn't a healthy reaction. "I'm Lyra."

"Lyra," Jayla nodded. "Way prettier than Lapis. You come up with it yourself?"

"Yes," I said, feeling oddly proud.

"Pronouns?"

"They/them."

"Kinda figured," Jayla said. "She/her for me. Got a place to stay?"

I opened my mouth and tried to make it say something that would qualify as a word, but instead just made an uncertain noise while my cheeks flushed.

"Kinda figured that, too," Jayla nodded. "No shame, Lyra. I've been there more than once. You wanna come back to my place?"

Her face fell as my eyes widened.

"Oh God, I didn't mean it like that!" she blurted. "Never said I was great at phrasing. Let's give that another shot: I have a place where I am staying with a group of my friends. Would you like to non-sexually stay with me there tonight?"

"S-Sure," I stammered, wishing that the floodlight would turn off and hide how bright pink I could feel my face was.

"Cool," she laughed. "It's a few blocks from here. You okay walking?"

"Absolutely," I said, my voice warbling in an unfortunate way.

"Okay, good," she said, with another laugh. "Take a few deep breaths as we walk, okay? You've had a hell of a night, but my friends are...let's say the cautious type, and if you walk in there humming with anxiety you're going to spark their anxiety, and...well, let's just have a calmer night than it already has been, 'kay?"

"I...I don't want to be a problem," I stammered as we walked. "If your friends—"

"Oh, pssh, don't worry about them," Jayla said, waving me off. "They'll love you. Eventually. After they act all big and scary. But the good news is that I'm the biggest and scariest of all of us, and I already like you."

I blushed again, glad that Jayla was a full foot ahead of me and couldn't see. Taking a deep breath, I reached out with a fragment of my anima and found Athena, who had followed us and was currently circling high over our heads.

"It's okay, friend," I said to her through the anima. "Come and see."

"Is there anything else?" Pastor Ben asked as we sat in his office, a modest room but with enough space for his particle board desk as well as a small round table with two chairs at which he conducted one-on-one sessions with the residents. For the sake of privacy, there were no windows, just built-in bookcases lining the walls with various theological and pop spiritual texts packed into them. Above his chair hung a large oak cross, behind which was a cloth banner printed with a rainbow and the phrase "All are Welcome."

"There is one other thing," I said, swallowing heavy. "Ren would like to go back to using he/him pronouns and...and using his birth name."

I have seen many hideous sights in my time on Earth, but none more vile than the smile that crept onto Pastor Ben's face.

"Well that's just fine, isn't it?" he said as I felt a gnawing in the pit of my stomach. "I had a feeling he might be coming to that conclusion soon. We've had some very productive discernment meetings in the last month. Praise the Lord, Lyra!"

"I...I'm not sure about that," I muttered.

"It's what we're here for, Lyra!" he exclaimed. "Helping these kids figure themselves out. They get so many messages from all sorts of sources, and they're so young they don't know who to listen to and who to tell to keep on walkin'. It's always cause for celebration when one of them discovers his or her truth."

"But...do you think that's really Ren's truth?" I asked. His smile thinned down from a crescent moon to a slightly curved line, sending a different kind of chill running down my spine.

"I knew you were going to ask that," he said, with half a laugh in his voice. "Absolutely knew it! Your presence here with us is a blessing, an absolute gift. I will never stop being amazed that you were the answer to my prayers. The Lord is good! You keep me honest, and I can honestly say that yes, yes I do think this is that young man's truth. But you're right to ask! I do doubt myself sometimes. Sometimes I even doubt our mission here. But this is, above all other things, a place for lost souls to find themselves. To find the truth, not to be forced to see it. You see all of these other pastors getting red-faced and screaming, and all it does is drive people away."

"But you draw them in," I said, the hairs on the back of my neck standing up.

"Yes, yes I do," he said. "Because I've worked with these folks long enough to know that all they've ever faced is judgment, and while there's a time for that, there's a time for embracing, too. Open arms can open ears. Of course, sometimes that won't work, either. Some folks have been too damaged by what they've gone through."

"Are you saying they're lost forever?" I asked, digging my fingers into my palms. "I thought no one was beyond the reach of the Lord."

"Of course not," Ben snapped, and then thought better of his tone. "I apologize. Of course not. No one is beyond the reach of the Lord, but sometimes I have to realize something very important: I am not the Lord."

He burst into laughter and watched for me to join in. He did not find what he was looking for.

"Well, anyway," he said, blushing. "It's very good to see the truth reveal itself to one of our lost lambs."

He paused and looked down at his desk, the top of which was taken up mostly by his ancient gray desktop, next to which were two pictures. The largest was of him and a generically pretty woman with golden blonde hair embracing and laughing on a sunlit beach. I'd never met Angie, the current Mrs. Holmes, but she looked like every pastor's wife I'd ever encountered in my years drifting silently through Rook Lake: attractive, pleasant, and far too trusting of her husband's goodness. But this wasn't the picture Pastor Ben's eyes turned to. I wondered if they ever did.

Instead, his eyes were fixed on the smaller frame next to the one of him and his wife, the one that held a portrait of a dark-haired woman with a warm, kind smile and painfully sad eyes.

"May I be very honest for a moment, Lyra?" he asked, his eyes still fixed on the photo of his first wife, Lia.

"You may," I said, trying to keep my voice steady as a feeling of dread fell over me.

"There were times before you joined us here that I had begun to doubt our work," he said, looking from the photo back up at me, tears welling in his eyes. "Were we being too lenient? Too permissive? Or the opposite? Should we have been so concerned with what the outside world would think of us? Was I playing politics when I should have been more concerned about bringing souls into the light? Was I becoming too reliant on the world, letting Russell Hausman's money have so much influence on our work?"

"What kind of influence?" I asked.

"It doesn't matter," Pastor Ben waved me off. "He is...he is a good man, but he is not necessarily a godly man. Which is why I was doubting. It was a painful, confusing time, and I had no one to turn to. Such is the burden of leadership, I know. But then you were delivered unto us. Your presence sanctifies us. Thank the Lord for healing all of my doubts!"

There was a long pause as he stared at me, and my heart sank into my stomach, knowing what was about to be asked.

"Lyra," Ben said, straightening himself up. "Please lock the door."

I could have ended him in that moment. I wouldn't have even had to extend my claws. I could have torn the anima from his vessel and let it dissipate like morning fog, joining the Everything, unable to hurt anyone ever again.

But the truth would go with him.

I nodded and stood, goosebumps raising across my body as I flipped the lock and, with one hand, began undoing the buttons of my lavender and white flannel.

"Thank you, Blessed One," Pastor Ben said, watching with rapt fascination as I let the shirt fall to the floor, leaving me standing in one of the low-backed tanks I had taken to always wearing under my clothes, knowing that any time we were alone together I could be asked to sate his grotesque appetite.

Wordlessly, I inhaled, and from my back grew two wings, one black, one white. I raised them as far as I could in the modest office, my anima assisting in lifting me from the ground until I was hovering three feet in the air.

"Holy, holy, holy are you!" Ben gasped, dashing around his desk and dropping hard to his knees before me, his fumbling hands flinging off my shoes without asking.

"I am your servant," he sputtered, pressing his face to my feet. "I am your chosen. Holy! Holy! Holy are—"

"There is but one who is holy," I said, disgust welling up in me as this pitiful man prostrated himself before me. "Confess, if you are going to confess. I am not here for your pleasure."

He looked up at me, a sickly sweet smell of shame and arousal wafting off of him.

"I am a sinner, Blessed One!" he gasped. "I have sinned!"

"How have you sinned, Benjamin Holmes?"

"I have looked lustfully on women other than my wife," he stammered.

"And what else?"

"I have not been a proper steward of the blessings given to me."

"And what else?" I asked again, as his hands groped up toward me, prompting me to hover just out of reach.

"I have taken what is not mine."

"And what else?"

His breathing grew heavy and hard, his face flushed. Lust howled through his anima, its stench radiating off of him.

"With shame I say that I have looked upon you, a holy angel of the Lord, with lustful eyes and had unclean thoughts. Please, please forgive me!"

Bile bubbled up into my throat. I reached my anima out and latched it onto his, felt the repulsive truth that his pious language had tried to hide.

I wanted so, so badly to pull the life from him, and even more to split him open and let it drain away in a bright, crimson torrent. I desired it as much as he desired me.

"And what else?" I forced myself to say.

"I..." he swallowed hard, and through the anima I could feel the turmoil inside of him.

"Benjamin Holmes...."

"I have made pacts with the ungodly!" he blurted.

"What kind of pacts?" I asked, keeping my voice calm and steady.

"B-Business deals!"

"What kind of business?" I asked, letting some frustration creep into my voice. "And what kind of deals?"

"I—I don't know!" he gasped.

"You don't know what kind of pacts you have entered into?" I snarled, catching him off guard. His fear was both good and right, and it pleased me more than I ever thought such a thing could.

"I—I don't!" he gasped.

"Liar!" I yelled. "Tell me!"

"I—I can't!" he cried, tears running down his cheeks.

"You lie!" I snapped back. I wanted him to tell the truth, I wanted him to tell all of his truths. I wanted to shred him like tissue paper and burn away his anima, leaving nothing for his apathetic god to collect.

But I couldn't let those desires rule me.

They were not mine.

Were they?

"No! No Blessed, I—"

"Tell me the whole truth! All of it!"

"I...I'm not ready, Blessed," he said, his face red and wet. I lowered myself to the floor and leaned down, putting my hand under his chin and bringing his eyes up to mine, which were blazing with blue flame.

"Then neither are you ready to be forgiven."

I let my wings withdraw and the fire in my eyes fade, snatching my blouse and shoes from the floor. Knelt on the floor, he watched me dress myself, tears streaming down his face, a disgusting bulge still risen between his legs.

I unlocked the door and left, sliding it closed behind me. The next time we saw each other, we would speak nothing of this. We never did.

I stormed down the hallway toward my quarters, my whole body shaking, tears welling in my eyes. I just wanted to get to my room, to my bunk. I wanted to pull the covers over my head and forget what had just happened, forget Benjamin Holmes, Agape's Rainbow, and the whole goddamn world.

As I passed by, Abby's door opened.

"Lyra?" she called, leaning her head out the door. "Lyra, are you okay?"

"Yes!" I snapped, not turning around. "No. I'm sorry. I'll...I just need some time alone!"

"Okay," Abby said, her voice worried but not hurt, even as I felt terrible for biting her head off. "I'll...I'll be here all night if you want to talk. I love you and I like you!"

"I love you and I like you, too," I muttered back, reaching my door and bursting into my room. Slamming the door behind me, I threw myself face down onto my bunk and let my anima free, drifting from my vessel and out the room's single window, floating across the street to where my truest friend sat perched on a streetlight.

"Fly, Athena," I begged as my anima joined hers. "Please."

And without hesitation, she took off, ascending over the vast and towering city, which still seemed too small to contain the breadth and depth of my hatred for Benjamin Holmes.

Behold

The Saint

"CHOSEN NAME AND PRONOUNS?" the person across the desk asked me as I sat there, my hair still dripping wet from the rain, my dress soaked and clinging to me in a way the elders would have called immodest. Because God made the rain, and God made me, but it was my fault for letting the rain drench me as I walked through downtown Seattle, where I'd never before been allowed to go unaccompanied, with nothing but my backpack full of earthly possessions (vanity, all vanity) and a card that I'd found pinned to a library bulletin board.

"She/her. Abby Tremaine," I mumbled. "Abigail I guess. No one calls me that."

"We can call you the name you are most comfortable with," they—Lyra, according to their name tag—said. They had a way of talking, an odd way, but not odd in a bad way. It reminded me of how I had talked when I was younger, before my parents yelled at me enough times for 'making people feel uncomfortable' by being 'weird' that I started mimicking my classmates until I achieved the coveted title of 'normal.'

Not that that lasted. Obviously.

"Thanks," I said, the word coming out barely audible. I wanted to pull my legs up to my chest and rock, but that was 'not normal,' and I didn't want to make a worse impression than I felt I already had. I'd stumbled in through the main door, dripping wet, just as a gaggle of the most beautiful human beings I'd ever seen walked through on their way to something or some such. They were adorned like gay royalty in crop tops, patch-covered vests, and leather pants, most of them with hair coifed into shapes my parents would have declared unholy and colors that probably didn't exist when Jesus walked the Earth. And there I was, dingy blonde hair plastered to my face, wearing a now-ratty floral dress that came up to my throat, down to my ankles, and looked like it had been made out of an old lady's couch. None of them said anything, of course, just a few muttered hellos before one, a long-haired girl with the most immaculate goth makeup I'd ever seen, told me she'd go get someone. And then she emerged with a tall, lithe, genderless deity with vibrant royal purple hair and eyes that momentarily made me forget my own name. And now said genderless deity was

sitting across from me while I dripped all over the floor, despite the very large and gloriously warm towel they had been kind enough to wrap me in.

"Phone number?" they asked, jarring my attention back from the path my brain had led it down. There had been a moment of silence, so obviously I started wondering if Lyra's haircut was what I'd heard referred to as a 'wolf cut,' which I was pretty sure it was, but then I couldn't remember where I'd heard that term, and also why did they call it a wolf cut when wolves don't really get haircuts and—

"Abby?" Lyra asked, leaning toward me.

"Oh, jeez, sorry," I said, shaking myself back again. "I can give it to you, but I have a feeling it's only going to last until the end of the month...."

I made it to the third digit before I burst into tears, catching myself by surprise as I thought I had been doing a good job pushing down my feelings but apparently not and now they were pouring out all over my face and probably weirding out Lyra who—

I looked up and saw them looking back at me with none of the disgust I thought I'd see in their eyes. Just care and concern. Slowly, they reached out and placed a hand just over my forearm. It took me a second to realize what they were waiting for.

No one else had ever asked before touching me.

I nodded furiously, sending tears spraying off of my face. They gently placed their hand on my arm, and somehow, everything felt...not better, there was too much wrong for anything short of God Himself to make it better, but...safer.

"Sorry," I said, gathering myself up again. "I'm so sorry, I've just...it has been a very long day."

"You don't have to apologize, Abby," Lyra said, and I think they meant it, too. "I need to step out for a second, but I will return momentarily."

"Okay," I mumbled, my cheeks flushing as they stood and left the intake room. Great. They definitely thought I was a freak and needed to go out there and take some deep cleansing breaths and probably tell their boss that under no circumstances should they admit me because I'd just freak out all the other residents with my weirdness and—

The door opened again, and Lyra stood there, an arm full of clothing over one arm, a steaming mug with a cartoon snail on the side of it in the other.

"Pastor Ben asks that we perform our intakes as soon as possible," they said, setting down the mug in front of me and holding out the clothing. "But it seems very unkind to make you revisit your trauma while you are soaking wet. These are probably not the correct size, but they were as close as I could find in our clothing closet. Let me know when you're ready for me to come back in."

"T-Thank you!" I blurted, the words finally finding their way out of my mouth as Lyra was closing the door again behind them. Peeling the sopping wet dress off of myself and hanging it on the hook on the back of the door, I paused for a moment to dry myself on a non-saturated section of the towel I'd been sitting wrapped in. Unfolding the clothes, I discovered that Lyra had actually guessed my sizes pretty well. The black and white checked flannel was a size too big, but the light blue jeans were actually spot-on and, as much as I hated to admit it to myself because I knew as an official queer (if that word was okay for me to use?) I should be above such things, but the larger shirt made me feel more comfortable. My mom had instilled in me that, though my chest would be "a blessing" for my "future husband," until that time it was my duty to conceal it as best I could so I didn't cause my brothers in Christ to stumble.

That stuff gets in your head, you know?

Buttoning the last button on the flannel, I took a second to appreciate how good it felt to be mostly dry again. I think some part of my mind had honestly decided that that was never going to happen, that I was just going to spend the whole of the rest of my life wet and clammy, as penance for my sins.

They always talk about washing those away; maybe they should talk more about drying them up.

"R-Ready," I stammered, leaning my head back out the door where Lyra was waiting.

"I am sorry that they aren't the most stylish," they said, coming back in. "When you are admitted, we do offer a small stipend to purchase more clothing if you did not come with any."

"Thanks," I said, "but I don't mind these. I mean...it's what you're wearing, too."

Lyra looked down at their red-checked flannel and dark blue jeans.

"I, also, am not the most stylish," they said, straight-faced, which made me smile.

Which was another thing I didn't think I was going to do again.

While they woke up their computer, I picked up the mug they brought me. When I looked into it, I saw a steaming, light brown liquid waiting for me.

Coffee. The forbidden drink.

"I put in cream and sugar since I wasn't sure what you'd like," Lyra said. "I can remake it if you prefer it a different way."

"No, no, this is perfect," I said, looking down into my sinful drink. In an 1833 revelation, Joseph Smith was told that we should abstain from all hot drinks. In the intervening years, this mostly got winnowed down to just tea and coffee, and occasionally herbal teas were given an exception, but in my household at least, coffee was still the devil's drink.

In my most defiant act since I wrote out an unsent letter to my best friend telling her I was in love with her, I placed the mug to my lips and drank deep.

It tasted terrible and beautiful at the same time, like sin and virtue wrapped together, and in that moment I decided I was now a coffee drinker, and I liked it exactly how Lyra had made it.

"If you're ready, and only if you're ready, I do have some more questions," Lyra said.

"I'm ready," I nodded.

"Excellent. Age?"

"Eighteen. Nineteen in a month."

"Any allergies or health concerns?"

"No," I said, taking another drink.

"Medications?"

"No."

"Emergency contact?"

I froze, staring at them like a deer in the headlights.

"It can be a family member, friend…." they said, trying to help.

"I…I don't really have any of those," I mumbled, looking down again.

God I wanted them to reach out and touch my arm again. They didn't, but they did the next kindest thing.

"Okay," they said. "Substance use?"

"No," I said, assuming they didn't count the caffeine that I had very recently become hopelessly addicted to.

"Alright, so…this next section gets into more personal questions," Lyra said, straightening up in their chair. "Feel free to answer as much or as little as you want, or to tell me to go fornicate with myself."

The laugh that came out of me sounded more like a blast of noise leaving my mouth in a giant glob.

"Gender identity?" Lyra asked, unfazed.

"Um…woman?" I stammered, getting myself back together. "Like, not trans…cis?"

"Cis female," Lyra said, typing it into their computer. "Sexual orientation?"

"That's…difficult," I said. "Because, like…I'm demi—demisexual—as far as, like, sexuality, but for, you know, romance and stuff, I'm—"

Up until half an hour before, I'd have said lesbian. However, this deeply intriguing human being sitting in front of me was distinctly neither a woman nor a man.

"Pan," I blurted, making a snap decision.

"Great," Lyra said, which I realized was probably just a way of acknowledging my answer but I chose to take as saying I'd done a great job of choosing my sexuality. Which I agreed with!

"Okay, here's the question that I don't want you to answer more than you wish to," Lyra said, looking away from their computer and back to me, their gloriously brown eyes once again making me forget all the words I knew and wonder if 'genderless' was far enough from 'woman' to get my parent's approval. "What brings you to Agape's Rainbow?"

Oof.

"Um, well, so...." I mumbled, looking down at the top of the desk separating us. "My family is...very, very Mormon? And I realized a while back that I am...distinctly not straight. I was just going to keep it inside, but I have this friend—"

I paused, my heart going 'plop' into my stomach.

"—had this friend," I corrected. "We'd known each other our whole lives, and I just...I caught feelings, I guess. And then I started getting this stupid idea that maybe she felt the same way? I realize now I was reading way too much into, like, little touches and glances. But I wrote this letter to her, because I tend to ramble when I talk and I wanted to get all of my words out and in the right order, and I wasn't sure I was even going to send it but apparently I didn't hide it well enough before room inspection and—"

"Room inspection?" Lyra asked. "Were...was this at a shelter or...?"

"No, my home," I said, not knowing why that was confusing. "But anyway, my parents found it and read it, and...yeah, things got messy."

"I'm so sorry," Lyra said. "Did they drop you off here or—?"

"No," I shook my head, a few remaining droplets of water flinging off of my hair. "They kicked me out like, right away. For about a week I stayed with a friend—a different friend—whose parents let me sleep on their basement couch, but then I made the mistake of saying that my friend looked cute in her new dress. And I did not *mean it like that, I was just trying to give a compliment like I used to give her all the time, but her parents freaked out and...and yeah. I spent the next night sleeping in a park and then when I was at the library the next day I found the poster for this place so...here I am. Ta da."*

"Ta da indeed," Lyra said. "I am so sorry for everything you've been put through. Thankfully, we have a bed available. You will be rooming with Lenora, she/her pronouns. She's the one who came and retrieved me when you first arrived."

"Oh, the goth girl?"

"Yes, but rest assured that her demeanor is much friendlier than her makeup may imply," Lyra said. "Your room is actually right next to mine."

"Oh!" I said. "I didn't realize—I thought you were, like, an employee and lived in, like, an apartment somewhere, or a house, but houses are expensive and—"

My brain's "YOU ARE JUST SAYING WORDS NOW" alarm went off.

"...and yeah."

"I...exist in a kind of netherworld," Lyra said, inhaling deeply. "I have been entrusted with certain clerical tasks around the center, but I am not compensated and I do live on site."

"I'm glad," I said, a moment before I realized the implications. "Not that you have to live here! Just that you do live here, because you seem cool and I'd like to...to talk to you some other time when you don't have to fill out a form and I'm not still lightly damp and—"

JUST. SAYING. WORDS.

"I look forward to that," Lyra said, to my relief. "You are welcome to stay as long as you would like. I'll give you a packet of information about meal times, curfews, and other schedule information. You are free to go whenever you would like, but we cannot guarantee that there will be a room available when you return. Though if there is, you are welcome to reoccupy it."

"T-Thank you," I stammered. I'd honestly expected a more vigorous admission process. To be even more honest, I expected to be rejected.

"If you are ready for it, I believe the other residents are gathering in the Fellowship Hall right now, along with Pastor Ben who will want to meet you," Lyra said, looking at the clock on their screen. "But if you would prefer, I can also show you to your new room and—"

"I...I think I'm up for going to the Fellowship Hall," I said. "And...and thank you. Like, thank you, personally. You're really nice."

The blush that spread across their cheeks was absolutely adorable.

"Y-You're welcome," they stammered, for once. "And...and thank you. Oh, if you hand me that dress from the back of the door, I can take it to our laundry facility."

I followed their eyes and looked at my old floral dress, hanging dripping from the door hook. I'd been given it as a graduation present, for job interviews and courtship. When I was ejected from the only home I'd ever known, it was one of the few items I'd grabbed, convinced that I'd need it to wear some day in the future when I tried to convince my parents to take me back.

"Actually, don't," I said. "I don't want it anymore."

"You sound certain."

"I am," I said. And for the first time, I meant it.

II

Hymn of Unforgivable Sins

"*WHAT THE ACTUAL FUCK, Jay?*" *a man's voice bellowed as we emerged from the darkness and into a dimly lit room full of laptop-strewn tables and four people staring back at me as if I had just fallen out of a spaceship, including the deeply irritated bearded man who had just yelled at us.*

"Calm down, Bob," Jayla groaned, stepping in front of me as Bob, who was one of the largest humans I'd ever seen, took a step towards us. "They just need a place to stay."

"And we're running a halfway house now?" Bob asked, veins raising across his enormous shaved head, his heavy brow furrowing so hard I thought his face would collapse in on itself.

"I'm so sorry about this," Jayla said, ignoring him and turning to me. "Some of us are just a wee bit paranoid."

"Paranoia keeps us alive, Jayla," his voice rumbled.

"It's okay," I told Jayla before turning to Bob. "I understand. Really."

I remembered the night Ezri brought Aiden Moser to our temporary shelter in Elodie's adopted father's office with a black hood over his head so he couldn't retrace his path to our hideout. My chest ached reflexively as I remembered how, later, after he had gained our trust, he put three bullets into me.

"Understanding is great," Bob said, leaning in at me. "Do you understand why I want you out of here?"

"Jesus Christ, take it down a notch, Bob," groaned a person with sienna skin and a bright red flopped-over mohawk. "They look like they'd wet themself if you said 'boo.' They're just a scared kid."

Being nearly eternal I bristled, but decided not to press the issue.

"I'm Clover, a fellow they/them unless I'm guessing wrong," they said, reaching out a ring-covered hand.

"L-Lyra," I said, cursing myself for choosing that moment to stutter. I took their hand and gave it a weak shake.

"Sit! Sit sit sit!" Clover said, gesturing toward a disjoined circle of chairs and a ratty red couch, the latter being where I finally settled.

"Thank you," I said, the old sofa groaning as I sat. "It's nice to meet you, Clover. And you, too...Bob?"

The woman on Bob's left burst into a fit of bleating laughter.

"It's a weird name, right?" she cackled. "Like, you've met Clover and Jayla, I'm Syn, the quiet old bastard in the back is Tavish—"

An older man with a thick silver-gray beard who looked more than a little like a children's book illustration of a wizard waved without looking up from the computer he was working on.

"—but then there's 'Bob.'" Syn finished. "Bob! Like the cartoon construction worker! Bob!"

"Bob is a fine name," Bob grumbled. "Just because I don't sound like a goddamn William Gibson character...."

"Bob!" Syn laughed even louder.

"I...I think Bob is a nice name," I muttered, not sure what else to say.

"Oh do you?" Syn asked, her laughing turning off like a faucet as her head snapped from Bob to me. She moved like a serpent toward me, her pale skin creating a contrast that made her brown eyes look like black voids as she approached. Her head was completely devoid of hair or even eyebrows, giving her a startlingly ethereal look as she wove across the sitting circle, stretching herself up over my lap, bracing herself with her arms on either sides of my legs.

"Y-Yes?" I stammered as her dark eyes pierced into me, all traces of joviality gone from her face, her lips pressed into a thin scowl. She leaned in close enough that her nose was almost touching mine, the scent of burnt coffee on her breath. She held her glare for a long second before jutting forward.

"Boop!" she declared as the tip of her nose touched mine, erupting into laughter again before I could process what had just happened.

"Jesus, calm the fuck down, Syn," Jayla groaned.

"I'm just teasing them! I—"

"Sit your ass down and pretend to be normal for five goddamn seconds, okay?"

Shoulders slumping, Syn retreated back to one of the chairs on the other side of the small circle. Clover slid themself next to her and wrapped an arm over her shoulders.

"Well, anyway, that's the group," Jayla sighed. "As you can guess, we don't socialize a lot."

"Yes, Jay," Bob grumbled. "Because, as you may remember, we are not a social club."

"Bob, I made a command decision. They needed a place to stay and—"

"Then send them to the shelter!"

"Fuck you!" Jayla snapped back. "You sound like a fucking cop!"

"Yeah, you kinda do, man," Tavish said from his computer, still not looking up from the screen.

"Jesus, Bob," Clover said. "Would you look at them? They look as lost as we all did when we came here."

"We all came here because we were vetted ahead of time," Bob retorted. "By the group. And I'm sure they're harmless, they look like they weigh less than their own shadow, and I don't think the feds are this good at disguising their operatives. But maybe their friends aren't harmless, and they go from here and start yabbing with them about the bunch of weirdos they spent the night with. And those people tell their shitty friends, and—"

"Get to your point, Bob, I'm bored," Syn sighed.

"My point is that we can't just start letting in everyone Jayla wants to hook up with!"

I have been surrounded by many deeply uncomfortable silences in my time among humans, and that one was at least in the top five.

"Oh fuck," Syn mumbled.

"They are scared, and they are vulnerable," Jayla said through her teeth, straightening her shoulders and staring an unbroken beam into Bob's eyes. "Just like you were when I brought you here. Tavish and Clover trusted me then, you can trust me now. And keep your speculations on my personal life out of your ugly mouth. We clear?"

Bob stared back, the deep wrinkles of his forehead looking like canyons on a forgotten planet. He stood at least a foot taller than Jayla and probably outweighed her by a hundred pounds, but everyone in the room could feel which direction the power balance was tilted.

"Yeah, we're clear," he grunted. "Don't fuck it up, Lyra."

"I'm not planning to," I said, borrowing the tiniest sliver of courage from Jayla. "Bob."

Syn started laughing again, and the ghost of a smile crept onto Bob's face.

"Okay, okay okay okay," he sighed. "I'm not trying to be a hardass, we just have enemies."

"Who...who are all of you?" I asked, looking around the group. "What is this place?"

"This place is an abandoned cell phone store that, by some miracle, hasn't had the power turned off yet," Clover said, gesturing around the large, dilapidated room as I noticed for the first time the slabs of plywood boarding up all the windows. "As for who we are...."

I could almost hear all the eyes in the room shift back and forth.

"We're activists," Jayla said, finally. "We work for the benefit of the parts of society that everyone else steps on or just plain forgets. And sometimes our work is to the detriment of those who are doing the stepping."

"Heh, 'sometimes,'" Tavish chuckled.

"Now, not to be all 'Bob' about it," Jayla continued, "but we're going to have to get to know you a bit better before we let you in on anything more than that."

"I understand," I nodded.

"Good," Bob said, sitting down on the other side of the couch next to me. "So, that's us. Tell us about you, Lyra."

My heart sank.

"Oh, me? I...there's not much to tell. What do you want to know?"

"Where are you from, how about?" Clover asked.

"I'm from Rook Lake, Oregon."

"Rook Lake? Isn't that the place where—?" Syn asked.

"Yeah!" Tavish said, finally looking up from the computer. "The lake! The lake vented all that CO2 and killed a bunch of people!"

"Shit, were you there for that?" Clover asked.

"No," I lied. "I left before then."

"Good break," Bob nodded. "Okay, so, how'd you get here?"

"I...followed a friend who was moving here."

"Oh no!" Syn groaned, drawing out both words. "A 'friend' huh? Oh, sweetie, it's okay; I am also a member of the 'followed a hot piece to a new city only to get my ass dumped a week later' club. Let me guess? Happened before you had a job and you found yourself on the street because this city is fucking expensive?"

"I—yes," I nodded.

"Fucked up, huh?" Syn shook her head. "You got family?"

"I...have a sister."

"Close?"

"Yes. Well, once."

"Here?" Jayla asked.

"No," I said, my heart sinking again. "Back in Rook Lake. We...haven't talked in a while."

"Shit," Clover said. "I got a brother. Same story."

"Yeah, that's me and my parents," Bob grunted.

"My sister tells her kids I died," Syn said. "Fuck biology, this is my family."

"Fuck biology is a good place to end this interrogation for now, I think," Jayla said, stepping between me and the rest of the group. "Lyra, we have some things to work on, but I can show you back to where we all sleep. We don't have a spare sleeping bag, but—"

"I'll be okay!" I blurted. "Anywhere is preferable to the park."

"Okay," Jayla smirked. "But if you end up staying long-term, we can go looking for one for you."

"Goodnight, Lyra!" Syn called, waving from Clover's lap as Jayla and I headed toward the back room.

"'Night!" the rest of them called as I waved back.

"They're a lot, but they're good folk," Jayla assured me as we stepped into the back room, where five sleeping bags had been arranged. "You doing okay? I know this is a lot all at once."

"I'm okay," I said, half-lying. "Thank you for...for taking me in. For all of this. I just wanted to say that I understand why Bob is worried, and—"

"If a pigeon sits on a lamp post across the street too long Bob thinks it's an FBI camera," Jayla said. "Not that we don't have our enemies. But I don't believe in pushing away friends preemptively. You can stay as long as you want, Lyra, but you also don't have to. I just ask that you respect the group's privacy while we're doing what we do out there."

"Of course," I nodded.

"Oh, and that thing Bob said? Look, I already told you I think you're cute, and I do, but I don't want you to think I just brought you back here because—"

"I don't!" I said, probably with too much volume. "I didn't think that."

"Good. Have you eaten today? We don't have a lot, but I could find something."

"I'm okay," I said. "Thank you, though."

"Of course," she said. "Now, you look exhausted. You should get some sleep. We'll try to not make too much noise when we all clomp in here in a few hours. Here...."

She walked over to a bright blue sleeping bag and removed the thick green blanket from the top of it.

"Take this. It's mine. It's not much, but it's soft, and I know the floor is better than the ground, but I can't look myself in the mirror if I let you sleep cold all night."

"Are...are you sure?"

"Of course I'm sure," she said. "We take care of each other here, and you're 'we' now. At least as long as you want to be."

"Thank you," I said, taking the blanket from Jayla's hands. It was softer than anything I'd felt in the last month. "Jayla?"

"Yeah?" she asked, one hand on the door back to the front of the store.

"Is there...is there anything I can do? For you or the rest of the group? I don't want to just take."

"We all take sometimes, Lyra," Jayla smiled. "It's okay. If you end up staying, we'll all do plenty. Right now, you just get some rest, okay?

"Okay. Goodnight, Jayla."

"Night, Lyra," she said, winking at me before stepping through the door. Alone in the darkened room, I wrapped the blanket she'd given me around my body and lowered myself to the floor, feeling safe for the first time since I came to Seattle.

On a different night months later, I found myself lying awake in the dark, staring up at the poster of the Sistine Chapel ceiling that Abby had given me to mount over my bed. I was the only resident to have a permanently private room, due entirely to Pastor Ben believing me to be a holy messenger from his God's heaven. I hated deception. Not only did it not come naturally to me, it felt corrosive, like it was burning away a tiny part of who I was every single day, like it was giving more and more of me over to—

It was necessary. He needed to believe that I was an angel of the Lord. If any of this was going to work, I needed him to feel that he had been blessed by a holy presence. That's why I let him see me the way I let him see me. That's why I tolerated his intolerable touches. That's why I read the book that was so important to him.

The clock on my nightstand rolled over to 3 AM, and I slid out of bed, grabbing two pairs of thick socks from my dresser and stretching them over my feet to muffle my footsteps. Though I would have preferred to travel through the center as unbound anima, unbound anima would not be able to accomplish the mission set before me. So instead I eased my door open and gently clicked it shut behind me, and then with slow, deliberate steps headed down Agape's main corridor.

At three in the morning, Pastor Ben would be sound asleep on the wealthy side of town next to his unloved wife, most likely dreaming of his ex or—the thought chilled me to the bone—me. But while that made him only a psychological threat, the three program aides assigned to the graveyard shift, tasked with monitoring the halls to guard against curfew violations or other misbehavior, were a more practical concern.

Monday's graveyard shift was a tired-eyed woman named Luisa, a young single mom named Macy, and Thomas, a theology student with a painfully smug face. From midnight until about 2:45 PM, the three of them would have been dutifully watching the security monitors or pacing the halls, ready to pounce on any of the residents caught outside their rooms. As an employee of Agape's Rainbow, I had special privileges that exempted me from the rules the other residents had to follow, but since disobeying curfew was the least of the sins I'd planned for that night, I needed to remain unseen. Fortunately, weeks of monitoring the Monday night trio informed me that by 3:00 AM Luisa would be sound asleep at the security desk, letting Macy and Thomas sneak away to the maintenance closet to have sex.

Pastor Ben liked to keep me close, and as such it was just a short walk down the hall to his office. I had been trusted with a key—of course I had: I was an angel, after all—which I slid from my jeans' pocket and placed in the lock. The latch turned gracefully but still echoed like thunder through the empty hall as I breathed a sigh of relief that my assumptions regarding the graveyard workers' nocturnal activities seemed to be holding true.

There were no windows in Pastor Ben's office, and the door was sealed well enough that no light crept in from around it, either. I was in a dark beyond darkness, engulfed fully, without even the faintest glow for human eyes to acclimate to.

Fortunately, strictly speaking, my eyes were not human.

Tapping into my anima, I began rebuilding the rods of my retinas, the room falling into focus as I drew light from darkness, the desk with its papers and photos suddenly visible, as was the cross on the wall, the rainbow banner, and....

And the shadowy figure in a hooded sweater dashing around me toward the door.

I moved like lighting as they shot by me, grabbing them around the waist and pulling both of us to the floor, their bulky frame landing hard on me but not breaking my grip.

"Who are you?" I hissed as they flailed against me. "What are you doing here?"

"L-Lyra?" a familiar voice yelped. "Lyra, it's me! Jesus, you're strong!"

"Ren?" I asked, releasing my grip enough to allow breathing but not escape.

"Um, well...well it's Nathan now," they reminded me. "Remember?"

"Oh. I'm sorry," I muttered. "What are you doing here?"

"Wait, no, can we go back to how strong you are?" they laughed. "Like, I used to wrestle at my old school, and—"

"No," I interrupted. "What are you doing here?"

"I was...I was just looking to see if Pastor Ben was here and—"

"Honesty," I demanded, with no less authority than had I sprouted my wings and hovered over them.

"Fuck," they sighed. "I...I was trying to get in to use Pastor Ben's computer. But not for anything bad! I promise!"

I released my grip the rest of the way and we both eased ourselves up off the ground.

"Then what for?"

"I...I wanted to see if there was anything on there about Jett," they mumbled to the ground. "I tried just asking, but Pastor Ben keeps saying he doesn't know and he doesn't know how to find out, that once they go to work for SafeHaus it's out of his hands blah blah blah. But, like...okay, look, I know he's not a bad dude, but I can tell when someone's not being honest with me. So, I tried contacting SafeHaus the other day, and I asked to speak with Jett."

"Did you?"

"No," they sighed. "The receptionist said that they can't connect people to individual employees, but then I pressed a bit harder and, you know, um...turned on the charm?"

"Did it work?"

"Yes and no," they said. "I got her to try to look him up, but she couldn't find him anywhere in the system. I even...fuck."

They looked down at the ground and turned away from me.

"I even had her look up his deadname," they whispered. "And I know, like, maybe they don't add interns to the employee directory because they aren't important enough yet? But I don't know, Lyra, something smells *wrong*."

"What do you think happened?"

"I don't know," they shrugged. "Best I can think is that Jett got to SafeHaus on his first day, discovered it sucked shit, bounced and then...and then I worry something happened to him before he could get back here."

"R—Nathan...."

"Look, I know, okay?" they snapped. "I know what they say: that this place is like Summer camp, and you promise each other you're going to keep in touch and you're best friends forever and then you leave and real life makes you forget. I know that internships are stressful and keep you busy as hell and no one who goes to work for SafeHaus really keeps in touch. And I also know what everyone is probably thinking, that Jett probably met some corporate hottie who made him forget about me and...and you know what? Maybe! Maybe he did! Jett's cute and charming as fuck, and there are way better options out there than a pudgy-ass island boy for someone like him. But he wouldn't just ghost me. That's not him. He'd at least let me know, even if it was just over the phone. Fuck, even if it was just by text! I know you didn't know him very long, but you had to pick up that that's not a thing he'd do, right?"

Sweat beaded on my brow. Jett had left for his SafeHaus internship shortly after I had arrived, well before I had become Pastor Ben's administrative assistant. I remembered his going-away party, how he clung to his partner like velcro the whole time, how hard he sobbed when it was time for him to leave, not wanting to go but repeating over and over again that he thought it was the only way to make enough money to afford a good life for the two of them. Ren was right; there was no way he would have forgotten them.

"This...this isn't the way to do this," I said.

"I know," they sighed, looking down far enough that their hair fell over their face. "And I'm sorry. I really am. I know this is fucked up. But I don't know what else to do! I've checked with all of Jett's friends, I've even talked to the police. I'm...I'm desperate, Lyra. It feels like there's this hole inside me. It's like...even if I found out he met someone else, even if he told me he never wanted to see me again, it would be better than this. It would hurt like hell, but at least I'd know, you know? I just...this can't be the end, Lyra! He saved me from myself. He loved me like I didn't think anyone could ever love me. It can't just end with him getting in a fancy SUV and driving off!"

"I'm sorry," I said, putting a hand on their back as they began to cry, trying to keep their tears silent, unaware that I could see in the dark better than they could. "I'm sorry, but I can't let you do this. But...but let me talk to Pastor Ben. Let me see if he can give me answers he can't give to you. I'll...I'll see what I can find out. I'm sorry, but that's the best I can do."

"Okay," they nodded, looking like the life had been drained out of them. "I'm really sorry, this isn't how I am usually."

"I understand," I said, feeling an awful pang in my heart for both of us. "I...I know what it's like to love someone from the other side of a vast chasm."

"Hell of a way to put it, but...yeah. Yeah, that's what it feels like. You know what the shittiest thing is, though?"

"What?"

"The shittiest thing is that...that if you actually find something and I get back in touch with him, he'll probably just get mad at me."

"Why do you say that?"

"Because..." they said, taking a deep breath, "because I'm not Ren anymore."

"Are you not?" I asked, leaning against Pastor Ben's desk.

"I...I don't think so. Maybe. I don't know! I talk with Pastor and it seems really clear. I'm Nathan, and I'm a man, because that's what God made me and God doesn't make people 'wrong.' There are only two genders in the Bible, and God knew me when I was knit together in my mother's womb. So I'm Nathan, and I'm a man. But then when I'm not in here, I just...the feelings come back, you know? The ones that say, 'No you're not, you know who you are! You know who you are!' And Pastor Ben says those are just the doubts talking, just the…you know, 'the world' talking, wanting me to rebel against my true nature. But I don't know! Shit, maybe…maybe it's best that Jett isn't here to see what a fucking mess I am."

I pushed away from the desk and walked over to them as they leaned against the door and slid down to the ground. I sat down next to them and put a hand on their shoulder. I wanted to link with their anima, to calm the storm inside them, but to do so without their permission would be to violate the trust they had in me.

To do so would make me no better than Elodie.

"He would not see a mess," I said. "I did not know him long, but I witnessed the two of you together. He does not love you for your name, or for your gender. He loves you for you, and the heart of you is the heart of you no matter what. And he would help you know yourself in ways that neither Pastor Ben nor I could ever do."

Tears poured down their face, and they were no longer able to keep them quiet.

"May I?" I asked.

"Yes," they said, their voice cracking. I reached over and put my arms around them, letting them bury their face in my shoulder and cry. If Pastor Ben's God did exist, I hoped he would damn anyone who would bring someone that much pain. Ren's whole body shook and seethed as their cries left them one by one. We sat there for fifteen minutes until the storm ebbed away, leaving them gasping for air in hard, heavy breaths.

"Are you…are you going to tell him?" they asked between breaths.

"No. I will not."

"Th-Thank you," they stammered. "For all this. I'm so sorry."

"You've dealt with enough sorrow for one night," I said, standing up from the ground and extending a hand to them, which they took. "Waste none on me."

"Thank you," they said as they stood. "You're…you're really awesome, Lyra."

"You should go back to your room, Na—"

"Hey, um," they interrupted. "Just for right now, could you, like, use the other name? Just this time?"

"You should go back to your room," I said, smiling in spite of myself. "Ren."

Ren put a hand on my forearm and held it there for a long heartbeat before letting go, opening the door, and sliding back out into the hallway.

It took a minute for my enhanced eyes to recover from the light that glared through while the door was open. I reknit them to be less sensitive as I crept around the desk, turning on Pastor Ben's computer, the screen's blue-white glow illuminating the whole room as the login screen—adorned with SafeHaus

Enterprises' minimalist dog-and-roof logo—welcomed me. I entered the password I had discovered on a sticky note attached to the underside of the desk on my first night at Agape's Rainbow.

Lia0620

I knew nothing of computers, but Tavish had shown me enough to know what I needed to do. Slipping the flash drive he'd provided me into a USB port, I started the process of copying Pastor Ben's entire file library. Soon, I hoped, both Ren and I would have answers.

I was on a mountaintop, looking out across a lake, a forest beneath me. There were villages in those vast woods, and people in those villages. The young, the old, the soft-hearted, the cruel, those who danced, those who toiled, those who cried, and those who laughed. Long tendrils of my anima bit into each and every one of them, and if I pulled, I could tear it all out in one pulsating mass. And with that mass, I could form a spearhead to drive into my parent's heart.

And so I did.

As every living being for fifty miles in all directions of the body of water that would one day be called Rook Lake gasped their last breaths and fell dead to the ground, I thrust their stolen anima deep into Cennend—who would now never be called Cennend—piercing through everything they were. The perfect being roared with hatred and agony as raw life force burned away their substance. I wondered at what moment they knew, at what second it became clear to them that death, that awful force that they had always thought separated us from the humans, had come for them, too.

Their pyre flared bright and my parent let out one last, mournful howl that faded into the void, meaningless and empty.

And then, I was alone.

But something was wrong.

It hadn't happened like that. I'd released the anima before taking it, deciding to prioritize the lives of the humans over the end of Cennend. I'd come up with a new plan, and only a handful had needed to die for it.

But that wasn't what was wrong.

Something was wrong, and I don't think it was anima or the nature of what I had been born that told me so. I think maybe it was something profoundly human, something built into my vessel. A sense that lays dormant until danger hovers just out of the range of all the others, a little voice that is neither little nor a voice, more a tuning fork struck inside your skull, vibrating with a tone your ears could never hear.

Something was wrong.

My eyes popped open, and I was no longer on a mountain top. It took me a handful of seconds to remember all that had happened the night before, and why I was on the floor of an empty cell phone store, under a warm blanket.

Something—

"Something's wrong!" Jayla yelled, bursting through the door from the main room. "Get up, we've got to go!"

"What's going on?" I asked, scrambling to my feet and reaching out with my anima, finding my answer a heartbeat before Jayla confirmed it.

"We're being raided. Come on!"

I stumbled after her, back to the front of the store, where Tavish, Clover, Syn, and Bob were frantically shoving laptops, papers, and possessions into backpacks.

"Throw them out the fucking door Jay!" Bob yelled as he threw his bag over his shoulder. "You really think this is all a coincidence?"

"Fuck you, Bob," Jayla snapped back. "They look like a cop to you?"

"They look like a snitch, and fuck me for not being louder about it earlier!" Bob retorted. "They look like someone who shows up right before five cops mysteriously arrive outside, because, oh yeah, that's what's fucking happening!"

"Seven," I interrupted as Jayla tossed me a pack to carry. "Five out front, two around back."

"How the fuck do you know that?" Syn asked, helping Clover with their bag.

"They were sleeping back there, probably heard them arrive," Jayla answered before I could. "Come on, we need to—"

"Building occupants," a deep voice that reminded me far too much of Sheriff Wexton barked through a megaphone, "you are on private property and are not authorized to be here. Please come out with your hands behind your heads."

"Um, does that not sound like the official SPD greeting to anyone else?" Clover asked.

"Yeah, that sounds like someone trying to sound like a cop," Tavish answered. "Like—"

"Fuck," Syn hissed, pressing an eye to a knothole in one of the plywood sheets. "We got Hounds!"

"Fuck!" Jayla spat. "Fuck, fuck, fuck, fuck! Okay, Lyra, you sure there are only two in the back?"

"Yes," I answered, reaching out first. "But four more just arrived in the front."

"They're right," Syn confirmed. "We've got to fuck off, like now."

"This way!" Jayla called out, gesturing toward the room I'd been sleeping in. Bob, Syn, Tavish, and Clover raced through ahead of me. As I turned to follow, Jayla's hand latched onto my forearm, holding me fast as her fingers bit into my skin.

"Bob's an asshole," she said, looking directly into my eyes, "but if you had anything to do with this, I'll put you down like a sick cat. Feel me?"

"I—yes!"

"Good. Come on."

"This is your final warning," the voice through the megaphone crackled. "Come out or we will be forced to enter and detain you."

"Okay, if there's still just two of them out there, we can rush them and run like hell," said Bob, adjusting his backpack straps and approaching the rear exit. "I guess I'm on tank-duty again...."

"We appreciate you!" Clover yelled to him, which got a smirk in return.

"Nah, you don't," he chuckled, putting his hand on the handle.

"Wait!" I yelled. "No, let me go first!"

Bob's brow furrowed as I pushed past him.

"What? Kid, you're tiny. No, get out of—"

The boom of a battering ram smashing open the building's front door cut him off before I could.

"No time for this," I groaned, shoving Bob aside and flinging the door open. "Stay behind me!"

"F-Freeze!" one of the two men guarding the back entrance yelled as both of them fumbled to bring their guns around. I leapt at him with a punch so clumsy it probably wouldn't even leave a bruise, which was okay because it was just cover for an anima snap.

"Kev!" the other guard yelled as his partner collapsed into a pile on the asphalt. "What the fuck did you do?"

My fist didn't even come close to making contact this time, but he still fell just the same, something I hoped was lost in the flurry of movement and the shadows of the back alley. Because if someone wasn't aware of anima and its workings, this would all look like planned theatrics.

"Ha! Fuck me! You brought us a scrapper, Jay!" Syn laughed as the group, not listening to my earlier instruction, ran around me and into the alley. I was too fixated on the fallen men to object. The others had been right; these weren't cops. Their uniforms were blue, but not the dark navy that Officer Nelson had worn. This was a deep blue that almost verged on teal, with silver badges that seemed to want to evoke the idea of a police officer's badge without actually being one. Moreover, neither of these men looked like cops. They looked like killers, and though cops killed all the time, they did so behind a veneer of law

and order to first and foremost fool themselves into thinking they were on the side of justice. You could always see it in how they held themselves, and there had been none of that in these two men.

These two just enjoyed it.

"Beta Team, what's your status?" chirped the chest-mounted radio on the second guard I'd snapped. "They aren't in here, did they come out your way?"

"This way!" Jayla called, rushing down the alley as the man on the other end of the radio repeated his question with more urgency. We dashed after her, stopping just in time to avoid the path of the black SUV that screeched across the alley's mouth.

"On it!" Bob sighed, charging into the driver's door like a locomotive as it opened, crushing the driver as he attempted to emerge, the man's cries of pain lost in the sickening sound of ribs snapping. From the other side of the massive vehicle, the passenger jumped out and ran to use the front of the SUV as cover, barely getting his gun drawn before Syn leapt like a panther and shoved a long, black-bladed knife through the right side of his throat.

I gasped as the man collapsed, blood spurting from his wound and drowning his dying screams as Syn withdrew the blade. The force of his sheared artery arced deep crimson bursts from the hole in his neck as he writhed on the ground. It was horrifying, grotesque, awful—

Beautiful.

"Gut up, kid, this shit's real," Bob yelled, opening the door on the barely conscious driver, slamming his massive fist into the prone officer's face with a dull crunch.

"Lyra, sweetie, we gotta go," Jayla said, grabbing my arm and pulling me away from the carnage, breaking my momentary trance. "I get it, you're having a hell of a day. Kinda got tossed into the deep-end. In case it isn't super obvious by now, those aren't cops, and they aren't interested in arresting us."

"Who are they?" I asked as we slid around the now unmanned SUV and ran out into the rain-soaked street, amid blessedly mild traffic.

"Hounds," Clover answered as we dashed across all four lanes and into another dark alley. "Private security force owned by Russell Hausman."

"Yeah, his own private death-squad," Syn added.

"Former military, mostly," Tavish said, catching his breath. "Dishonorable discharges well represented. Along with some cops whose apples were just a little too 'bad' to be swept under the rug."

"Monsters, every last one," Clover said. "But I know it still can't be easy to see someone get stabbed in the throat and—"

I barely registered the gunshot before I saw Clover's body fling sideways in a macabre, twisting dance toward the ground, a bright red stain blossoming on the left side of their abdomen.

"Morning, Lyra," Toby mumbled to me through mouthfuls of cereal as he sat looking half dead next to Sage and Nova, both of whom also looked as if they hadn't slept in over a week.

"Good morning," I said, studying the three of them. Had they been up wandering the halls of the center the previous night, too? Was I not the only one who had paid attention to the graveyard shift's unofficial schedule?

"You'll have to start a new pot of coffee," Nova grumbled, massaging her temples. "Sage is a terrible person and took the last cup without refilling it."

"We're all terrible people this early in the morning," Sage grumbled, looking down into zir mug, which was emblazoned with the Agape's Rainbow logo. "But yeah, if you were going to start another pot, Lyra...."

"Have you all been sleeping alright?" I asked, mustering up my Agape's Rainbow employee voice. "You seem...tired."

I did not have to have been observing humans for several thousand years to notice the lengthy, howling pause before Toby responded.

"Yeah," he said, less convincing than a single word had ever been said. "Sleeping great, just—"

The world's most perfectly-timed yawn burst from his lips.

"Jesus Christ, Toby," Nova sighed. "They're not an idiot. We...we stayed up a bit late. But we didn't break curfew! We were still in our rooms."

"We were just texting," Sage blurted. "See?"

Without being asked, Sage produced zir phone and opened a group chat with all of the other residents, holding it out for me to inspect.

"O...kay?" I said, narrowing my eyes as I scrolled with my finger, noticing certain words appearing frequently. "What's Sorcerer Street?"

"It's a TV show," Sage answered, maybe a half-beat too quickly. "Super nerdy, but we're all hooked."

"I've never heard of it," I said, though, admittedly I was only familiar with the shows the various residents had introduced me to. Mainly Abby, who wanted me to watch everything with her. Abby, whose name was in this group text and yet had not begged me to sit down and binge Sorcerer's Street....

"We all just discovered it," Toby blurted. "That's why we spent all night talking about it."

"Yeah, it's, like, not from here," Nova said. "It's from, I think, like, Europe somewhere?"

Europe. Somewhere.

"We didn't think you'd like it," Saeed's voice said as he entered the dining hall behind me. "It's so nerdy, and you're, like, you know, cool."

I could honestly say that no one in all of existence had ever referred to me as cool. Something was up, and I needed to decide if it was worth devoting attention to.

"What's it about?" I asked, all four staring back at me with momentary panic in their eyes. They were very, very bad at this.

"Oh, it's, like, about this evil sorcerer," Sage said, finally.

"Who lives on a street!" Toby blurted.

"Jesus Christ, Toby," Nova grumbled.

"He lives in a village, is what Toby means," Saeed jumped in. "And he has these pet ogres that guard the gates, and the heroes are always trying to escape. Oh, he also has this talking snake that is, like, his best friend."

"But the talking snake is nice!" Nova added. "Really, the talking snake is the best character."

"Oh, yeah," Lenora said as she entered. "Everyone loves the talking snake. Big fans."

Talking. Snake.

"I feel the need to move this along before my feelings get further damaged," I said, through my teeth. "So. You've developed a coded way to speak about Pastor Ben and me and you hoped that either it would be too opaque or we would be too stupid to figure it out during cellphone checks?"

Four wide-eyed, slack-jawed faces stared back at me, trying to form words.

"Oh no, y'all, somehow Lyra broke your secret code," Ren said as they entered. "How did they do it when it was so brilliant and uncrackable? They must be a wizard!"

"No," I said, as Ren laughed at the others, "I'm a talking snake. And I saw your name in that group chat as well."

"I did *not* sign off on the talking snake," Ren said, approaching the coffee pot. "Oh, shit, there's no coffee?"

"Lyra was going to make some," Sage said.

"Snakes can't make coffee," I said, deadpan, which actually got a laugh.

"Okay, okay," Sage said. "When...when we say it out loud and you're, like, here looking at us and stuff, it seems kinda...mean, I guess."

"You guess."

"But we do all like the talking snake!" Nova blurted. "And you!"

"I thought I was the talking snake?"

"You...were," Ren said.

"Yeah, so, it all started as us shit-talking this place and Pastor Ben," Saeed admitted. "Who we also like! Really! But then it just kinda...I dunno...."

"We started getting away from that and doing one of those, like, round-robin story things from grade school," Lenora said, cheeks blushing. "It's stupid."

"Stupid fun," Toby corrected. "That's why we were up all night. We—the heroes were making a plan to overthrow the wizard and...um...okay, maybe it's kinda stupid."

"Nah, you were right, it's fun," Leonora shrugged. "I'll admit it."

"That's really the only part Abby ever got into," Nova added. "So, like, don't be mad at her. Honestly, I think she's why we switched from shit-talking to storytelling."

"Yeah, we were kinda bumming her out hard," Sage said. "But...yeah. Sorry."

"Yeah, sorry," Saeed mumbled.

"Sorry," Nova and Toby said at the same time.

"Sorry for being bitches," Lenora said.

"Forgiven," I said. "But you need to let me read your story at some point. I hear I feature prominently in it. Now, you are all fortunate that I, too, desire coffee."

"You're the best, talking snake!" Sage called across the room as I went over to the coffee maker and started filling the filter.

"Do not forget it," I called back. "Also, where is Abby this morning?"

"Oh, she went out for a walk," Lenora, Abby's roommate, answered. "She's so fucking excited about this stupid internship."

"Stupid?" I asked, pouring water into the machine.

"I mean...like, for me it would be stupid," Lenora blushed. "I'm happy for her, really. I'm just going to, you know, miss her and shit. She was a good roommate."

"I wish she wouldn't go," Sage said. "I mean, honesty time? I wish she wouldn't take that internship period, even if she was still leaving."

"Why's that?" I asked.

"Look, don't get me wrong, I get why someone would want to go make bank working for Evil Corp. I really do," Sage said, leaning back in zir chair. "But you can't work a place like that and not lose your soul, and Abby has more soul than anyone I've ever met. Can you imagine her working down the hall from, like, SafeHaus' private prison office? Or eating lunch next to a bunch of sociopaths who are in charge of Russell Hausman's 'private defense contractors'? Shit, that place is going to eat her alive, or it's going to assimilate her, which would be even worse."

"Oh come on, give Abby some credit," Nova rolled her eyes. "She's spacey but she's not a dummy. She'll get out when she realizes how evil the place is, and by then hopefully she'll have enough money to open a....shit, I don't know? Puppies and ice cream store?"

"Yeah, that sounds right," Toby nodded, as everyone made vague noises in agreement.

"While I think Abigail would excel at a puppies and ice cream store, I do believe it would be a waste of her talents," Pastor Ben said as he entered. "And please don't believe everything you read online about SafeHaus. They are a corporation, and it's true that it's almost impossible to make it in corporate America without getting your hands dirty, but I've met Russell Hausman and he's a good man trying to do better with what he has."

"Sorry," Sage mumbled.

"You are forgiven," Pastor Ben said. "There are a lot of very convincing voices out there on the world wide web, on all sorts of topics. Speaking of, I wanted to go over Agape policy on internet usage...."

My skin crawled with every word Pastor Ben spoke, the sense memory of his sweaty hands on my feet as he made his gasping, obscene confession was still too fresh for me to be in the same room with him. Hitting 'brew' on the machine, I slid back across the room and out the door to the hallway without anyone noticing. I would get coffee at a later time.

I was about halfway down the hall when I heard Matthew's booming voice.

"They're full of shit, you know that right?" he said, walking up behind me. I ignored him and kept going.

"They talk shit about you all the time," Jason added, apparently finding the loathsome courage he had lacked during our last encounter.

"They think you're a pathetic kiss-ass," Matthew called out, his footsteps getting faster. "They all like *your* ass, though."

"W-Who wouldn't?" Jason laughed, his momentary stutter betraying him.

"Leave me alone, and get back to work," I said, without turning around, stopping in the middle of the hall. I didn't want to go all the way down the dormitory wing with them still following me. I didn't want them that close to my door.

"Once again, Lyra, you are not my boss," Matthew said, and then placed a hand on my shoulder and spun me around.

I almost did it. Right there. I wouldn't even have thought twice about it if I hadn't heard the main door open and shut.

"Matthew and Jason!" Abby's voice called out. "Best boys! Good morning!"

Both men's faces softened, Matthew giving me one last eyebrow flare before he turned around.

"Good morning, Abby!" he boomed, Jason parroting him a moment later.

"And Lyra!" Abby beamed. "All the best people! God, I'm going to miss you all so much. I have to say, I've always envied you all getting to work together, hanging out, having fun. I hope my new coworkers are like you all are."

"We're going to miss you, too," Matthew said, as Jason gave her a lecherous head to toe and back again look.

"Goodbye hug?" Jason asked, spreading his arms.

"Actually, Abby, I wanted to talk to you about something," I said, pushing between Jason and Abby and guiding her by the shoulder down the hall. "Let's walk and talk."

"Oh, uh, sure! Okay!" Abby said. "I'll catch you two later, guys!"

Matthew and Jason grumbled something in return, which I ignored.

"Sorry about that," I said as we walked.

"No worries," Abby shrugged. "So, what did you want to talk to me about?"

I am the child of an omnipotent being, I have moved across this world for thousands of years, and I still could not think of a single convincing lie.

"I...um...I honestly don't remember," I mumbled.

"Oh wow, I'm glad I'm not the only one that happens to," Abby laughed. "Good ol' auDHD brain, huh? Well, I'm glad I saw you anyway, because I wanted to ask you if you were...you know...okay. After yesterday. You seemed really upset, and I didn't want to push, but...."

"I'm okay," I said, pressing my lips into a thin smile. "You are very sweet to worry. Or even notice."

"Aw, Lyra," Abby said as I suddenly found myself being hugged again. "Of course I noticed! Why would you think I wouldn't notice?"

"Not...you, specifically," I mumbled, embarrassed that I'd said anything at all. I didn't care about being liked. It wasn't important. It wasn't why I was here.

"Oh...oh no, did you find out about the sorcerer thing?" Abby asked, her face falling. "I told them not to! I told them it was mean, and they were being unfair and—"

"I know," I said, trying to sound reassuring. "They told me, but I kind of knew anyway. That's...not like you."

"I should have just left that stupid group chat," she huffed. "I did get them to stop, though."

"I heard about the round-robin story."

"It's actually pretty good," she said, blushing. "And...and I really pushed back against you being a snake, I just got outvoted."

"I'm curious," I said, as we reached her room, "what animal would I have been represented by if you had had your way?"

"Um…okay, well, I can actually answer that in a weird sort of way" Abby stammered, grabbing for her messenger bag. "I, uh, was going to leave this for you as a gift because I was hoping it would make you feel better, but…."

She reached into her bag and carefully withdrew a colored pencil drawing of a luna moth in beautiful, delicate greens and yellows, its wing-tips forming a gentle swish down the page.

"It's nothing, really," she mumbled, fidgeting with the zipper pulls of her jacket.

"It's amazing," I said, tears forming in my eyes as I looked over the moth's gentle lines.

"I just…when I think of you, I think of transformation, and grace, and…."

She muttered another word that I missed, which I think was her hope.

"I just wanted you to know you're not a snake," she said, looking down. "Not to me."

This time I was the one to put my arms around her.

"I hope you like it," she said as I released her, both of us blushing now.

"I love it," I said, looking once again at the moth that represented me. "Thank you."

"Of course," Abby said, blushing harder. "Just…just don't get used to it, okay? I'm good for like one decent drawing a year."

We both laughed and said our goodbyes. She waved as she closed her door, and I headed back to my room and sat on the edge of the bed, resting the moth drawing on the bedspread next to me.

This was why I was here.

"Clover!" Syn screamed as Jayla and Bob both drew guns of their own, Tavish dropping down to the ground where Clover was bleeding out onto the wet asphalt.

"Put 'em down, folks," a deep, amused voice ordered from behind us as Jayla and Bob trained their guns on the four Hounds in front of us, all of whom had their own weapons pointed right back.

"I have good news," the speaker said, approaching out of the shadows and staying behind the row of his men. He looked even less like a cop than any of the rest of them. His face was smooth-shaven, his dark hair perfectly coiffed. He had the kind of blue eyes that those who found men attractive might have

described as handsome. But his smile was haunting. It wasn't evil, or smug, or cruel...

It was authentic. Standing there in a dark, wet alley with his death squad holding six people at gunpoint while one of them bled to death on the ground, he was the perfect picture of happiness.

"We need at least one of you alive to answer questions," he continued. "Bad news is, we don't need any more than that. So...which one of you is Jayla?"

"Sure hope it wasn't the one I just wasted!" one of the men on his right joked, getting a smattering of snorts and laughs from the others. I ignored them all as best I could and dropped down next to Tavish who was pressing his own wadded up jacket against Clover's wound as Syn knelt on their other side, holding their hand and sobbing.

"Kid, take over for me," Tavish hissed, gesturing with his chin at the blood-soaked jacket. "My hands are old and we need to keep the pressure on."

"Me," Jayla said to the Hound's leader. "I'm Jayla."

I placed my hands on Tavish's jacket as he let go and moved back, a coppery smell hitting my nose as blood oozed up through the fabric and onto my fingers. They were losing too much.

"Ly...ra..." Clover mumbled, barely holding onto consciousness.

"Yeah, that looks like her," the man who had joked about shooting Clover said, holding his pistol in one hand and his phone in the other, then turning it around for the smiling man to see. "Well, kinda. Joe, she looks hotter in her mugshot, right?"

"I...I need you to trust me," I said, to both everyone and no one, yanking the bloody jacket away and pressing my hand to Clover's wound.

"Are you fucking crazy?" Tavish yelled.

"Lyra! No!" Syn gasped. "You'll—"

I looked up at both of them, my glowing blue eyes knocking the words out of their mouths.

"So you're Jayla, huh?" the smiling man—Joe—said, taking a step closer to our group while still staying behind his men, more of whom had appeared at the other end of the alley, boxing us in. "You're a real pain in the ass, you know?"

I inhaled and linked to Clover's anima.

"That's the idea," Jayla said. "Now just let everyone else go and I'll come with you, okay? They're just some dumb assholes I hired as muscle. You know all about that, right?"

"Cute," Joe laughed. "How about this: I let you keep one. You can even pick which."

I was only half-aware of the stand-off above me, the rest of me lost in the maze that was Clover's damaged vessel. I remembered Janna, Elodie's *mother, and how hard my sister had fought in vain to save her. This wasn't like that, though. Janna had laid wounded for too long before we reached her. The damage had not yet spread through Clover, but I still needed help.*

"Lyra," Clover mumbled, their head lulling up. "What's…going on? I feel…warm…."

"Syn," I said, reaching out toward her. "Give me your hand!"

"Hey!" one of the new soldier yelled approaching from the back. "You three, get up!"

"Don't worry," the man with all the jokes laughed, "your friend will still be down there waiting for you!"

Ignoring the men and giving me a terrified look, Syn reached out and grabbed the hand I'd stretched out to her.

"What's—?" she started.

"Do you love her?" I asked.

"Yes!" Syn blurted. "Of fucking course I do! I—"

"I said get up!" the soldier, still approaching, barked.

"Better tell your freaks to get on their feet, Jayla," Joe said. I could still hear the smile in his voice.

"Then hold on," I said to Syn, linking my anima with both her and Clover, becoming a conduit, the mingling of our three animas flowing through Clover's body.

"You…you never said it before," Clover mumbled, a soft smile on their lips as their injured side knit back together. As the wound finished closing, I felt the spent bullet expel itself under my palm and fall to the ground….

Right as another one shot clean through my shoulder.

"Lyra!" Syn and Clover both screamed as pain exploded through the right side of my body. Jayla and Bob both opened fire, the two of them sprinting in opposite directions to draw the Hounds away from the rest of us as Syn drew her knife and Tavish shielded Clover and me.

The pain erupting from my shoulder burned like being branded with a hot iron, and as I struggled to my feet, I remembered how powerless I'd felt the last time I'd been shot, the day Aiden Moser betrayed us and unloaded three bullets into my chest. I was so weak then. I had barely had my vessel a single day, and already a small, pathetic man had tried to take it away. And now more small, pathetic men were trying to do the same, to take away what was mine, to kill the five people who had been kinder to me than anyone else had since I'd left Rook Lake.

"Get down, Lyra!" Tavish yelled as bullets whistled through the air all around us. Jayla moved like liquid with a beautiful, terrifying grace, dodging in untraceable patterns, dropping two Hounds without pausing, the first not even

making it to the ground before her second bullet was tearing into the next. Bob, on the other side, had none of Jayla's grace but moved with a speed that I had not expected from such an enormous man. He bowled into one of the Hounds, knocking him backwards and into the path of a bullet originally meant for Bob's skull. One of Jayla's bullets dropped the shooter from across the alley before he even knew what had happened.

But still more came. There were too many of them. I knew it, and I imagine the rest of our group did, too. As if to underscore my point, a bullet fired by the joking man struck Bob's left elbow, shattering bone and flesh. He staggered a few steps and fell, howling in agony as his gun clattered to the ground.

"Shoulda stayed in the jungle," the Hound laughed.

Aiden Moser had failed. And when, aided by my parent, he tried again, he failed again. But there would always be another pitiful little man who dreamt pitiful little dreams of being powerful.

"Not joining the party, huh?" the joker's voice called out as he approached us through the chaos. "Too bad...party's gonna come to you!"

Without warning, Syn sprang up and jumped between him and us, slashing wildly at him. He stumbled back at the last minute, and then again, dodging swipe after swipe until he gained enough footing to leap forward—

And right into my hand, which closed like a fist on the front of his shirt and lifted him off of his feet.

"Fucking let me go!" he screamed, kicking and writhing as he tried in vain to free himself.

I could have anima snapped him. I could have anima snapped all of them.

But I didn't want to.

I inhaled and ripped away enough of the man's anima to heal my wounded shoulder, but not enough to let him lose consciousness. This man, this pathetic, awful little man had watched Clover bleeding out on the ground and he'd laughed. He'd hurt these people, the only people who'd even thought of helping me, and he'd laughed.

Talons grew from my fingertips, just like I'd learned from Elodie. Elodie, whom I'd lectured about not giving into her own darkness, Elodie, my sister, made from the same substance, who had butchered an entire sheriff's department. Elodie, who had looked at me with eyes full of regret and sorrow when I chastised her and told her she had been as wicked as our parent, just because she could.

Elodie, to whom I owed an apology.

Elodie, whom I was not.

"Let go you fucking bitch!" the man screamed, his bravado gone as he kicked pointlessly at me. My free hand drew back, talons ready. It's what Elodie would have done, had I not shamed her.

But I was not Elodie.

Under my lips, my teeth grew and shifted, elongating into needle-like fangs, moving to make room for more and more, growing so long that they wrenched my jaw open, my lips sliding back over the maw of jagged enamel.

"H-Holy fuck!" the man I held shrieked. "Holy—"

His next word was lost as I sank my fangs into his throat, a gurgling, wailing scream his last living sound as my mouth filled with warm, coppery blood. I wrenched my head back, teeth still embedded, tearing out a wad of sinew, tissue, and blood and spitting it onto the ground, where I dropped the rest of him a second later.

He didn't seem to find it very funny at all.

The shooting had stopped, and every eye in the alley was on me now.

"L-Lyra...." Jayla stammered.

I inhaled and burst my wings through my back, igniting the blue flames behind my eyes.

"Come," I said, blood still running down my fangs and over my chin. "And see."

The screaming and the shooting restarted all at once. I moved like lightning, pouncing from one vile little man to another as they fired wildly after me.

I had once stood on a mountain top, and spared the lives of everyone below.

What a fool.

A bullet whistled by my head as I bit into the neck of the last Hound still on his feet. Tearing my teeth free and dropping his lifeless body to the ground, I spun around and found Joe sprawled on the ground, propped up on one arm, trying to aim with the other as his wounded, bleeding body trembled. He tried to fire again as I locked eyes with him, but his gun made nothing but a dull click.

Joe was no longer smiling.

"H-H-Holy Mary, Mother of God," he stammered as I advanced on him, my steps slow and deliberate, blood dripping from my fangs and talons. "P-Pray for us s-s-sinners now and at the hour of our deaths. Pray—"

I reached down and picked him up by the throat, hoisting him into the air, his hair matted and his face caked with blood, tears streaming from his eyes.

He, the man who had hunted a group of homeless people like animals. He who had told Jayla she could choose which of us would live while the others died. He who smiled when he thought we would be his prey, who delighted in our fear...

...was finally afraid.

I looked into his eyes and he trembled in my grasp. In that moment he was Aiden Moser, was Sheriff Wexton, was Maria Quinn, was Mayor Prine, was the whole Juniper Society, was every heartless person who glared at me, spit on me, or threw trash at me as I slept on the street, every 'good' person wearing a crucifix or a rainbow pin who had refused to even look at me, every cop who kept the unhoused from a moment of peace, every politician who criminalized poverty, every preacher who called wealth a virtue and destitution a sin, every 'good citizen' who demanded that the undesirables of society be kept far from their neighborhoods, everyone who found joy in pointless acts of cruelty, callousness, or just plain meanness, and everyone who stood by and let them happen.

He was them, and they were him. And they would all be afraid.

I carried him by the throat to where Bob lay on the ground bleeding. He was afraid, too.

"I-I'm sorry!" the man in my grasp blurted. "Holy Mary, Mother of God—"

"I don't know her," I hissed, slamming him to the ground, grabbing Bob's shattered arm with my free hand. Before either could react, I tore the anima from Joe's body and channeled it into Bob, a man who had been unkind and rude and callous toward me, who didn't like me, didn't trust me, but at least had had enough human decency to not deny me a place to lay my head.

As the anima burned from Joe's body, Bob's arm mended, bone and muscle twisting back together, both men screaming at the top of their lungs until, suddenly, neither was.

Silence.

Jayla approached first, the only one of the five who didn't look terrified. The others stood at a distance, Syn bracing Clover, Tavish gesturing for Bob to join them as the big man struggled back to his feet.

"Lyra," Jayla whispered, "what...who are you?"

I'd told Elodie once that we are the sum total of our actions, and the us who loves is the us who hates, and that if she killed because she could, that was, intrinsically, who she was.

All at once I felt the weight of all I'd done crashing down on me, combined with three healings and a gunshot wound. My wings vanished, as did my talons. My new maw of fangs reduced back down to 32 human teeth. My knees buckled and, around the edges of my vision, the world grew dark.

"I am," I said, my words slurring, "who I am."

I felt myself collapse, down,

down,

down,

into the deepest, blackest darkness.

III

Hymn of Angels Above and Below

THAT NIGHT NEVER STOPPED haunting me. I had killed the Hounds, each and every one of them. Humans. Men with lives and hopes and dreams and families. I'd slaughtered them, one by one, with my claws.

And my teeth.

In quiet moments, I swore I could still taste the blood.

But the part that haunted me the most was that I couldn't force myself to care. I would do it again. And it would be easier than the first time, and the time after that would be easier still. Isn't that what I told Elodie? Isn't that what I'd discovered so many millennia ago, when I played with the lives of the early humans as if I was a god?

I had certain things to do in this world, certain purposes to fulfill. The residents of Agape's Rainbow still needed me, and maybe Ezri did, too. Elodie certainly didn't, even if she thought otherwise. But once I'd done all the things I was still meant to do, maybe the best thing for me to do would be to go to the primeval forest where my parent languished, unmake the beautiful vessel Elodie and I had crafted, and finally let my anima disperse on the wind.

This world did not need another god.

But until that day came, I still had work to do, both in a broader, more metaphysical sense and also in the sense that I had emails piling up in my inbox. It was the latter that was occupying my mind when Pastor Ben came walking back down the hall toward my desk, whistling some insipid contemporary worship song, looking absolutely ridiculous in his khaki cargo shorts and lime green polo.

"Good morning, Lyra!" his voice boomed from down the hall. "You left breakfast before I got a chance to say hi."

"I apologize," I muttered. "I wanted to get started early."

The lies that were impossible to summon for Abby flowed like a mighty river when talking with Pastor Ben.

"And I appreciate your work ethic," Ben said, with a broad smile that turned my stomach. "But you shouldn't feel bad about taking time for camaraderie with the other residents. You are a positive influence in their lives, and sometimes I think you have more sway over them than I do. Which, I guess makes sense, given...your nature."

I truly don't know if he meant angelic or agender. Either way, every word was still hitting like a wad of saliva. Pastor Ben's 'confessions' were always a disgusting affair that left me feeling violated afterwards, but none had affected me as much as his most recent one. Maybe it was because the longer I spent at Agape's Rainbow, the more I realized what a truly vile human being Pastor Ben's facade of holiness and congeniality masked. Maybe it was because he stubbornly refused to discuss the one thing I needed him to confess to. And maybe it was because Abby's time left at the center was now measured in a number of days that could be counted on a single hand, and that meant I was moving closer and closer to needing to do something truly vile myself.

"Speaking of, Pastor, I wanted to talk to you about something," I said, swiveling my chair toward him, fighting the bile back down my esophagus.

"Of course, of course," he said, looking at his expensive smart-watch. "I do have a phone call in about ten minutes...."

"It won't take long," I assured him. "I just wanted to pass on something from the group. Some of the other residents have been upset that they haven't heard from some of their friends who left to work for SafeHaus. They were—"

"Ah, you've been talking to Nathan, huh?" Pastor Ben chuckled, Ren's deadname hitting my eardrum like a needle. "I feel bad for him, he obviously had some pretty strong feelings for Jett, but that's young love, isn't it?"

He leaned in, looking around conspiratorially.

"I feel weird saying that to you, looking like you're all of eighteen yourself," he whispered with a lopsided grin. "But I know you're probably older than this whole planet, and have probably seen all manner of heartbroken teenagers. Never gets easier, though. My heart always goes out to them. It all feels so *real* and *important* at that age. Honestly, it's what made it so hard with my first wife, Lia. She was about, well, the age you look when I met her. I was just a little older, really, in my later-twenties, and I certainly didn't have everything figured out, but I was glad I could guide her through it all. You would have loved her. Complete sweetheart. Troubled, certainly, but...."

"Pastor," I said, trying to wrestle the conversation back to the topic at hand, my skin crawling anew as I got a fresh glimpse into the loathsome man's past, "I hate to cut you off, but I know your time is limited. Would it be possible for you to contact your connections at SafeHaus and at least ask Jett—and maybe some of the others—to, I don't know, send a message to the current residents? It doesn't even have to be a long one. Just something to let their former friends know that they're okay. We could even ask if they could make an endorsement video for the center, or talk about what the internships are like, or—"

"Lyra," Ben interrupted, in perhaps the harshest tone he'd ever used with me. "I'm afraid that wouldn't be possible, no. Why are you suddenly so interested in the SafeHaus internships?"

"Because," I said, choosing my words carefully, "I care about our residents, and this is something that has been causing them concern and upset. I worry it is becoming a distraction, I—"

"Lyra," he interrupted again, "why are you lying?"

There was no one else around, and I was sick of being talked to like this man's inferior.

"Correct your tone and remember who you are speaking to," I said in a low, dark voice, igniting the glow behind my eyes. "I have told no lies, and what a brazen accusation from one who is, himself, keeping the truth hidden. What is it about the SafeHaus internships that makes you so defensive? What is it you are hiding from the Lord, Benjamin Holmes?"

Pastor Ben did not seem nearly as fazed as I expected him to be. He swallowed deeply, and then spoke

"I have hidden nothing from the Lord," he said, keeping his voice steady, though it was clearly taking a considerable amount of effort. "The Lord sees all; it is impossible to hide from him. Angels, however, are not omniscient."

"I suggest you make your point, Benjamin," I said, digging my nails into my own palms. This wasn't the Pastor Ben I was used to. Something had changed in him, and all I knew was that he was too small of a man to bring it about in himself.

He had spoken to someone.

"My point is, and I truly mean no disrespect," he said, his voice quavering, "that the Lord already knows my sins, and if he has not illuminated them for you, then he must have a reason for not wanting you to know."

Someone who had emboldened him. Someone who had whispered him sweet, pretty words. Someone who was going to be a problem.

"So, again, with all respect due to a being such as you," Pastor Ben said, sweat beading on his brow, "I would request that, to honor the wishes of the God we both serve, you stop inquiring."

Without wanting to tell me anything, he told me two things:

One, there was, most certainly, something sinister going on at SafeHaus Enterprises.

And Two: There was, most certainly, someone doing everything in their power to keep it in the shadows.

"Now," Pastor Ben continued, as the blue glow faded from my eyes, "as I said, I have a phone meeting that I really can't be late for. Good luck with your emails, Lyra."

I made no effort to respond, nor did he wait for me to, instead walking past me and into his office.

Unfortunately for him, doors mean little to 'a being such as me.'

While half of my anima remained with my vessel, seated at my desk and wading through spam emails advertising ministry kits and mission trip opportunities, the rest of me flowed under the door and into the office where Pastor Ben sat at his desk, fidgeting with the collar of his polo as if his appearance mattered on a phone call.

The ringing of his desk phone made him jump as if a gunshot had just echoed through his office. His hand trembling, he picked up the receiver, and my anima moved between it and his ear.

"Hello, Benjamin," a high but stern voice said from the receiver.

"Oh, Co—Ms. Emerson," Pastor Ben stammered. "I'm sorry, I thought I would be talking with Russell today."

"Don't feel bad, many people have made the same mistake over the years," the woman whose last name was Emerson, apparently, said. It was impossible to not hear the disdain oozing off of every word. "But Mr. Hausman is currently in Hong Kong and, even if he wasn't, not to be too blunt about it, but this would be beneath him. Frankly, it is beneath me as well, but he made me project manager for this endeavor, and he pays me too well to say no. So. What happens to be on your mind *today*, Benjamin?"

Pastor Ben's face was reddening by the minute, and I kept expecting him to tell her to use his title. But he didn't.

"I…I just had a few questions," he said, trying to deepen his voice.

"Shocking," Ms. Emerson sighed. "Alright, what can I not answer for you this time?"

"It's nothing, really," he said, fidgeting with a pen on his desk. "I just…the residents are asking questions. About their friends who have joined the internship program."

"I see," Ms. Emerson said. "What kind of questions?"

"Just…they haven't heard from them since they left," he said. "Any of them. And…and I haven't, either. I tried texting a few of them that I had…grown close with…and never received a response. In a few cases, it seems like their phone numbers had been reassigned."

"Benjamin," Ms. Emerson said, "are you under the impression that I manage the social calendars of our teenage interns? You do remember who I am, right? Right hand to one of the most powerful businessmen in the world, *not* 'child wrangler'?"

"I—of course, of course," Ben stammered. "I'm sorry, I didn't mean to imply—it's just that they're getting more insistent and—"

"And that is a you-problem," Ms. Emerson interrupted. "And you-problems need to have you-solutions, because if they become me-problems, then Mr. Hausman and I are going to start questioning what the purpose of *you* is, exactly. Do I make myself clear?"

"Yes. Yes of course. It's just that…they've started asking my angel to intercede for them."

I almost threw up at being called his, but at least I hadn't had to wait long to learn who had been coaching him.

There was a long pause on the line before Ms. Emerson spoke again.

"Well, that *is* a bit more concerning," she said. "But also a you-problem. How have you addressed it?"

"W-With scripture," he answered, swallowing heavily. "Ma'am."

"Hmm. Well. I hope that means more than it sounds like it does," she said, before another long pause. "Continue on as planned, but I'm going to speak with Mr. Hausman about this."

"T-Thank you," Pastor Ben said, wildly misreading the tone that even I could hear in Ms. Emerson's voice. "I appreciate it. I think if we could get *some* transparency—"

"Oh, I'm sorry," Ms. Emerson said, with an airy, disdainful laugh. "I feel maybe I was unclear: I'm going to speak with Mr. Hausman about whether or not you are still worth the effort or if we need to take the whole endeavor from your overly sweaty hands before you fuck it six ways from Sunday. Are we clear now, *Pastor*?"

Pastor Ben's hands were clenched into fists, his face bright red with sweat pouring down his brow. I wondered if any woman had ever spoken to him this way before.

"Y-Yes."

"Wonderful," Ms. Emerson said. "We'll be in touch."

"Okay," Pastor Ben said, clenching his teeth. "God bl—"

The call ended, and Pastor Ben flopped back in his chair, wiping at his face with his forearm, mopping up a mixture of sweat and now tears.

Back outside his office, at my desk, my cell phone buzzed in my pocket.

Can you talk?

Jayla's number.

Yes, I typed in reply. *Give me a moment to get outside.*

She replied with a 'thumbs-up' emoji. I started to get up when one of my emails caught my eye.

FINAL NOTICE the subject line read. Opening it, I scrolled down to the bright-red text in the body of the message.

"Our records show that payment for the policy for AGAPE'S RAINBOW MINISTRIES is now overdue. We will have no choice but to cancel your coverage if payment is not received by—"

The date of the very next day followed. With a single click of my mouse, I sent the email to the trash, which I then opened, and with a second click emptied.

Not all power comes from Heaven above.

Warm.
Sore.
Under me, something soft. But just barely.
Crisp air. Like water. Like we were near water.
Sound.
Low sound.
Whispers.
Voices!
"Oh, shit, Jayla! Jayla, they're waking up!"
I fought to remain in the darkness, to stay in that inky black cocoon, but it pushed me up through itself and spat me out into a dim gray room. Suddenly, Syn and Clover's faces burst into view.

"Lyra! Are you okay? How are you feeling?" Clover asked as I felt them take my right hand into theirs.

"Do you need anything?" Syn asked, eyes full of concern. "Water? Food? A drink? Weed? I've got good stuff with me."

"I brought you tea!" Bob declared, rushing into my field of vision holding a Starbucks cup with a string and tab dangling out of it. "It may be a bit cold now, but my mom always gave me tea when I was sick, so...."

"T-thank you," I said, sitting up and immediately regretting that decision. My head was throbbing and my bones felt like gelatin. I took the cup from Bob and placed it to my lips. The tea was barely warm and too strong by half, but it hit my raw throat like a balm.

"Okay, okay, give them some space," Jayla said, pushing her way forward. Tavish followed behind her holding a bagel half-wrapped in a paper towel which he pressed into my hand.

"How are you feeling, Lyra?" Jayla asked.

"I'll...I'll be okay," I said, between bites of the bagel, which tasted like salvation.

"Yeah, we assumed that based on the, you know, wings and shrugging off gunshots and stuff," Jayla said, sitting next to me. "How are you now, though?"

"I'm sore," I said. "And tired. Like I'm...."

"Coming down?" she asked.

"Yes. That's a good way to put it. I...imagine you all have some questions."

The floodgates opened.

"Are you an angel?" Bob.

"Are you a vampire?" Syn

"Where do your wings go?" Tavish.

"Can you make me a vampire?" Syn, again.

"H-how did you heal me?" Clover.

"You're fucking awesome! More of a comment than a question." Syn, a third time.

"Our questions can wait!" Jayla said, glaring daggers at the rest of the group. "Let's not come at them like the fucking paparazzi."

"It's okay," I said, getting my bearings. "I'm not an angel, Bob; at least not in any conventional way. Tavish, my wings get made and then unmade every time I need them. Clover, I used a mingling of your anima, Syn's anima, and my own anima to mend your wounds. Syn, I am not a vampire and, as such, cannot make you a vampire, either. But thank you for thinking I'm awesome. I...I don't feel awesome."

"Lyra, those blue-shirts would have killed all of us," Bob said. "You did—"

"Don't," I put up a hand. "Please. Next question."

Bob nodded and stepped back.

"Okay, so, I want to ask this in a way less asshole-ish way than I did the first time," Jayla said, putting a hand on my back. "But...."

"What am I?" I finished for them.

"Yeah. But, again, like...the non-asshole version of that."

"It's okay," I said, looking down at my hands, which were just soft flesh again. While I was unconscious, someone had washed them, cleansing away the stains of the blood I'd shed. Gentle enough to not have woken me, thorough enough to remove every spot.

I looked up at the group. They had taken me in when I had nothing to offer them. More than that, they had taken me again after they'd seen what I was, after, by all logic and reason, they should have left me behind and run far, far away.

"I...I can tell you," I said, choosing every word carefully. "But I...I want to make sure you want me to. If you do, I'll tell you things that will make you see

everything—me, the world, yourselves—differently. I'll tell you things you can't unknow. Things that won't leave your mind. I don't have to, though. I won't, unless you want me to."

"You don't have to," Jayla said. "You never have to share more than you want, and I know you just met us, but...."

"But you saved our asses, Lyra," Bob said.

"You saved the person I love," Syn added. "Yes, Clover, I love you; don't get a big head about it."

"You made Syn admit she loves me," Clover said. "And you saved my life."

"You fought for us when you had no reason to," Tavish said. "You could have run off. Or flown, I guess."

"You're part of the family now, Lyra," Jayla said. "Tell us as much or as little as you want, it won't change that. And it's not like anyone here is unfamiliar with the idea that the world is fucked up beyond belief."

The group nodded. I didn't want to tell them. Not because I didn't trust them. They could have left me behind to be found by the police, or the next group of Hounds. But they didn't. I didn't want to tell them because no human should have to bear that knowledge. But I had to. I'd already shown them too much for them to ever believe in the world they thought they lived in before they met me. They deserved to know the rest.

"O-Okay," I said, taking a deep breath. "The universe is not like what you think it's like. It—everything—exists in the firmament of my parent, who my sister calls Cennend...."

I told them. All of it. About Cennend and Elodie, the Juniper Society and Rook Lake. About anima. About Ezri. About the battle in the Heartwood, and the truth about what happened after. About me.

When I'd finished, they all stared at me, eyes wide and faces stunned.

"I'm...I'm sorry," I whispered.

There was a long, silent pause before Bob finally broke it.

"Well, shit," he said. "Sure as hell ain't going to let my grandma guilt me anymore about not going to church."

"O...kay, yeah, that was...a lot," Jayla said, shaking her head. "But...here we are. So, Cennend is trapped now?"

"Yes," I nodded. "Elodie is maintaining their bonds."

"And Ezri...Ezri is the friend you mentioned when we first met?" Syn asked.

"Yes."

"You should, like, tell her," Clover said. "Give her her memories back."

"No," I said, shaking my head. "Not yet. Not now. She has a new life, and, every time I've checked in on her, she seems happy. I can't take that away. I...I worry, too, about what would happen to her brain. She has created a new truth* *around the holes in her memory. I don't know what happens if that collides with reality."*

"Kinda fucked what your sister did," Syn said. "Like, yeah, I get it, but...."

"Shit, Lyra, what we're doing here must seem meaningless to you," Bob said, eyes still wide, looking down at the floor.

"No," I shook my head. "Not at all. This...this all matters. When I lived as anima, everything was theory and philosophy and abstractions. But I've been human long enough now to realize the seriousness of this earth. I've slept on the street. I've seen people suffer. I've watched people die. I've watched the cruelty, the callousness, the apathy. What I've learned is that this—all of this—doesn't matter less because of the reality of the world. This all matters. There is no big picture and small picture. It's all the same picture. If...if I'm family now—"

"You are," all five of them said at once.

"Then...then what do I do? How can I help?"

"Fly to DC, find nine old fuckers in black robes and tear them all in half," Syn laughed. "Please and thank you."

"Yeah, not that," Jayla said. "As cathartic as it would be. So, I guess if I'm going to answer your question, and if we're all being honest with each other here, we should tell you who we are. We call ourselves No Affiliation."

"No Affiliation? Why?"

"Because it fucks with the cops records," Tavish chuckled. "They got a box on their stupid little forms that says 'gang affiliation,' and it's a dumb computer, so if they enter 'no affiliation' then it can't distinguish between us and, you know, people with no affiliation. Not going to keep us safe or anything, but I like the idea of giving them headaches."

"I...see," I said, though I didn't. "So...."

"So, what do we do?" Jayla finished for me. "Well, like I said when we met, we fight for the persecuted, the discriminated, the impoverished, the vulnerable, the abused. For them and against those doing the persecution, the ones who created and uphold the systems that keep vast subsets of humanity under the heel of the rich and powerful. Only, we don't do it through voter registrations and raising 'awareness.' We're, well...."

"We're domestic terrorists, Love," Tavish laughed.

"That's what they *call us," Jayla retorted.*

"I'm reclaiming it," Tavish shrugged.

"We do what needs to be done," Bob said.

"And we make great friends along the way!" Syn added, smiling like a crocodile.

"The system was designed to be oppressive, Lyra," Jayla said. "The political 'good guys' don't want to help the suffering any more than the 'bad guys'

do, they're just better at knowing all the right grunts and frowns. Systems of oppression won't save us from themselves. We have to do it ourselves or no one will. So...that's the macro-view, I guess. Bet you're wondering about those blue-shirts, though, right?"

"Yes. The...Hounds?"

"Stupid fucker name," Clover rolled their eyes. "Russell Hausman and his 'haus' bullshit. Dude is lucky he wasn't named Cochran. Hound, like the protectors of the 'haus,' get it?"

"I do, though I feel it may not be worth getting."

"It's not," Jayla confirmed. "I don't know how much you know about Safe-Haus, but the happy little security apps? The browser that's probably on your friend Ezri's phone? The cute dog mascot? The humanitarian bullshit? It's all to distract from Hausman's real money-makers: his military and private prison contracts."

"The Hounds are part of that," Bob said. "Private security contractors. Been spotted in Iraq, Afghanistan, Palestine, Yemen, Venezuela, all the biggies."

"Also at every major protest in the United States for the last five years," Jayla added. "They have a real knack for making people disappear. Which brings me to our current operation and how we got all of their beady little eyes on us. Here, check it."

She turned her phone around, showing me a website bedecked in rainbows. A large image of a very modern building with a dove flying under yet another rainbow on its front door dominated the screen.

"Agape's Rainbow?" I asked, reading the top of the page.

"It's a shelter and religious center for LGBT youth," Jayla said. "Very respected in town, a real example of good Christians standing up to help queer youth in defiance of the bigotry that has come to be associated with their religion."

"That...sounds nice?"

"It does, doesn't it? Only, that's all bullshit. It's a goddamn conversion therapy roach motel."

"I...don't know what conversion therapy is."

"It's using Jesus and emotional torture to try to make someone think they're not queer," Syn said. "It's toxic, abusive, and utter bullshit, but don't worry, in this state, it's illegal."

She and Clover threw their heads back and laughed like hyenas.

"All that law did was make them be more subtle," Clover said.

"The stealthy conversion shit was enough to put them on our radar," Jayla said. "Then we discovered something even more fucked up. Got them our undivided attention. See, Agape's Rainbow has a partnership with SafeHaus. Hausman plays it up in the media, because Seattle is a liberal city and helping

queer youth is good PR. The place is well respected, even by other queer groups who don't bother doing their research like we do. Part of that partnership is an internship program that Agape residents can be selected for. They get job training, room and board, even a stipend. Sounds nice, huh?"

"I am going to assume that, once again, it is actually not."

"Ding ding ding," Jayla said. "See, here's the thing: once they leave for the internships, no one ever hears from them again. At all. And another thing we discovered is that, weirdly, only the residents who aren't swayed by the conversion therapy seem to ever be selected. Then, poof! Into thin air."

"That's...that's awful. But their families, don't they—?"

"Lyra, these kids don't have families," Bob said, somberly. "Not real ones. Most of their families booted them out the second they discovered they were queer."

"If they knew what happened, they'd probably be thrilled," Syn muttered. "Mine would be."

"So they're...they're preying on people they know are alone and afraid?" I said, feeling the same fire I'd felt in the alley begin rekindling in my chest. "For...for what?"

"Human Trafficking? Slave labor? Organ farming? We don't know, Lyra," Jayla said. "But while trying to figure that out, we got sloppy and accidentally tipped off Hausman's goons to our existence."

"And since they're willing to frag us all because of it, I doubt they're taking them out for ice cream," Bob said.

I was back, back in that bright red place. I could feel my claws trying to harden. I wanted to reach back in time and disembowel the stupid, naive, arrogant, sanctimonious version of me I'd been when I lectured Elodie about non-violence. I had thousands of years on her, but the vastness of what she had known that I had not could have filled galaxies.

"May I see that again?" I asked, gesturing at Jayla's phone. She showed me Agape's Rainbow's website once more, its rainbows seeming blasphemous this time. I scrolled down to where the address was and memorized it. I knew Seattle well, I'd walked and flown it over and over again since I'd arrived. I could find this place. And then I could leave no place left to find.

"I will return," I said, standing and manifesting my wings as I walked toward the door.

"Um..." Clover said.

"Uh, Lyra?" Bob objected as I walked past him.

"Oh, fuck," Syn muttered.

"Hey! Wait up! Lyra!" Jayla called after me. "Lyra, what are you thinking? Come on, talk to me."

"I can fix this," I called back, not turning around.

"Oh, oh, you can fix this? Well, geez, why didn't we think of that?"

"I can do things you can't," I said, unlocking the front door of whatever dead store our new shelter had once been. "I can stop them. I can end them."

"You can end them, huh?"

"You've seen what I can do!"

"Yeah, I have. Lyra," Jayla said, through her teeth, grabbing onto my shoulder. "After what we've been through, like I said, I consider you family. More than that, I consider you a friend. May I say something, as a friend?"

"What?" I snapped. The rage was an inferno inside me. My eyes were illuminated blue, my claws extended. People were suffering—people were being hurt by other, awful, vindictive, hateful people. And I could stop it. I could use the gifts of my nature to put an end to the oppressors and—

"Okay, well, as a friend," she said, looking me in the eyes, "sit your motherfucking unbearably white ass down and listen for one goddamn minute!"

I was in full effect, wings, eyes, claws, fangs. Law men, murderers, and mercenaries had all trembled before this form. She had seen what I could do. She knew what I was.

And yet I had never seen a human being less afraid.

"They're hurting them!" I objected.

"Do you not think I know that?" Jayla yelled back. "How do you think this fucking house of horrors came to our attention? My brother went there, Lyra! He's trans and he was lost and scared and we'd had a fight, so he went there. He went there, and he's a bullheaded asshole, just like his sister, so he told that deranged pastor to fuck off with his god and—hey, whatdya know—suddenly he's a perfect candidate for the SafeHaus internship, and then he's fucking gone. You think you could ever feel a fraction of the abject hatred I feel for these people, Lyra? You think it never occurred to me to march my ass down there and light them all up? I don't have claws and wings, but I got guns. Lots of them. Do you truly think this is an original thought you're having?"

"I—"

"You are white as fuck is what you are," she sighed. "And yeah, I know you made this body for yourself, but you sure picked the right color for you. Rushing in here like you've got all the answers. You told us you aren't an angel, I'm telling you you sure ain't a savior either. But sure, go ahead, go kill that asshole who runs that place. Hell, blow the whole building up! Quick question, how you going to keep them from rebuilding it? Bigot Pastors are a dime a dozen, and Russell Hausman has, rounded to the nearest billion, all-the-money. Buildings are what he buys with his pocket change. So, what? Kill him, too? Great! Go ahead, I won't cry! But oh, wait, another question: How far are you willing to

go? Because I saw you when you took that bullet. It hurt you. I know you're big and bad, but I don't think you're invincible. So how far do you get into this killing spree before they bring you down and then show up here and paint the walls with all of our brains? Oh, and of course then show up at about a dozen other activist organizations along with the actual cops because you just declared war on all our behalf? Oh, yeah, and what about all those kids in that bastard's church now? Gonna be like, 'good news! I saved you! You get to be homeless again! You're welcome!' Big fucking question, Lyra: Do you want to help people, or do you just want vengeance?"

I stared at her with my eyes still burning, the anger in my heart scalding my insides. I hated her in that moment. I hated that every word she said was true, and I hated that I couldn't make them be untrue. I was a child of the outer darkness, a being of forged anima, fury and violence incarnate, and yet I felt as powerless as a newborn left in the desert.

"Well?"

I looked into her eyes. There was anger there. Fury. Maybe disgust. But no malice. My eyes dimmed and my wings and claws retreated.

"I want to help people," I whispered.

"Good," Jayla said, her face still hard but her voice softer. "Then sit down and listen, and we'll see about getting you some of the other thing, too."

"Okay, so, bear with me," Jayla said as we sat opposite each other on a series of crates that were much less comfortable than the couches and chairs at our last safe house. "I was coming up with a lot of this plan while you were still unconscious, so I'm having to incorporate new information on the fly."

"You were making plans while I was unconscious?" I asked, looking around the circle at the rest of No Affiliation.

"We're always making plans, Love," Tavish shrugged. "Just kinda how we have to live."

"Of course these particular plans hinged on you not waking up and immediately sucking the marrow from our bones," Syn said.

"Syn!" Clover snapped.

"What? I thought we were all being honest with each other?"

"Children!" Jayla groaned. "Adults are talking. But, yeah, Lyra. We were making plans. Because, like Tavish said, we kinda have to. And I'm going to

be honest, we need a new plan now more than ever. Because we're hitting a wall, Lyra. Agape's Rainbow has the kind of firewall you usually see protecting NORAD, and so does Pastor Benjamin Holmes' private residence. We can't get in. We've interviewed a few former residents, but the ones who would talk didn't know much."

"And that's how we fucked up," Bob added. "The kids who come out of there come out brainwashed. One of them ratted on us."

"We've tried a handful of other tricks, too, but nothing has panned out," Jayla sighed. "And meanwhile, while we're sitting around figuring out fuck-all, more kids are disappearing."

"It has been five so far," Clover said. "That we can confirm."

"My brother Lincoln was the first," Jayla said. "I'm disgusted with myself that he wasn't the last. We've tossed around the idea of having someone infiltrate the center, but we didn't have anyone the right age who we'd trust and, well, none of us look like teenagers."

"Hey!" Syn objected. "They take up to twenty-one and I'm only twenty-two! I still get carded!"

"Yes, Syn, but there's so little chance of you not getting kicked out within the first five minutes that we may as well try sending Tavish," Jayla said, rolling her eyes.

"Ow!" Syn snapped. "Just because it's true doesn't mean it doesn't hurt!"

"Anyway," Jayla groaned again, "while I now know that you are older than everyone in this room and the planet we're standing on, when I first met you I put you at twenty, tops."

"So...you want me to infiltrate this place?" I asked.

"Yes, but that's not it," Jayla said. "Bob, computer."

"How about 'Bob, please get the computer'?" Bob grumbled as he opened his laptop and faced it toward me, displaying a photo of a white man with sandy brown hair and a broad smile who looked to be in his mid-forties. Behind him was a large backdrop with a white cross under a rainbow.

"Meet Pastor Benjamin Holmes," Jayla said, ignoring Bob. "Lead Pastor at Agape Ministries, beloved local minor celebrity, founder of Agape's Rainbow. Pastor Ben, as he likes to be called—never Pastor Holmes, or Ben—is a transplant from Spokane where he had his own church for several years before having to resign due to a minor scandal involving these three...."

Jayla reached over and double-clicked on an image file that opened and displayed a photo of three women huddled together, all of them smiling. On the left was a tall, medium-skinned woman with bright blue hair, on the right a ghostly pale blond with an enchantingly crooked smile, and in the center was a dark-haired woman whose eyes were brimming with joy.

"Specifically, the woman in the center," Jayla said. "That's Lia no-longer-Holmes. Inexplicably, she was married to Pastor Ben for several years before having a teeny-tiny awakening and leaving him to go be in a polycule with these two."

"They...they all look so happy," I said, absently as I looked at the three women.

"Oh, they were adorable together," Clover said. "They had a YouTube show. Realm of Hauntings. You should check it out, it's a lot of fun."

"The blonde one's my favorite," Syn added. "Because...well, look at her."

"Anyway," Jayla said, "after that happened, Pastor Ben tailspun for a while, especially after Lia passed away."

"Oh," I said, being hit harder than I expected by the news that someone I'd never known beyond a single picture had died. "She—"

"Cancer," Jayla sighed. "Just like my mom. But here's the thing: About that time, Pastor Ben resurfaced. Started blaming Lia's death on her sinful lifestyle."

"Please," Syn laughed. "If being railed by two hotties gave you cancer, I'd have been dead years ago."

She held out a hand for Clover to high-five, which they did with great enthusiasm.

"He pedaled his story on some Christian websites, but was still laying low in the three-dimensional world up until about three years ago when he reappeared in Seattle with a bunch of mysterious seed money for a new church and his not-conversion-but-yeah-conversion center," Jayla said. "Which is a story in itself, but here's the thing: we discovered that, during his time off the radar, Pastor Ben was having a mini crisis of faith."

"We found some burner accounts on various websites we were able to trace back to him," Tavish interjected. "Not atheist sites or anything, but like...the opposite of that."

"Sites for people looking for miracles," Jayla said. "More specifically, looking for signs."

"Signs?" I asked.

"Words from the deceased," Bob said. "Messages from God."

"Angels," Clover added.

"Yeah, that," Jayla said. "That was his focus. He became obsessed with the idea of being visited by a 'holy messenger' who could 'tell him his purpose in life.'"

"Dude was all fucked up," Clover said. "Guess that's what happens when Jesus doesn't keep your wife from leaving you for two women."

"So, I'm guessing you can see where we're going with this," Jayla said.

"You want me to infiltrate Agape's Rainbow and pretend to be an angel," I said. "Yes."

"Yes?"

"Yes, I'll do it," I said.

"You…you don't want to think about it?" Jayla asked, raising an eyebrow.

"This man is doing something that is making vulnerable people disappear," I said. "I repeat: Yes, I'll do it."

"Lyra, it's going to be rough in there," Bob said. "Like, psychological torture rough. I appreciate the enthusiasm, but…but we just want you to know what you're in for."

"There is nothing that small, pathetic man can do that can match what I've already endured."

"Well, that I believe," Jayla said. "I want to be clear, though, the angel thing is a…pardon the term, Hail Mary. Hopefully you can just infiltrate and find what we need to know as, you know…the way you look now. But, if that doesn't work…."

"If that doesn't work, then you will have another weapon in your arsenal," I said, standing and walking over to where Jayla was pacing. "I understand, Jayla. And I know it won't be easy. But…let me do this. Please. In Rook Lake, I failed. I failed hard, and a lot of people lost their lives. I…I know it won't make up for that, but I just…."

"I get you," Jayla said. "And okay. But we're going to have a whole lot of training for you first, and even more safety nets. And if at any point you want out—"

"I won't."

"Yeah, I know," Jayla sighed.

"Um, I have a question," Syn said, raising her hand like a child in a classroom.

"An on-topic question or a deeply inappropriate one?" Jayla asked, glaring over at her.

"On-topic. And ouch!"

"Okay, go," Jayla shrugged.

"Okay, so, you talked about how Elodie tore the memories out of Ezri," Syn said, stretching to her feet as she spoke "What's to stop you from just, you know…."

She extended her arm and placed her palm against my forehead, making a vaguely electric sound with her mouth while her body shook.

"You're asking if I could take Pastor Ben's memories?"

"Yeah, that," Syn nodded, and then looked over at Jayla. "On-topic enough for you?"

"Actually, yes," Jayla said. "Well done. So...?"

I took a deep breath, and the memory of rebuilding my wing haunted my thoughts.

"Yes," I said, finally. "But please don't ask me to."

"Why not?" Bob asked.

"They don't have to do anything they don't want to!" Jayla snapped. "But...if you'd be willing to explain...."

"So, it's not as simple as Elodie or I thought it would be," I said, looking out at all the eyes fixated on me. "Anima doesn't...stay put. It takes on qualities of other anima it's mingled with. A small thing like healing a wound won't matter much, but something like taking someone's memories...."

I looked back over at the computer, where, behind the photo of the three women, Pastor Ben's smiling face peered out at me.

"I don't want part of that man to become part of me," I said, tears welling in my eyes at the thought. "Please. I...I know it could work, and if I have to—"

"No," Jayla said, putting a hand on both of my shoulders. "Hell no."

"Fuck no," Bob said.

"Seconding that fuck no," Syn added.

"Thirding," Clover said.

"And it's unanimous," Tavish said.

"We'd never ask that," Jayla said. "That man is vile beyond what you can imagine, and no one deserves him in their head. That's not how we're going to do this."

The rest of the group clamored in agreement, leading to Jayla giving a more exhaustive version of her plan while the others chimed in throughout, adding their input whenever their area of expertise came up. My eyes kept drifting back to Pastor Ben, looking out from behind the photo of his ex-wife and her partners.

I hadn't met him yet, and all I knew was what I'd been told, but I'd never, ever been so certain that I hated someone.

And soon, he would hate me, too.

Pastor Ben hadn't emerged from his office after his phone call with Ms. Emerson, which made it all the easier to slap the "Out to Lunch" sign on my desk and retreat to the alley behind the center, where no one but me ever came. Despite this last fact, I reached out with my anima as I made it to my usual phone call spot, confirming that, aside from a few pigeons and a seagull, I was alone.

I pulled my phone out of my pocket and checked my texts. I had three messages. The first was from Syn and simply said "You :)" over a cartoon woman dressed in a red trench coat and matching fedora. I had no context for who the cartoon woman was, so I sent back the "smiling while sweating" emoji that had become my generic response to most of the inexplicable things Syn sent me.

The second message was from Bob and was actually two messages. The first said "pics?" and was followed by another that said, "Shit, that sounds creepy. You know what I meant." To which I responded, "Soon."

The third was the one from Jayla, which I'd already responded to.

Her number rang five times and then picked up to dead air.

"What is dark within me, illumine," I said into the silence.

"Hey, Celestial Hottie," Jayla responded.

"I continue to request a new callsign," I grumbled at the moniker Syn and Clover had bestowed upon me.

"And I continue to inform you that you may have one as soon as you come up with one for yourself," Jayla—who was Boomslang on calls—laughed while I cursed my deficient creative abilities.

"Anyway, I have some news," she continued. "You're alone, right?"

"Yes," I said, pulsing my anima outward one more time, just to make sure.

"Good," she said. "So, Deadhead grabbed the flash drive from the drop point this morning. Thanks for getting it out there so goddamn early."

The last three words were yelled with her lips facing away from the phone.

"Paranoia saves lives," Tavish yelled back, somewhere in the distance.

"Anyway," Jayla said, "it's a goddamn treasure trove. Pious motherfucker never deleted anything. And I mean *anything*."

"Anything in there about the interns? Or the program?"

"Nothing useful. Some emails back and forth between the pastor and Russell Hausman's assistant—"

"Ms. Emerson?"

"A bit formal, but yeah, Cora Emerson," Jayla said. "Been doing some research of your own on Daddy Warbucks?"

"No, she just—she and Pastor Ben just had a phone call."

"Oh really," Jayla said. "Shit. You find anything out?"

"No," I said, my mouth dry. "I don't think Pastor Ben actually knows what's going on with the internship, either. Or at least he doesn't know everything."

"You think he knows *something*?"

"Yes," I said. "And he's being very, very secretive about it. He told me to stop asking."

"He did what? Shit, aren't you an angel of the Lord?"

"Yes," I sighed. "But I am not the Lord himself. And...and I think that Cora Emerson knows about me."

"Wait, what?" Jayla snapped. "Shit, okay, do we need to extract you?"

"No!" I gasped, not intending to. "No. I...when I say that I think Cora knows about me, I mean that I believe Pastor Ben has told her that he is in the presence of a holy angel. I'm not sure that he has gone further than that, or that she knows that said angel is me, specifically."

"And she, like...just rolled with that?" Jayla asked. "I'm wondering because Cora Emerson is on the record in several interviews as being slightly more atheist than Christopher Hitchens. Which could be bullshit, sure, but she doesn't strike me as just being cool with one of her subordinates babbling about angels unless she had some reason to believe he's actually telling the truth. Fuck. I don't know what this means, but it worries me. Are you sure you don't want out of there? I know you want to help, but—"

"No," I said again, my voice steadier this time. "I need to stay."

"Ly—Celestial, I'm sure it has occurred to you that if Cora Emerson knows about you, there's a chance she knows about, you know, everything. You said her boss was in Rook Lake. I don't know if that's connected or not, but I don't want you in danger if—"

"I need to stay," I repeated.

There was a long pause.

"You have someone there you care about, huh?" Jayla said. "Like, not just in a generic way."

"I have seven people here I care about," I answered. "But yes, one in particular who is...very dear to me, and who will be leaving for her internship on Monday."

"Oh, oh fuck," Jayla said. "Okay, yeah, you need to stay. We'll try to speed up going through these records. Like I was saying, everything between the pastor and Emerson is all innocuous shit. At least so far. Deadhead is still digging, and we'll all start helping to get through it faster. Meanwhile, what we *have* found is every piece of financial data for the church since its founding. Dumbass pastor got some fancy military-grade firewall from his corporate overlords and started thinking he was invincible. If we can time this like we're trying to time it, we can have everything go down before a credit card or bank statement comes his way. You're still handling all the emails, right?"

"Correct."

"Good, because you're going to start seeing some payments made and some transfers being initiated. Probably some new subscription notifications, too. You feel me?"

"I do."

"You've been awesome, CH," Jayla said. "We started you on hard-mode, but you've kicked ass in a major way. But...how are you doing? I know this has to be a lot. Like, just being there has to be a psychic bomb."

"I'm okay," I lied.

"Come on. The truth will set you free. Go ahead, I've got spoons for a good long venting."

"I—" I almost lied again, but what purpose would that serve?

"I'm not doing well," I said, not expecting my voice to tremble as much as it did. "This place is...grotesque. It's like a mockery of something that could be pure and beautiful, a place where people cast out by society and their families could come and grow and discover themselves. But it's...*this*. It's all lies, pretty lies wrapped in spirituality, taking advantage of kids! And they're good kids! I wasn't lying before, I care about all of them and I just want them to have a chance to be the people they're meant to be and love who they love and—and why the fuck is that so fucking offensive to these people?"

"You picked a great time for your first f-bombs, CH," Jayla said. "I wish I had answers. I mean, I do: Greed, sanctimony, homophobia, lack of empathy, lack of humanity, compulsion toward conformity, capitalism...all the greatest hits, sure. But if you're looking for an answer that will make any sense out of this steaming pile of shit, I'm sorry."

I didn't know what more to say, so I just sat silent on the line, feeling very alone.

"Hey, so...we miss the hell out of you here," Jayla said. "Like, I know that may be weird since you weren't here that long before we sent you out on this mission, but we all miss you. Even Black Mr. Wizard, who still insists we call him that."

"Don't be mad that I have the best callsign," Bob yelled back in the distance.

"Anyway, Stabby and One-Zero have decorated your corner of the safe-house to the point where it may literally be the gayest thing in the known universe," Jayla continued. "Deadhead is bursting at the damn seams with pride over how fast you took to technology—"

"They're a goddamn prodigy!" Tavish yelled.

"What he said," Jayla laughed. "And I...I miss our talks. So...you able to sneak away tonight?"

"Yes." I said, without pause.

"Cool. Meet me at the place around eleven. That work?"

"Yes." I said, trying not to betray the enthusiasm that was making me feel like a pot left on boil for too long. "Yes, absolutely."

"I'll see you then, Celestial Hottie. Oh! Black Mr. Wizard wanted me to remind you about—"

"The photos. I'll get them before tonight."

"Great. Take care, and I'll see you at eleven. Peace."

The phone hung up and for the first time since I came to Agape's Rainbow, I felt joy brimming up inside me. Nothing had gotten better, not really. In fact, things were worse than they ever had been. But tonight, tonight I was going to get to put it all behind me for a few hours. Tonight I was going to see a friend.

I still had one last thing to do, though.

I crept back inside. There was no rule against me being out in the alley, but I didn't want to invite either questions or suspicions. Thankfully, the hallway was empty. I darted down it, around the corner to the large metal door labeled "Maintenance: No Admittance."

Fortunately, my stolen key could not read.

The maintenance room was dank and dim, even with the lights flipped on after I closed the door. The hum of the heating system and the trickle of the plumbing competed for dominance. Sliding my phone from my pocket once again, I switched on the camera and took almost fifty photos of the furnace, the pipes, the fuse box, the wiring...

...and the fire-suppression system.

Behold

The Guardian

"So…so now you know."

"Heh, 'now' I know," I laughed, trying to keep my smile warm so it didn't seem mean. "I think I've known longer than you have."

"Well shit, Jayla, could have told me or something," my brother laughed next to me, still shivering under the blanket I'd wrapped him in. Michael and Sarah, whom I refused to call mom and dad, had literally tossed him out their front door with a light jacket, his school backpack, and a string of slurs. Just like they'd done with me five years prior, except at least with me it was late April, not mid-December. To their thinking, they'd picked us up from the trash, they could throw us away, too.

Offend a white savior's sensibilities too many times and you'll realize they're only one of those things. They *never will, though.*

"Thought about it," I nodded, handing him a cup of hot chocolate. "Probably should have. I dunno, couldn't come up with anything other than, 'Hey, so…you know you're a dude, right?' Didn't seem like it would land."

"Might have," he shrugged. "Thanks for answering the door."

I was just glad I had a door to answer. No Affiliation had a few safe-houses back then, but we weren't to the point of hiding in dead phone stores yet. I was still living in a shitty apartment that I was probably not going to be able to afford soon on my bartender salary plus tips. It was roughly ten miles from the only 'home' the two of us had known growing up, though the psychological distance could only be measured in lightyears.

They hadn't let him grab his wallet with his bus pass in it. He'd walked.

"Always, kid," I said, leaning over and kissing his forehead, like I'd been doing since childhood. "I don't stop being your big sister just because you're my little brother now. What do I call you, anyway? Name-wise."

"Um, well, I haven't really decided," he stammered, looking away from me and down into his cocoa. Which I knew meant he had absolutely decided but thought whatever he'd picked was stupid. "But I was…um…see, I was thinking…."

"Spit it out, Bro," I ordered.

"I was thinking about Link!" he blurted, suddenly looking like a deer in the headlights. And in that moment he was eight again, getting caught by our adoptive 'parents' sneaking out of his room to watch Adult Swim. *But this time I wasn't the one stepping between him and the big, scary adults. This time I was the big, scary adult, just by virtue of being someone who lived outside of his head.*

"That was the first time you said that out loud, wasn't it?" I asked, feeling myself tearing up. My brother.

"Y-Yeah."

"It's a good name," I said, leaning over and hugging him. "Like, short for Lincoln?"

"Naw," he said, shaking his head. "Like, um...well...remember when we were kids and they gave us Da—Michael's old Nintendo? I—"

"Like the videogame character?" I laughed. "Oh thank God! I wanted to be nice, but if you're going to name yourself after a white man, at least make it a magical one. We gotta replay those games now."

"If you can find a working NES, I'm down," Link laughed.

"Pfft, I got a guy," I said, waving him off. If I'd texted him at that moment, Tavish probably could have had me a NES with controllers, light-gun, and that stupid little robot within the hour.

"So, um...so you're really cool with all this?" Link asked.

"Link..." I said as my heart broke a little. "Yeah. Yeah of course I am. I'm...I'm sorry you ever thought I wouldn't be."

"I'm sorry," he said, looking away. "I know it's stupid, and you're, like, bi and shit, but—"

"Yeah, but even if I wasn't, you're my brother," I said, putting a hand on his back. "That doesn't go away. It's been you and me from the beginning, it's gonna be you and me until the end."

"I know," Link nodded. "It's just...."

"It's just that that's what Michael and Sarah said, too," I snorted. "Family until the end. More like family until they got sick of their fucking Diff'rent Strokes *LARP. I ain't Michael and Sarah, Link. You were too small to remember but...but do you know what the worst three months of my life were?"*

"N-No?"

"I think you were like two, which made me like eight," I said, holding back my tears and taking a deep breath. "Which means mom—actual mom—had been gone a year and we'd been in the system just a long. Fucking social workers were starting to give up on the idea of placing us together. Everyone wanted you, because you were just a cute little lump, but I was a surly little bitch going

through complex trauma with zero support. So they...they placed us with two different families."

"Jesus, Jay, I...I don't remember any of that," Link said as tears I couldn't stop rolled down my face.

"Well, like I said, you were two and you'd also gone through trauma you probably couldn't process even as well as I did," I shrugged. "You got placed with Michael and Sarah, too, so there was no second transition for you. I was placed with this creepy ass Christian couple. Like, not Michael and Sarah's kind of Christian, like the 'we don't celebrate Christmas' kind of Christian. And for the first month I was an absolute terror. I think I tore a Bible in half."

"You tore a Bible in half?" Link laughed.

"Well, down the spine," I laughed back. "In my mind, they'd taken my brother away, and if I could get them to toss me out, I'd get to see you again. That's how my kid-brain worked, at least. Screamed for you constantly. I didn't know anything could hurt as much as losing you. It...it hurt more than when we lost Mom. I kept having this nightmare that I was running through the streets yelling your name, and I could hear you yelling mine back, but you were getting quieter and quieter no matter what direction I ran, and—anyway. The next month I tried doing the opposite. I tried being sweet as pie, following all their stupid rules, saying all their stupid little prayers. I thought maybe I could earn being placed back with you. Nope, they just bought me uglier and uglier dresses as 'rewards.' Real ugly shit, you'd hoot and howl."

"I guarantee you I would," Link said with the million-dollar smile that always got him out of trouble. "So, what did it? What finally got you out of there?"

I looked at him for a long time without answering. But he was my brother.

"Sometimes my foster mom would go to women's Bible study, and my foster father would take care of me, because he was an involved dad, you see. Well...you know how I have trouble trusting men?"

Link's face slowly fell.

"Jesus, Jay, I...I didn't know! Fuck, I'm so sorry. I—"

"This ain't the time for that," I said, holding up a hand to stop him. "I'm not going to shit on your parade."

"My parade?" Link asked, shooting me a deeply incredulous look from within his blanket-nest. "Jay...."

"This day sucked hard, and fuck Michael and Sarah, and fuck the December cold, and fuck the foster system," I interrupted. "But today you claimed yourself. You took a name and said 'this belongs to me.' And today, I got a brother. Officially. And that's what I was getting at. Ask me what the most traumatizing part of the foster system was for me, and even with all the other horrors I had

to go through, it was being forced away from you for three months. You and I have had our fights and our rough times, and I'm sure we'll have some more. But there is not a thing you could be or do that would make me not open that door."

Link's face quivered for a second before he launched himself out of his blanket and pulled me into the fiercest hug we had ever shared.

"I love you, Jay," he sobbed into my shoulder.

"I love you, too, Link," I said, gently stroking his hair and noticing a familiar gold chain around his neck. "I'm glad you grabbed mom's necklace."

"What? Oh," Link said, moving his head from my shoulder. "I mean, I never take it off, so...."

He reached under his collar and pulled up the little gold angel pendant that our mother had worn every day of her life, one of only a handful of her personal effects that had made their way to us after she died.

"Glad you still got your guardian angel," I smiled, wiping away some of my own tears.

"Yeah," Link, said, looking at the little pendant between his fingers. "I mean, maybe."

"Maybe?"

"Yeah, like...okay, I know you don't believe in...anything...anymore," he said, looking away. "But, like, I know what God says about...about people like me, and—"

"Sir," I said, putting a hand on each of his shoulders and moving so I could look him in the eyes. "Michael and Sarah are not God. That shitty church they took us to isn't God, either. And yeah, while I do believe in plenty of things, God is no longer one of them. But if I'm wrong for the first time ever, then he made you like this, so he can't really get mad at you for being the way you are. And if you really do have a guardian angel beyond the one around your neck, then she's been with you your whole life and probably knew what was what before even I did."

I paused.

"She? I forget, is your angel a she?"

"I could never tell," Link said, examining the pendant. "Like...it has long hair, but so does Jesus, so...maybe it's supposed to be a he?"

"Oh, suddenly you respect 'supposed to be' when it comes to gender?" I laughed, getting one out of him, too.

"Okay, fine: My angel is nonbinary now," Link laughed. "I'm being watched over by a they/them angel."

This time he paused.

"Huh. Okay, so, I started this as a joke, but that's actually kinda comforting."

"Makes sense," I nodded. "I mean, shit, even back when I believed, I never thought you and I would get the boring angels."

"Oh for sure, they were always going to give us the gayest angels," Link laughed. "Gayngels?"

It was a stupid ass joke, but we both laughed ourselves to the point of almost blacking out. When we finally regained our composure, we started talking like we always had, about every little thing and nothing of meaning all at the same time. I offered to connect him with some trans friends of mine so they could all talk shit about cis people without worrying about offending me. He asked if we could set up a little Christmas tree, which I acquiesced to. At around one in the morning, he fell dead asleep mid-sentence while telling me about some graphic novel he was obsessing over. I brought a pillow and a second blanket from my room and gently laid him down on the couch, tucking him in just like when we were kids.

I would always be his big sister.

IV

Hymn of Pride Unfallen

June 30th went from the loudest day I had experienced at Agape's Rainbow to the quietest in a handful of seconds. Being both a Sunday and the day of Seattle's Pride festival, the whole building was abuzz with anticipation, the residents all waking up around five in the morning to start getting ready, drawing the ire of the overnight staff, who were used to a quieter end to their shifts. Pastor Ben arrived around six to practice his sermon in the chapel, where he would not be presenting it later. On Pride Festival Sundays, Pastor Ben held an 'inclusive, welcoming, affirming, non-denominational Christian service' at Seattle Center, amid the revelers, vendors, and corporate sponsors.

I mostly stayed in my room. I had already endured a battery of questions from the residents as to why I would not be attending the festival, and my answer that, while I appreciated the message of the celebration, the combination of giant crowds, loud noises, and late June sun sounded overwhelming to me received responses that ranged from "c'mon!" (Toby) to a whispered "my friends can get you something that will make you not even know there are other people there" (Nova). I declined. Pastor Ben, on the other hand, took me aside later and, unprompted, told me that he fully understood why I would not want to be present at 'an event like that,' which was actually the closest I came to changing my mind until I remembered that choices made for spite rarely pan out well.

I heard the other residents leaving at about nine in a cacophonous mass, led by Pastor Ben and the center's staff, who would be manning Agape's booth at the festival and handing out free lanyards and pins with our logo. I didn't go out to see them off, afraid of having to fend off last minute pleas to join them, but instead watched from my window as they all climbed into the church's fourteen-passenger van. There was a joy pouring off of them that I both admired and envied. Nova led the group, her hair spiked up and freshly dyed a brilliant purple that almost matched mine, dressed in a patch-covered battle jacket, a rainbow scarf, and a kilt with alternating pink, white, and blue pleats. Ren followed behind her, wearing their usual cargo shorts and sandals but with a rainbow tye-dyed t-shirt with "First Pride!" printed on it. Lenora and Saeed were laughing together as they boarded the bus, which was something I couldn't remember ever seeing the two of them do, Saeed with his hair gelled and slicked back into a shell-like pompadour and wearing a rainbow-printed keffiyeh, Lenora dressed in a black t-shirt that said "Proud but not into rainbows" in white letters. Toby came next, wearing an exceptionally bright rainbow tuxedo that he'd found at a thrift store and, despite it being at least a size too small for him, he insisted on buying. And Abby...

...wasn't there.

I craned my neck to see if I had missed her in the mass of residents and staff, but realized that neon-pink hair would be relatively hard to not see. I pulled out my phone and texted Lenora asking if Abby was with them, getting a response that she was not, due to waking up not feeling well, followed by three sad-faced emoji and one that indicated vomiting.

There were many uses of anima which I would consider unethical to perform upon someone without their knowledge. But I remembered how excited Abby had been for the past month about attending Pride, and I couldn't think of anything unethical about soothing an upset stomach. The festival went on into the night and wasn't far, she could easily take a bus and still enjoy most of it with her friends.

Leaving my room for the first time that morning, I headed into the kitchen and used one of the keys Pastor Ben had trusted me with to open the medicine cabinet, producing a bottle of Pepto Bismol that would make a good cover for some light anima healing.

It took three knocks on the door before she answered.

"Hey, Lyra," Abby said, significantly less enthusiastic than usual, her hair in disarray and her eyes red, wearing an oversized gray hoodie and sleep shorts.

"Hi, Abby," I said, holding up the pink bottle. "Lenora let me know that you hadn't been feeling well, and—"

"That's really sweet," she said, her lips pressing into a weak smile. "God, that's so—"

Suddenly she broke into tears, turning away from me and hastily pulling her hood over her head.

"Abby? Are you—?"

"I'm...I'm sorry," she blurted. "I'm sorry, but...but can you go? I just need to be alone right now. I'm sorry. You're really sweet but I need to be alone."

"Oh," I said, unprepared for how hard that hit the center of my chest. "Of...Of course. I'm sorry. I'll be next door if you...I'm sorry."

I took a step back and pulled the door closed, feeling my face flush and wishing that I, too, had a hoodie to retreat into. Instead, I just settled for rushing back into my room and flopping down on my bed, curling up into a small ball while feeling deeply foolish. There was nothing wrong with Abby needing time alone. I knew that. She did not owe me her time. I also knew that. I was a nigh-immortal being forged of pure life force who should be beyond being hurt because my friend didn't want to see me. I knew that, too. And yet, there I was, fighting back tears of my own. Maybe it was because I felt sad that I wasn't going with the others to Pride. Maybe it was because I'd once again had a stupid, half-cooked plan to make everything 'better' that blew up in my face. Or maybe it was just because my friend was hurting, and I couldn't help her.

I reached out my anima and tried to find Athena, thinking it might be nice to fly with her over the parade and at least see it from the air. Unfortunately, my avian friend had also departed for parts unknown, probably fishing in the Sound or trying to get away from the street noise. I thought about trying to do some recon in Pastor Ben's office. It would have been the perfect day for it, none of the staff being on the premises and the only other resident confining herself to her room, but I'd already done all that I knew to do, and I doubted I'd find anything I hadn't already uncovered. So I just laid there, alternating between staring into space and feeling sorry for myself.

At about ten-thirty, I was jarred out of my trance by a light tapping on my door. I jumped out of bed and stumbled over, opening the door and finding Abby standing there.

"Hi," she said, barely above a whisper, looking at me for a second and then darting her eyes away. She was still wearing her hoodie but had brushed her hair and her eyes had faded from a harsh red to a soft pink.

"Hi," I said, not knowing what else to say.

"I'm...I'm really sorry about before."

"You don't need to be sorry. You did nothing wrong."

"I...I know, but I didn't have to snap at you," she said. "You were being really sweet, and...I just wanted to make sure that, you know, we're okay. Your friendship means a lot to me, and I...I wouldn't want to mess it up by being a bitch because I'm having a hard morning."

I was, again, taken aback by Abby, who had just used the harshest word I'd heard her utter since she came to the center.

"I forgive you," I said. "I was never mad, but I forgive you. I'm sorry I interrupted your alone time. And that you're having a hard morning."

"It's okay," Abby said, shrugging. "On both counts. I don't...I don't really want to talk about it. But...could we just, like, hang out for a while? If that's okay! You can say no. I know you probably have work to do or...."

"My tasks today have involved laying in my bed, staring at that wall, and then turning over and staring at that other wall."

"Oh, wow, second wall? You've been way more productive than I have," Abby said, with the ghost of a smile. "Show off."

"I would love to hang out," I said, feeling myself smile. "Did you want to watch something...?"

"You know, not today," she said. "Actually, could we...could we just have some coffee and talk? I feel like it has been a minute since we got to just chat."

"Of course," I said, wishing I'd worn something nicer than torn jeans and a flannel over a camisole. I hadn't expected to be social, and while Abby was no fancier in her hoodie and shorts that occasionally disappeared under it, I still felt that I should have worn something that I hadn't found in a long discarded backpack under a bridge.

"It's amazing how quiet this place becomes when it's just two of us here," Abby said as we walked down the corridor to the Fellowship Hall. "Is it kinda weird that Pastor Ben didn't leave someone to, you know, watch us."

"I, um...I think I'm the officially sanctioned adult today," I said, blushing.

"Oh, that's funny," Abby laughed. "You're, like, what? Twenty?"

I didn't know how to respond to that. Technically, I was nearly timeless, but in another way, I was roughly one year old, and my existence as a human could not have been more different than my existence as anima. So, sure, I supposed that could average out to twenty.

"Is it, like, weird for you?" Abby asked as I flipped the Fellowship Hall lights on. "Being both staff and a resident, I mean."

"It's...complicated," I answered, flipping on the coffee maker. "I am, first and foremost, a resident, but Pastor Ben does sometimes talk about me like I'm his second in command, which is both untrue and...I fear puts up a wall between me and the rest of you."

"I...hope I've never made you feel like that," Abby said, her face falling. "I—"

"No, you never have," I assured her. "And it could just be my own perceptions."

"No, I can get how that would be weird," Abby said, sitting down at the table as I poured water into the machine. "Oh, hey...not to be ridiculous, but can you grab me the mug with the snail?"

"Of course," I said, not that she needed to ask. Everyone in the center knew that the mug with the purple-shelled snail that said 'I break for coffee' was unofficially Abby's. I grabbed it and my unofficial mug (a much less whimsical unadorned navy blue), along with the coffee grounds, which I poured into a filter and set the machine to brewing.

"I...definitely can get feeling a weird vibe with the rest of the residents," Abby said, looking nervous as she did. "They're all really nice, but...but sometimes I don't think they know what to do with me."

"I'm sorry it seems like that," I said, sitting down next to her as the coffee pot filled. "They all speak very highly of you."

"Oh, I don't think they don't like me or anything," Abby said, shaking her head. "Sorry, I didn't mean to make it sound like that. I just...I think there are a lot of differences between our queer experiences, you know? I think I was way more sheltered than any of them, and they don't give me any guff about that or anything, but I can tell sometimes they feel like they need to censor themselves around me. And I probably don't help since sometimes when they get talking about, like, their relationships and sex and stuff I kinda flounder because I'm demi and—"

Her eyes got wide for a second and then she shook her head.

"Anyway," she said, "my main message is I definitely get it, but it's not you."

"I'm going to repeat back to you your statement," I said. "I hope I've never made you feel like that."

"No, never," she assured me this time. "You're pretty much the only person who hasn't."

"Same," I said, hearing the coffee finish brewing. I got up and filled the cups, then looked in the fridge for creamer.

"All we have is hazelnut," I muttered, picking up the bottle.

"I like hazelnut!" Abby declared. I had no strong feeling either way, so I poured a healthy amount of the creamer into both mugs and then returned to the table.

"Thank you, Mx," Abby said, taking her mug from me. "So, Lyra...can I say something I've noticed?"

"I...imagine so?"

"So, you're an amazing listener," Abby said, looking across her coffee mug at me with an impish grin. "Like, I know I can talk. And talk and talk and talk. And that most people just kinda tune me out after a while, but not you. But while that's awesome and something I love about you, I noticed that you kinda use being a good listener to cover for not talking much about yourself. Which is fine! But...okay, so, this is probably weird to say, but I feel like you're the person I'm closest to in this whole place, and yet I know the least about you."

"I'm sorry," I said, blushing, and then found words that I'd have never said to anyone else falling out of my mouth. "What would you like to know?"

"Not a sorry situation," Abby assured me. "And you don't have to tell me anything. But I just really like you and, like I said kinda awkwardly earlier, I value your friendship and just...if there was anything you'd like to share...."

"Such as?"

"Such as...okay, so, I know you came to Seattle from Rook Lake, and I know you were following a friend who ditched you—which, as an aside, how dare she?—and that's how you ended up homeless, but...but what about before that?"

Oof.

"There's no real easy answer to that one," I said, being both truthful and opaque at the same time. "I lived in Rook Lake my whole life before I came here."

"How did you like it?"

"I didn't," I said without hesitation. "I liked the nature. I liked the lake, and the forest. But the people...it was a town built on elitism and cruelty."

"That sounds terrible," Abby said, sipping her coffee. "Any friends?"

"Only the one I followed here," I admitted. "And, if I'm being honest, she was more my sister's friend."

"Oh! See, I didn't know you had a sister. Did you tell me at some point you had a sister and I just forgot? Are you two still in contact?"

"No," I shook my head. "We...went our separate ways. Ezri—the girl I followed to Seattle—was her girlfriend—"

"Oh!" Abby blurted. "And she brought you to Seattle instead? Yeah, that'll drive a wedge!"

"Oh! No, nothing like that! They...they broke up before that, and I just wanted to make sure Ezri was safe. There was never anything like that with her and me."

"Yeah, but...you kinda wanted there to be, didn't you?" Abby asked, with that same impish grin.

"No, I...."

She tilted her head and narrowed her eyes.

"I...I don't know," I mumbled.

"Crap, I made it awkward, didn't I," Abby said, blushing. "Great job, Abby. Really sorry, we can—"

"No," I said, words starting to pour out of me. "The situation made it awkward. And...and the answer is, yes, yes I think part of me did. She was an amazing person and she was the only one not directly related to me to be kind to me and...yes, I think I did want there to be more between us, and I was probably considerably jealous of my sister and...and honestly it feels good to say that out loud, so thank you for asking. You did not make it awkward."

"Do you still?" she asked. "Have feelings for her, I mean?"

I paused and pondered the question, which was one I had kept my brain from asking. It was hard to tell with my mind being constantly muddied by Ezri's stolen memories, but...

"No," I said, finally. "No, I don't think I do. I care about her, and I hope she is having the life she always deserved. But I'm not going to be a part of that, and that's okay."

Setting down her mug, Abby leaned over in her chair and hugged me, which was the exact amount of comfort I needed.

"I...I get that," she said. "It's how I feel about Miriam. I'm not mad, and I miss her, but...but not like I want her back in my life. It's not that I 'got over' her, it's just that...I'm trying to think of how to say this: Have you ever watched a movie or read a book or something, and you think 'wow, I really enjoyed that, I hope they don't ruin it by making a sequel'?"

"I understand," I said, even though I didn't relate to her specific analogy.

"So... " Abby said, looking down again, "as long as we're saying things we've never said to anyone before, want to know why I didn't want to go to Pride?"

"I am curious," I said, tilting my head, "but only if you want to tell me."

"Because it wouldn't have been my first Pride," she said, looking down into her mug. "I went last year, too."

"Oh? I thought—"

"Oh, I didn't go to celebrate," she said, turning slightly more away from me. "My church youth group was sent to...well, they would have said to share the Gospel and help lost souls see the light."

"I...see."

"Yeah, messed up, huh?" she said, looking down past her mug and at the carpeting. "Even more messed up is that I already knew I was gay. But I was determined to keep it inside or, if I was ever going to come out, that I wouldn't be 'one of those' gays who is loud and demanding attention."

She looked up at me, her eyes full of tears.

"Do you want to beat the shit out of me?" she asked. "It's okay to want to beat the shit out of me."

"I do not."

"That makes one of us," she said, looking back down. "So there I am, singing our stupid songs—which I thought were stupid even back then—and saying our terrible slogans, and I start looking around at everyone celebrating and it's just...they were just having fun and loving each other. And they were all so happy! Until they heard us. I watched faces fall and smiles vanish because...because of the words I was chanting like one of those goddamn dolls that tells you when it has crapped its pants! And then this woman walked by, and she was tall, and poised, and had this amazing mane of brilliant rainbow hair, and all I could think was she was the most beautiful human being I'd ever seen, and she looked right at me—not at our group, at me—and yelled 'You're the reason I left the church! Fuck you and fuck your god!'"

Abby fully turned away, her voice barely audible.

"And she was right," she said. "My friends started yelling back, and she just gave them the finger and walked away. She was right about that, too. And

everything started spinning, and I felt like I was going to throw up and had to go sit down on the grass until my parents—who really loved being in the middle of a Pride Festival, let me tell you—could come and pick me up. Pride is this joyful, beautiful celebration of love, and friendship, and life and I'd brought pain, and shame, and judgment in with me. I just...it didn't feel right for me to go back."

I stood up and crouched next to her seat, where she had her back to me and her legs drawn up to her chest.

"I hurt people, Lyra," she said, through tears as I put my hand gently on her back. "It doesn't matter if I was just parroting words, or if I was brainwashed or whatever, I hurt people. I don't get to say 'oh but I had a good heart' because...because that doesn't matter! What matters is what we do, how we treat people, and I...I hurt people. That's who I am. I'm someone who hurts people. I don't belong at Pride."

I remembered standing in a dingy, abandoned office, giving my sister essentially the same speech while she cried. I thought it was the words she'd needed to hear in that moment, but maybe it was just the ones I'd needed to say.

"I didn't know you then," I said, trying to choose these words more carefully. "I didn't know that Abby. Maybe we wouldn't have been friends. Maybe we wouldn't have even wanted to be in the same room as one another. But I don't think so. You weren't 'brainwashed,' you were abused, hurt, traumatized, and taught for eighteen years to hate yourself and everyone like you. And yet, when you saw that you were passing that onto others, you realized it for what it was and turned away. You did those things, and you can't undo them. I'm sorry. But then you stopped and turned away. That Abby didn't belong at Pride, you're right. But then you became—you made the choice to become—this Abby, the one who makes us all feel cared for, supported, and loved. That's who you are, and you belong at Pride."

Abby turned back toward me, tears streaming down her face, and lunged, throwing her arms around me in the fiercest embrace I'd ever been a part of.

"Thank you," she said into my ear. "Jesus Christ, thank you. You...don't know what that means to me."

"Abby," I said, carefully, putting a hand on her back as she clung to me, "I'm glad I could help but...but you know I'm not the god of Pride, right? You didn't need my permission. Or my absolution."

"No, but I needed someone's," she said, with a sad laugh. "And honestly—like, real honestly—I don't think I'd have believed it from anyone else. But you're you, and—"

She released me and slowly drew back, wiping her eyes with her sleeve.

"God," she said, with a warbling laugh, "I wish we'd talked before everyone left. Oh well, hopefully I'll still look cute in the outfit I picked out when we go next year."

Her eyes went wide.

"I...I mean if you want to go to Pride with me next year," she stammered. "I know you didn't want to go this year...."

"I didn't. But I will absolutely go with you next year."

"So, why didn't you want to go this year?" Abby asked. "And don't say the crowds. You are a terrible liar."

About the little things, maybe.

"I...also do not feel I belong," I sighed, returning to my chair.

"Why not?"

"I...I don't think I've ever felt I've belonged anywhere," I said, looking down at my now-empty coffee mug. "Which, sounds like I'm being self-deprecating but it's just true. I always feel like I'm a half-step behind everyone, like everyone is talking in some secret code that I only get ninety-percent of, and—"

"And like the key to people not thinking you're a freak is lost in that myste-rious ten-percent?"

"Yes. Exactly that," I said.

"Well hello, fellow unsuccessful code-breaker," Abby said, putting a hand on mine and then quickly darting it away like it was red-hot. "I, um, I may have some experience with that. "Ever do that thing where you get so lost in thought that you just stare into space without realizing you're actually staring at someone?"

"I was yelled out of an encampment for doing that exact thing."

"How about when someone tells a joke and it isn't funny so you don't laugh and somehow the joke being unfunny becomes your fault?"

"Frequently."

"Uh huh," Abby nodded. "I've gotten pretty good as masking that one. Same with 'you asked me what I was thinking and I told you but now you're mad because I was supposed to just say something about, like, the weather.'"

"A man at a shelter asked me how I was, and I told him, which was apparently not what I was supposed to do."

"Been there!" Abby laughed, wiping away the last of her tears. "Yeah, so, if you ever get insurance, you may want to go get evaluated and see if we have something else in common, too. But until then, if it makes you feel any better, you're only as weird as I am."

She crossed her eyes and stuck out her tongue, which made both of us laugh.

"It actually does," I said, finding words challenging to form. "Thank you for being weird with me. It may be the only time I've felt normal."

She looked at me for a long heartbeat, a shy, serene smile on her face.

"Yeah, same," she said. "Hey, so, Pride isn't far, we could definitely still go. I have bus money."

"We…we definitely could…."

"Or…or!" she said, jumping out of her seat and gesturing for me to take her hand.

"Or?"

"Or, we could make use of a completely empty building and have our own Pride!"

Hesitantly, I took her hand and she pulled me from my seat.

"I…don't know what that means, but I trust you," I said.

"Good," she winked. "Come with me."

She bolted off down the hall, my hand still in hers as I tried to keep up.

"Okay," she said, face beaming as we reached our rooms. "Go change!"

"Change?"

"Into something for Pride!" she said. "Our Pride. But still Pride."

Before I could ask clarifying questions, she dashed into her room and closed the door. I went to my own bedroom and changed into a nicer pair of black jeans, a new black camisole, and a maroon and black flannel I'd purchased at a thrift store, on which I affixed a rainbow button that I'd found left behind in my room by a previous resident.

Deciding I was relatively pleased with my appearance after running a comb through my hair, I stepped out into the hall and immediately changed my opinion.

Abby stood there, wearing rainbow socks that came up to mid-thigh, denim shorts, and a black crop top with glittery rainbow angel wings on it, her makeup done, including her customary eyeliner 'wings', and her hair flawless and radiantly pink.

I opened my mouth and unsuccessfully attempted to make a coherent series of words.

"Lyra? Pride, remember?" Abby laughed. Still trying to make even a word, I gestured to my pin.

"Oh, oh dear. Okay," Abby said, leaning back into her room. "I wasn't going to wear this because we're inside, but…you need it more than me, anyway."

She leaned back out holding what could possibly be the most ridiculous article of clothing in the known universe, a rainbow-painted straw cowboy hat with a hat-band that said "PRIDE" over and over again in black letters.

"There," she said, placing it on my head. "Pride!"

There wasn't even a part of me that considered objecting.

"Perfect!" Abby declared. "Pride selfie!"

Before I knew what was happening, she swung around next to me, put her arm around me, pressed close and took a photo with her phone, followed by two more in quick succession.

The third one, by which time I'd figured out what was happening, turned out well.

"Okay, check that off the list," Abby said, practically bouncing, the clouds from the morning long parted. "Now...we Pride!"

"Okay!" I said, as enthusiastically as I could. "How...do we do that?"

Abby smiled so wide I once again couldn't form words.

"Well...."

From just before noon until about 1:45, we connected Abby's phone to the Fellowship Hall sound system and blasted music that she assured me was "very very gay" while she danced and I approximated movements that may have been a reasonable substitute for doing so. Around 2:00, we switched from dancing to singing karaoke using her phone for lyrics, which culminated in the two of us belting out a version of the song Like a Prayer that was far more cathartic than I anticipated it would be. From 3:00 to 5:00, we played a very involved board game borrowed from Lenora's collection about a team of investigators trying to solve a mystery in a haunted mansion (when I asked how this counted as a Pride activity, Abby informed me that, as we were both queer, everything we did counted as Pride activity, which I found hard to argue with). At around 6:00, the pizza we ordered arrived, which we devoured in record time.

After that, we talked. We talked about some of the shows we'd watched together, and we talked about the music she'd shared with me. We discussed what it was like to be queer in a big city versus a small town (during which I drew largely on what I'd observed of Elodie and Ezri's experiences), and may have gotten slightly less than kind in venting about some of the things that annoyed us about our fellow residents. We then felt bad and spent even longer listing all the things we liked about them. By the time 9:00 rolled around and the sun had largely disappeared from the sky out the windows, we were both exhausted and collapsed together on the couch at the far end of the Fellowship Hall, looking out through the windows into the darkened city.

"It's a shame we're not higher up," Abby said, her head resting against my shoulder.

"Why's that?"

"Oh, just because they're doing a drone show around the Space Needle," she answered.

"What's a drone show?"

"It's what they do instead of fireworks now," she said. "This'll be the first year they do one for Pride. They put LED lights on a bunch of drones that fly

around in formation making pictures and words and stuff. You can see it for like four miles, but I don't think unless we could get up to the roof—"

"I can get us up to the roof!" I blurted.

"Wait, you can?" she asked.

"I have keys!" I declared, somewhat weirded out by how proud my voice sounded.

"I mean, that would be awesome, but I don't want you to get in trouble or...."

"I won't," I assured her. "Trust me."

"Absolutely!" Abby laughed. "Okay, lead the way!"

I led her through the darkened building, turning on lights as we went, through a locked 'employees only' door and up a staircase to the second floor, which was almost entirely storage. Shuffling around boxes of seasonal decorations and sports equipment, I led us to a ladder which ascended to a hatch that unlocked after two attempts during which it felt like my key was going to break.

"I...don't think anyone has been up here in a while," I said, pushing open the hatch which groaned in objection. Abby emerged behind me, wide-eyed as her face was illuminated by the city lights. In the distance, the Space Needle shone like a beacon, illuminated with rainbow lights and bright even among the rest of Seattle.

"It's beautiful," she said, staring out over the city. "Thank you so much for bringing me up here!"

"Of course," I said as she walked toward the edge of the roof.

"And...thank you for today," she said as I joined her. "All of it. I really thought this whole day was going to suck when I woke up this morning."

"Thank you, too," I said. "Thank you for...for being weird with me."

"Anytime," she smiled, and then looked back out at the city. "Oh! It's starting!"

In the distance, a fleet of tiny drones ascended and began shining intense, multicolored lights, first in the form of a rainbow, which then morphed into the word Love, and then into a frog for some reason. I knew all the true things. I knew that those drones were probably made by SafeHaus Enterprises, and were probably originally invented for much more sinister purposes. I knew that my mission to bring down Agape's Rainbow had neither completed nor disappeared. But I had just spent an entire day not thinking about it even once, nor had Cennend or Elodie even crossed my mind more than in passing. That day I'd just been Lyra, and for the first time ever, I considered the possibility that one day I'd get to just be Lyra again.

As the drones flew into a dazzling series of spirals, I felt Abby's hand close around mine. She didn't let go this time.

"Happy Pride, Lyra."
"Happy Pride, Abby."
And it was.

"The Place" that Jayla asked to meet at was the corner of University Avenue and Ravenna, the outer boundary of the Seattle micro-neighborhood known as The Ave, which extended off of the UW campus. Being so close to the college, most of the shops—the locally-owned ones, at least—were open well into the early morning hours. So at 11:00 PM the street was still occupied by young people milling down the sidewalks as I stood as nonchalantly as possible, waiting for Jayla to arrive.

Leaving Agape's Rainbow had not been an issue. While I was technically in violation of curfew, the netherworld I existed in by being both a staff member and a resident was so undefined that none of the other workers were really sure which rules applied to me and which didn't. I doubted even Matthew would have the courage to tattle on me, for all of his bravado. It was perhaps the only benefit to being Pastor Ben's right hand.

"Psst! Hey, Celestial Hottie," Jayla whispered from behind me. "Just kidding, we can use real names."

I turned around and, in the instant our eyes met, all the weight that had been hanging on my shoulders lifted off. We'd only spoken over the phone since I was sent to live at Agape's Rainbow, using dead-drop sites to transfer any physical items that needed to change hands. I'd spent months crafting, molding, and living a lie that I had to maintain twenty-four hours a day. It took seeing the face of someone who knew me—the real me, all of me—to realize how much living in deceit had been eroding me.

"Jesus, it's good to see you!" Jayla said, grabbing me into a powerful hug and lifting me off of my feet. "The others send their love. Athena has been doing great, too. She spends a lot of the day away from us, though. Is she visiting you?"

"Sometimes, yes," I said, my smile so wide it was starting to hurt.

"Good, that's what I hoped," Jayla said. "Heads up that Syn keeps trying to rename her 'Adora' for reasons she insists I'm a Philistine for not understanding. Anyway, how are you, Lyra? Like...for real, how are you?"

"Bad," I said, not even considering putting on a brave face. "Really, really bad. It's awful, Jayla."

"I'm so sorry," she said, hugging me again.

"It's just...it looks so nice on the outside!" I said. "And when it's just me and the residents, I...I can forget. Because *they* aren't awful. They can be jerks sometimes and call me a talking snake, but they can also be kind and supportive and—and then Pastor Ben walks in. And he just...breaks them down! He tells them God loves them just as they are, but then he asks them 'oh, but are you sure that's what you're feeling' and 'do you really think that's how you were made?' and chips away at them until they don't even know what 'just as they are' means anymore!"

"And anyone who resists gets sent off to SafeHaus like a family pet going to live on the farm where they can run wild and free," Jayla added. "Fuck. I'm so sorry, Lyra."

"Every time," I said, my eyes growing wet, "every time I think I've seen the depths of human cruelty, seen all the different ways they can hurt one another...."

"I...I know this isn't going to help," Jayla said, "but we're going to stop them."

"There's a girl there," I said, looking up at the dark black sky, every star eaten by the city lights. "Her name is Abby. She's sweet, and bright, and full of joy and energy, and no matter what Pastor Ben did or said, she kept becoming more and more herself."

"She the one you were telling me about? The one who is scheduled to go to SafeHaus on Monday?"

"Yes."

"Tell me more about her."

"Why?"

"Because," Jayla said smiling at me, "it sounds like she's your bright spot."

"She...yeah, I guess she is," I said, stepping to the side out of the path of two oncoming students. "She's...she's an artist. A really good one, though she thinks she's terrible. She loves all of these, if I'm honest, terrible TV shows, but what I think she likes even more is guessing what's going to happen next, writing her own little stories about the characters and...and she always gets sad when the show has them do something different. She's one of those people who no one wants to disappoint, not because she'll be unkind or even tell you that you disappointed her, it's just crushing to know you made her sad. She has this way of making you feel like the world is brighter just by her, like, being in it and—"

"So, if I can interrupt for a clarifying question," Jayla said, with a crooked smile, "does Abby know you're in love with her?"

I felt the blood drain out of my face and stopped dead, which made Jayla laugh loud enough to draw the attention of several other pedestrians.

"I—she's—it's not—" I sputtered.

"Well, my second question was going to be if *you* knew that you are in love with her, but I think you just answered that," she said through laughter.

"I—I don't think about her *like that*," I stammered.

"I didn't ask if you knew you wanted to have sex with her, I asked if you know you love her," Jayla said. "Because you clearly do, and I know it sounds like I'm giving you shit about it, because I guess I am a little bit, but honestly, good for you."

"I...don't know that it is," I said, trying to grapple with this new information. "I don't even know if I do! I just—"

"Okay, well, how about this," Jayla said. "Let's pretend for a second. Let's pretend that when you get back, good news, Abby got out and is going somewhere guaranteed to be safe and far away from Pastor Ben and SafeHaus, but bad news, you'll never see or hear from her ever again and—okay, you're already crying. Shit, shit shit shit, I'm sorry!"

"Shit!" I agreed, wiping my face roughly with my arm. "Jayla, I...I think I love Abby?"

"Yeah, pretty sure you do," Jayla said, handing me a packet of tissues from her jacket. "How you feeling about that?"

I just glared at her and gestured at my face.

"Yeah, that was a dumb question," she said. "I'm...shit, I'm sorry to drop a truth-bomb on you out of nowhere. You were just getting this dreamy look in your eyes and...and I thought you knew!"

"Clearly I didn't!"

"I mean, look, I don't know her, but I know you, and I'm going to guess there is more than an outside chance that this isn't a one-sided feeling you're experiencing," she said, gently elbowing me.

"Jayla," I said, pursing my lips. "She doesn't know me. Not the real me."

"How fake are you being in there?" she asked. "Like, are you putting on a whole personality, or is it just the 'not being open about being a nearly-immortal being' thing?"

"That's not a small thing!"

"Oh, yeah, absolutely it isn't," Jayla said. "Boy howdy it isn't. But I'm going to take that response as a 'no' to the first thing. And yeah, you being...what you are...is kind of a big deal. But on the other hand, fuck it. You've also been human for, like, what, a year?"

"A little less."

"And I'm going to guess it's kind of a trip. Kind of like what she's going through becoming who she actually is. Of course, for her it's less claws and wings and more 'girls and other not-dudes are hot,' but you get my point, right? And hell, if Elodie and Ezri can make it work...."

"Well...."

"Okay, but before that part. Lyra, if you've been you in there—and I don't mean the claws and wings part, I mean the person you—then she knows you plenty. And look, as a fellow former fanfic writer, I can say that we don't share our fics with just anyone. She's at least sweet on you."

I looked up at the sky again. It was still starless, but somehow seemed brighter.

"I...I love Abby."

"No shit," Jayla said, elbowing me again. "We're going to save her, you know that, right? We were going to anyway, but now we're going to make damn sure."

"Have you found anything in the files?" I asked. "Where they're taking the 'interns,' or what they're doing with them?"

"We're still waist-deep in the data, but so far not finding anything," Jayla sighed. "Pastor Ben is a stupid motherfucker but Cora Emerson isn't. Of course, the other possibility is that she didn't tell him *anything* and he's as clueless as we are. Which I think would be even more fucked up, honestly. I don't know, but this is kind of our last ditch, especially if he's shutting you out, too. I want to give Tavish and the others another day or so, but if Sunday rolls around and he still hasn't found anything, I'm good calling in the burn."

"But...but the ones who have already been taken—"

"Lyra," Jayla said, putting her hands on my shoulders and looking down at the ground. "I...I don't think it matters for them anymore."

"But...your brother."

"What matters now is saving the ones who are there at the center, and the ones who would come after them," Jayla said. "Link...Link is gone."

"Jayla...."

"I'm okay," she waved me off. "Made my peace a long time ago. Anyway, I didn't just invite you out here to bum you out more and give you a minor existential crisis. I wanted to show you something. I think it'll make both of us feel better. At least a little. Follow me."

I did without hesitation. She took me back down University, down the main drag of The Ave. We walked under bright street lights and colorful storefronts, college students wandering all around us.

"This place depresses the fuck out of me sometimes," Jayla said as we walked. "Not to sound old as hell, but when I was a kid, The Ave was all record stores, independent coffee places, and head-shops. Now look at it! There's a fucking Target! Shit. Good for depositing bricks during protests and nothing else. Anyway, here we are!"

She stopped us in front of a black painted storefront with a large, vibrantly colored sign over it illuminated by giant blacklights.

"Trash-Muse Tattoo?" I read.

"Yep. With a name like that, right?"

"Why are we here? Do...Do you want us to get tattoos?"

"Well, not tonight," Jayla laughed. "No, I want you to meet some folks."

She pushed open the door and beckoned me through with her, the bell in the jamb announcing our arrival to the two women in the surprisingly cozy waiting room. One was a tall, striking woman with emerald green hair and a sharp face who was organizing the magazine racks and gave us a long, appraising glance. The other woman, who stood at the counter, was quite possibly the most stunningly beautiful human being I'd ever seen.

"We're closing in like thirty seconds, so unless you're just here to pay a deposit I'll need you to come back tomorrow," she said, not looking up. I marveled at how her chestnut hair fell all around her face in perfect waves.

"You sure?" Jayla asked, with a smirk that came through in her voice.

"Yes I'm—Oh my God! Jay!"

"Wondered how long it would take for you to look up," the green-haired woman laughed.

"You could have told me!"

"This was more fun."

"Well, anyway, like I was saying, oh my God, Jay! So happy to see you! And you brought an adorable friend with you."

"Calli, Abra, meet Lyra. Theys and thems," Jayla said, gesturing to me as I accidentally made eye-contact with the woman at the counter and my face immediately flushed. I was unaware eyes could be so vivid!

"Lyra," Jayla continued, "this is Calli, and that green-haired space goddess over there is her wife, Abra."

"It's so nice to meet you," Abra said, standing and coming over to the rest of the group.

"It's nice to meet the two of you, too," I said. Which it was, even if I was still not entirely aware of why we were there.

"Calli's the top tattoo artist in Seattle," Jayla said. "Just about every musician who comes through the Emerald City has some of her ink on them."

"Pfft, top five maybe," Calli waved Jayla off.

"Don't be modest," Abra said, putting her arms around Calli's waist from behind and kissing her wife on the cheek, the whole act of which fluttered areas of my vessel that had seldom fluttered before.

"Modest? I'm not modest!" Calli scoffed. "I brag all the time, just about things that are true. I'm in the top one percent of OnlyFans accounts. See? Bragging. Thank you for your...new subscription...by the way, Jayla."

I had no knowledge of what was being spoken of, but I could make some inferences based on the tone. Though the water was somewhat muddied by all three of them bursting into laughter.

"So what brings you in so late?" Calli asked. "Looking to set up an appointment or...something else?"

"Something else," Jayla said.

"Then we can assume that Lyra is...?"

Jayla nodded.

"Let's head to the back," Abra said, gesturing us all through the door to the studio, a large, bright room with six black tattoo tables and art on the walls that ranged from stunningly beautiful to terrifyingly erotic.

"So, what's up?" Abra asked, closing the door between rooms.

"Mainly I just wanted to introduce y'all," Jayla said. "Lyra is our person on the inside at Agape's Rainbow."

Abra and Calli's faces fell.

"Oh...oh my God, you poor dear," Calli said, wrapping me in a hug that was not the least bit unpleasant. "I don't even want to imagine the things you've seen and heard in that hell."

"You're doing an amazing thing, Lyra," Abra said, looking at me with her own vivid eyes. "People in the queer community have been trying to ring the bell on that place for years just to be told that we were being 'antitheists' or 'gatekeepers' or some shit like that. Honestly, I can't wait to watch that torture factory burn. Still just seven residents?"

"Yes," I said, furrowing my brow. "How did –?"

"We know all, young one," Calli said, waving her arms in a slow arch over her head.

"Abra and Calli are...well, not members of No Affiliation per se, but they're family," Jayla said. "Abra, why don't you tell Lyra what your job is when you aren't helping Calli with the shop?"

"I run Prismatic," she said. "It's a queer community center here in the U-District. Small, but we hope to grow."

"Small and pure," Calli added. "Fuck corporate money."

"We founded it a few years back," Abra continued. "We both came from this tiny little deeply homophobic town in central Washington. Thing is, the same loneliness and exclusion we felt there still exists even in big ol' liberal Seattle. So, I wanted a place where people could come to be safe. But the more I listened to the people who came to us—especially the young people—the more I realized that it doesn't matter if I make a safe space if I just send them back to the wolves at home. So, I made some off the books things happen."

"Now she's the one being too modest," Jayla said. "Abra and Calli founded a damn queer underground railroad."

"We prefer clandestine hospitality network," Abra said. "Less appropriative."

"Oh, for you, yeah. I can say the other thing, though," Jayla laughed, elbowing Abra. "It's a network of queer folk who have residences that they are willing to share to provide temporary housing for queer folk in need."

"Usually it's things like giving someone somewhere to stay while they are on the run from an abusive family, or providing a safe space for a trans person recovering from surgery who has no other place to go. Things like that," Calli said. "But Abra worked some of her magic and was able to find seven of her angels willing to provide more long-term housing for the residents trapped in that repulsive place."

"Well, I found six...and then us," Abra said.

"Hell yeah!" Calli said. "Some lucky queer is going to get to have these two hot bitches as their awesome transbian aunts!"

"Wait," I said, looking between the three women. "You mean...?"

"Yep," Jayla nodded. "After we bring down Agape, your friends living there will have places to stay, warm meals, and good, kind, vetted people to care for them until they are ready to move on. That's why I wanted you to meet these two. I wanted you to know that those kids you've spent all this time watching over won't be forgotten. I just...I know you see a lot of ugly in there, and I know you've seen even more of it out here. And far be it from me to be the 'look on the bright side' bitch. But there are good people out here, too. I don't know if that helps, but...but I hope at least it makes the rest of your time in that shithole a little more bearable. I hope it helps you understand what we're trying to do."

I didn't know what to say. I could feel their anima pulsing around me, and there wasn't a hint of deception. I felt tears welling in my eyes.

"You...thank you. Thank you all."

"Thank *you*, Lyra," Calli said as both she and Abra hugged me. "I can't imagine being brave enough to do what you're doing. When this is all over, set up an appointment and I'll tattoo you for free. If you want. Anything you want. I have some suggestions. Again, if you want."

"We should be going," Jayla said, giving both women a hug after they released me. "I'll be in touch as shit gets real."

"Be safe out there," Abra said, releasing her. "Both of you."

"You, too," Jayla nodded.

The night air seemed warmer as we stepped out of Calli's shop and back onto The Ave.

"Thank you for introducing me to them," I said as we walked. "I...I really appreciate it."

"Of course," Jayla said. "Abra and Calli are good folk. They're part of the family, just like you. And when all of this is over, we're getting all of us together and having a proper family meal. Because this is going to end. There will be a day after Agape's Rainbow."

We walked and chatted some more, Jayla giving me a rundown of the web of relationships within the No Affiliation family (Clover and Syn were obviously a couple but not exclusive, which meant that Syn was fine that Clover occasionally slept with Jayla and Clover was fine that Jayla occasionally slept with Syn and neither minded that Bob and Syn sometimes hooked up, but neither Syn nor Bob ever felt great about that afterwards and, meanwhile, Tavish was asexual and aromantic which meant mainly he just laughed at everyone else). The longer we stayed out, the warmer the night felt, and the more Jayla's words meant to me. She was right; there would be a day after Agape's Rainbow.

And we'd all be there to see it.

I'd make sure.

"Mom, please! I just...I just want to come home," the hushed voice pleaded from behind one of the decorative hedges at the side of the center. "I can't do that! I can't be someone I'm not! I—"

I rounded the corner, still holding the trash bag I was on my way to deposit in the dumpster. The person crouched behind the bush was our new arrival, a quiet girl who came with a ratty floral dress, a Bible, a Book of Mormon, and her cell phone. That was it.

"No. No, I get it. I get it, Mom!" she said, now fully crying. She hadn't seen me, and I didn't want to embarrass her during a call she was clearly trying to have in private, so I shuffled as quietly past her as I could, depositing the bag of garbage and attempting to scuttle back.

"Fine," she said, her voice gathered enough that the tears pouring down her cheeks were inaudible. "Fine. Okay. Yeah, goodbye. I love—"

She looked down at the phone and sighed, sinking down to the ground as her sobs grew louder and more desperate.

"H-Hi," I said, calling out from the pathway. I couldn't just walk by. If she wanted me to leave, I'd leave, but no one should be forced to suffer like that on their own. "Abigail?"

"Abby," she nodded. "Only my grandma called me Abigail. I...I'm sorry. I know I'm not supposed to be over here. I'll go back to my room."

"It's okay," I said, holding my palms up. "I'm...I'm not here to get you in trouble. I just wanted to make sure you're okay and see if you maybe wanted someone to talk to."

"I'm definitely not okay," she shook her head. "And no offense, but I don't think I'm really ready to hear a sermon."

"And I would be very ill-equipped to give you one. I can go if you'd like."

"No," she said, her voice verging on pleading for a brief moment. "It's okay. You can stay if you want."

"May I sit?"

She nodded and I lowered myself to the cool ground.

"Do you have parents?" Abby asked. "I mean, not, like...like duh, everyone has parents. But...."

"I have one," I said, folding my legs under me.

"Mine stuck together, unfortunately. They shouldn't have. Is it your mom or dad?"

"Neither."

"Oh. That must be awesome," Abby said with a rueful smile. "Nonbinary parent. How'd you end up here?"

"My parent has many, many reasons to be disappointed in me that have nothing to do with my gender identity."

"Oh. I'm sorry."

"It's okay. We don't speak."

"Sometimes I wonder if that's the way to do it," Abby sighed. "I was just on the phone with my mom. My dad won't even talk to me. I still think he's the one who's least angry, though."

"I...take it the conversation didn't go well?"

"It's okay," Abby said, "I know you must have heard. You don't have to pretend."

"I heard some. I heard that you want to go home."

"Oh. Yeah. That," Abby blushed. "I'm...I'm really sorry. It's not that this place isn't nice, it's just...I don't know where I fit in. Like, I feel like a beginner queer. I'm not even sure if I'm allowed to use that word yet. Everyone else here is, like...master's degree queer. And Pastor Ben is nice, but I'm LDS and he's...some kind of protestant? I don't know, I just...it's not even that I want to go home.

Home was never that happy, even before my parents discovered my letter to Miriam. I just want something, like, familiar, you know?"

"I understand," I said. "Miriam was your best friend, correct?"

"Yeah. That was the worst part. After they found the letter—which I wasn't even going to send—my parents called her parents to 'warn' them and ask if they knew of anything 'immoral' happening in their house. So...her parents told her."

"Oh. I'm—"

"She was really sweet about it," Abby said, fresh tears falling from her eyes. I put a tentative hand on her back and she leaned in and rested her head on my shoulder. "I knew she would be. She's really sweet. About everything. Told me she didn't feel the same way but that I was her best friend and that would never change. But...then it did. Her parents forbid her from seeing me and she just...didn't. That was about the same time my parents kicked me out."

"So...you lost two homes."

"Yeah. Yeah, I never thought about it like that, but yeah. She was my home. We'd known each other since we were four. Then poof! Gone. My parents will take me back, you know?"

"Oh? It...did not sound like that from what I'd heard," I said. "Does that mean you will be departing from us?"

"No," she shook her head against my shoulder. "I won't do the thing they'd require."

"Which is?"

"Pretend I'm straight. They even put it like that. Pretend. It's like, they know I'm gay. They don't even seem to think I'm faking for attention or that my mind has been perverted, they just want me to pretend so none of their stupid friends will think they messed up their kid. And I know like, I'm technically an adult and it doesn't matter because I can be free of them but...but they're still my parents, and I can't pretend they're not. Just like I can't pretend that I'm not the person I am."

"That's...truly terrible," I said. "I'm glad you won't do it, but I'm sorry that means you have to stay."

"It's...it's not like that. I don't mean to be down on this place. I don't know where else I'd go. My first day here I had this stupid idea that I'd do really well and, like, impress them into taking me back. Like I could ever impress them. Maybe if I get one of those internships. Money equals impressive, and impressive equals worthy of love. Maybe working for a big giant tech company could outweigh being pan."

"You...you said that you missed familiarity," I said, trying to change the subject away from the potential horrors I was investigating. "Is there anything I—we—could do or get to make things more...familiar here for you?"

"You're sweet," she said, flashing her first real smile since I found her. "I'll be okay. It's not, like, an article of clothing or a piece of furniture or anything. If I'm going to be honest, it's not even really a person. I miss the little things that made me happy. Watching the sunset through my bedroom window. Coming downstairs in my nightshirt on a winter morning and standing over the best heat vent in the house. Having Pagliacci's with Miriam during a sleepover, and then sneaking up early to eat the leftovers for breakfast."

"I'm sorry, what are Pagliaccis?" I asked.

Abby jerked her head up off my shoulder.

"Lyra! Have you not had Pagliacci's? They're the best pizza place in Seattle! You have to go get some! Like, on my behalf!"

"Oh! I have had pizza," I said, remembering a mildly warm slice a kind woman had bought me from a gas station when I was homeless.

"No. Not like this. Seriously. As soon as you can, go try some. They're, like, everywhere. Any toppings. They're all good. I command it!"

Her tears had stopped and she was actually smiling.

"Alright. I will," I said. "I promise. If you'll make me a promise."

"What?"

"Promise me that if you ever need or want to talk, you'll find me. No matter what time it is. I would never say I understand your journey, nor would I say that I will always know how to advise you, but I...have some experience with situations not dissimilar to yours, and I will always listen."

Before I knew what was happening, I found myself in a tight embrace.

"You're...you're really awesome," she said, face buried against me. "I'm sorry if I was rude before. I just know you're, like, Pastor Ben's second-in-command and it's not that I don't like Pastor Ben, but—"

"Abby," I said, "I may do some office work for him, but if there is one thing I can assure you of with one hundred percent certainty, it is that I am nothing like Pastor Ben."

That made her laugh. She thanked me another half-dozen times and then stood, brushed herself off, and went back inside. I lingered for a second before reentering the building myself.

"Lyra, just the person I wanted to see!" Pastor Ben announced before the door even closed behind me. "Would you please join me in my office?"

My heart clenched. It had only been a week since I'd revealed my 'true' nature to him, and in that time he'd called me into his office on six different occasions to beg for redemption. Every time he told me a little more without telling me what I needed to know, and every time I refused him the forgiveness he craved. As if it was mine to give in the first place.

"I...I'm sorry," he said as we entered his office and he locked the door behind us. "Knowing who—what—you are, I feel blasphemous speaking to you in such casual ways, Blessed One."

My insides crawled like they were filled with maggots.

"You may speak to me however you wish out there," I said. "It is not the time for others to know me as you do."

"Yes. Yes, of course. May...may I give confession?"

I wanted to reach over and snap his neck. I had since the moment I'd met him.

"You may."

I had not yet been able to acquire the low-backed camisoles that would later allow me to display my wings in a more dignified manner. But I could feel the lust burning in his anima. I knew he wanted me like he had never wanted anyone or anything in his entire pitiful life. I would deny him every joy I possibly could.

Lifting up the back of my shirt only, I manifested my wings, releasing the fabric and letting it rest on top of where my feathers met my skin.

"Holy, holy, holy," he whispered, dropping to his knees as I rose into the air.

"If you have sins to confess, confess them," I said, unable to keep the disgust from my voice.

"I have thought lustful thoughts!" he blurted, which was always his opening volley.

"And what else?"

"I have spoken in anger against others."

"And what else?"

"I have failed to keep our Lord's commandments!"

"And what else?"

He stared up at me in silence, the first time such a thing had happened.

"I..." he started, and then paused again, looking down. "I failed my first wife."

"Failed her?"

"Her...her name was Lia," he said, still unable to meet my eyes. "She was beautiful and kind, but she had a weak will and...and sometimes her big heart led her to be taken advantage of by bad people."

"She is the one you speak of to the residents," I nodded, remembering the briefing Jayla and the others had given me.

"Yes. Yes, Blessed One. I tell myself that I conceal from them that we were married because it's best to maintain a barrier between us, but the truth is that I'm embarrassed. I'm embarrassed that I couldn't do more for her. We had

a good and loving marriage, and she was happy. But these two women—no, one whore and one man pretending to be a woman—who called themselves her 'friends' seduced her away from me. Convinced her that she wasn't happy. Drove her to the point of attempting suicide, and then after her attempt used her fragile mental state to manipulate her into leaving me and destroying our entire life together. But I can't put all the blame on them. I should have done more. I was too permissive. I should have insisted she sever ties with those vipers the second I saw their true nature. I failed her, Blessed One. I was too lenient, too permissive. A husband is supposed to be to his wife as God is, and I failed. I always thought she'd come back to me, but then she got sick and...I worry for her immoral soul. I...I hope she saw the error of her ways before she passed over. Could you...could you tell me if...?"

I had never been more disgusted with a human being in my entire existence.

"No. I will not tell you the fate of her soul. You should be ashamed for even asking."

"I'm sorry!" he blurted, tears streaming down his face. "I'm sorry!"

"You were already confessing."

"Y-yes, Blessed One. I...I confess that I overstepped my boundaries. Please, please forgive me."

"Have you told me all you have to confess?"

"Yes. Yes, that's all."

My eyes narrowed.

"You are a liar, Benjamin Holmes."

"No! I...I...."

He trailed off into silence.

"I am sorry."

"You are not yet forgiven," I said. "Return when you are ready to truly unburden your soul."

"Yes. Yes, Blessed One. May...may I ask a favor, a favor that I have no right asking?"

"You may ask."

"I...the reason that I bring up Lia today is that this would have been our anniversary," he said, fidgeting with his hands. "If...if she is where, where...you know...where you can be in touch with her, would you please tell her that I love her?"

I don't think he saw me move before he was aware that he was being lifted up into the air by his lapels.

"I am not your messenger!" I bellowed, letting my eyes flame blue for a single heartbeat. This man, this terrible, horrible little man, this hateful agent of pain and shame...I despised him. I despised his arrogance, his entitlement,

his sanctimony. I never met Lia, but there was no doubt in my mind that her life under his thumb had been as cruel and ugly as anything I'd seen in my thousands of years in existence.

"I'm sorry! I am sorry, I am so sorry!"

"Be more so," I sneered. "Never ask such a thing of me again. Never desire such a thing again. We are finished now."

He stayed on his knees as I lowered myself and unmade my wings. I turned and left before he could stand again. I made it all the way back to my room before it all came out of me. I grabbed my pillow and shrieked into it until my vocal cords burned like fire, then healed them and screamed some more before flinging my pillow across my spartan room, knocking my phone off of its charger.

Gritting my teeth, I went and picked it up, a thought occurring to me as I held the little black rectangle. With my other hand I flipped open the Bible I had been provided with, recovering the sheet of paper where I'd scrawled the center's credit card number.

Forty-five minutes later, I stood in the hallway, knocking on a door.

"Just a second!" Abby called, moments before the door opened. "Lyra! Hi! You—oh my God!"

"Hello, Abby," I said, holding out a square cardboard box that smelled like joys not contained even in the heaven Pastor Ben preached. "I am told that this pizza is superior to all other pizzas. Will you share it with me?"

She started to cry right away, and so did I. She ushered me into her room and we sat on the floor eating the best food I'd consumed since I'd taken physical form. I wasn't like her; in this form, I was a new being, born into a world in crisis. She had almost nineteen years of experience as a human, and I had not yet even had one. I had no traditions, no rituals, nothing of my own. I had no 'familiar.' But she did, and on that uncomfortable floor, our faces still streaked with tears, she was kind enough to let it become mine, too.

It is fortunate that I do not require much sleep, as I had none that night. I tossed and turned for a while in my uncomfortable bed, running through the night's events and, as always, continuing to roll the details of our plan over and over and over inside my skull. It was about three in the morning when I gave up on the illusion of slumber altogether and went outside to walk around the grounds.

The night air was surprisingly crisp, raising goosebumps all over my skin as it hit me. I had been through enough during my brief time in physical form to become jaded about a great many things, but I still hadn't ceased to be amused by all the foibles of my human vessel. I had very little time to muse on such things, however, before my phone buzzed to life in my pocket.

"Call when you wake up."

It was Tavish, who never texted just to talk. Moving myself from the glow of the security lights and into the shadows, I dialed his number and repeated the pass phrase into the silence.

"Hey, Celestial," Tavish said. "I'm just going to call you Celestial, okay? Using the rest of it feels weird when you look young enough to be my granddaughter. Jesus, you're up early."

"I...don't really sleep," I said, darting my eyes around the night to confirm that I was still alone.

"Yeah, I guess you wouldn't, right? Anyway, I wanted to let you know that I got through all of Pastor Ben's files. Religion is some fucked up shit, huh?"

"Did you find anything about the internship program, or what happened to the people selected?" I asked, ignoring his theological commentary.

"Zilch," he sighed. "Not a damn thing. Which is weird, because this dude keeps everything. I found some messed up stuff. Letters to his first wife after she divorced him. Some confessions of sins that are all like a 2.5 at best but still may give Jayla a bit more to work with. A draft of a novel he seems to be writing about a traveling preacher who romances an angel..."

In addition to forming goosebumps, my skin was also capable of crawling like it was filled with millions of tiny worms.

"...but nothing about the internship, the selected residents, or even much about SafeHaus at all. The most I could find were a few emails from way far back from Russell Hausman's assistant setting up what looks like an initial meeting with Pastor Ben, and then a yearly one about the donation SafeHaus makes to the shelter. But that's really it."

"You think he deleted everything related to SafeHaus? Could that mean he knows someone is onto him?"

"I don't know about that last part, but I don't think he deleted them," Tavish said. "I think they weren't there to begin with. Someone wanted to keep there from being any kind of trail, and Pastor Ben doesn't seem smart enough for that."

"Which means that Hausman...."

"Yeah," Tavish said. "For a guy who runs a tech company, he's working pretty damn hard to keep this non-electronic. Which means—"

"Which means the thought of whatever he's hiding seeing the light of day scares him."

"Yeah, that's one way to put it. It also means we're SOL, kid. Unless you can get him to spill the beans during one of your confession sessions."

"He has been reluctant to share anything of that nature," I said, my stomach turning over at the thought of another confession from Pastor Ben. "I...may have other ways, though."

"I mean, there's the obvious. You said that one of the residents there is going to be shipped off into the abyss on Monday, right? We could tail them as they leave and—"

"No. End of discussion. We will not place her in danger. I want this whole operation done before that even becomes an issue."

"I hear ya," Tavish said. "And Jayla agrees with you. I just hate the thought of leaving all those kids behind, the ones out at 'the program' I mean."

"I'm not giving up on them," I said. "I...have other ways of finding out what we need to know."

"Really?" Tavish said, drawing the word out. "What do you have planned? Pulling his nails out? Threatening his family? No judgment, kid, whatever works."

"I have other ways," I repeated.

There was a long pause.

"Lyra, no," he said. "Please, kid. We'll find another way."

"I fear the time for other ways is running short."

Another long pause.

"Fuck. Fair enough," he sighed. "I...I won't tell Jayla. I suggest you don't, either. Well, let us know what you find. And take care of yourself."

"You, too."

"Peace, Celestial."

"Peace, Deadhead."

I hung up the phone and continued my walk around the building. I felt foolish. I should have done what needed to be done right away, but I thought I could collect the information about the internship program in better ways. But now it was technically Friday, and the time for better ways was done.

"We're wasting our fucking lives here, man," a rough voice said from the bubble of light fifty feet in front of me. It was Macy, one of the night workers, who was leaning up against the door that led from the outside into the kitchen, a smoldering cigarette between her fingers.

"So you don't believe in Pastor Ben's 'mission'?" Thomas, her sometimes lover, asked, leaned against the wall next to her.

"Fuck his mission," Macy said. "Fuck him. Wasting all this time and money trying to save a bunch of fruit loops. They're the way they are because God doesn't want them."

"Don't blame him," Thomas laughed. "Fucking obnoxious little faggots. 'Boo hoo, you called me the wrong pronoun! I'm not a girl, I just have huge tits! You're problematic!' Seriously, my generation is fucked up."

"Oh? Is that why you like the older gals?" Macy asked, flicking her cigarette onto the pavement and putting both arms around Thomas's waist. I turned and headed back the way I came, into the darkness. I did not need to be more disgusted with humanity.

I spent the next few hours sitting in the darkness in my room until the morning alarm went off, at which point I relocated to the Fellowship Hall. Sage was the first to emerge from zir room, making a beeline for the coffee pot which I, as the first person up, had dutifully made sure had already brewed.

"Lyra," ze mumbled in acknowledgment of my existence as ze sat down at the table.

"Good morning," I said, not getting a response. Ren came in next, about five minutes later, and took a similar path to the coffee before joining us at the table. Toby shuffled in next, followed shortly by Abby and Lenora together, then Saeed, then finally Nova. I greeted each of them by name, but only got a real response from Abby, who said good morning but wouldn't meet my eyes. I sat with them as they sipped from their mugs, making stilted small talk with one another. With the exception of Sage, I had known all of them long enough to have learned their routines, their foibles, their tells. And something was off.

No, something was *wrong*.

They were all running like a malfunctioning cuckoo clock, going through the motions without any purpose behind them. Each of them seemed like they had something deeply troubling on their minds, and I got the distinct feeling that it was the *same* deeply troubling something. The hairs on the back of my neck were standing up—another foible of my human form—as I addressed the group.

"Not to rush you all, but I wanted to remind you that we have peer group in ten minutes," I announced. Usually such declarations were met with grumblings and the wet, smacking sounds coffee being gulped down, but this time there was only silence.

"Actually, I think we're good to start now," Sage said. "if you're okay beginning early."

"O-Oh," I said, glancing around at the others. "Is...Is everyone ready?"

I received a chorus of five affirmatives, with Abby nodding and looking away.

"Alright, well, let's begin, then," I said, adrenaline pumping into my synapses. Something was wrong. It was positively radiating through the anima of everyone in the room.

"O-Okay," I said, trying to get my voice to stop shaking. "So, Pastor Ben wants us to start with—"

"Person," Sage snapped, "I don't actually give a fuck what Pastor Ben wants. Toby, Nova...now."

On cue, Toby and Nova bolted from their seats and slammed the double doors of the Fellowship Hall, Toby using his immense size and Nova using her piercing eyes to block the way out. I stood up to say something, only to find the rest of the group suddenly on their feet, too, encircling me.

"What's going on?" I asked, steadying my voice. "What's this about?"

"What's going on is we want some fucking answers, and what this is about is you giving them to us," Sage said, taking a step closer to me. Ze stood at least a foot taller than I did, and the intensity behind zir eyes told me that there would be no moving zem unless I was willing to extend my claws.

Which I was not.

"Does ze speak for all of you?" I asked, looking around the circle. The rest of the group gave affirmatives again, though tears were running down Abby's cheeks.

"Alright. And what answers are you looking for?"

"Cut the bullshit, Lyra!" Saeed snapped. "You know what we want to know!"

"Do I?"

"We...we want to know what happened to Jett and...and the others," Ren said, desperation all over their face. "Please!"

"We know you know, so don't pretend like you don't!" Nova yelled from the door she was blocking.

"I see," I said, keeping my voice low and cool. "And what shall you do if I cannot or will not provide you with the answers you are seeking? Will you hurt me?"

"No!" Abby blurted.

"Maybe!" Toby called from the door, his voice shaking.

"No, we won't!" Abby yelled, moving to stand in front of me. "You promised! You promised you wouldn't!"

"Look," Sage said, shooting both Toby and Abby diamond-hard glares. "We don't know what we'll do. But we've all fucking had it, Lyra. This place is fucked up! Please tell me you see that! This isn't a 'queer-affirming church,' it's a fucking conversion camp that knows all the right words to say! And worse than that, it's making people disappear!"

"You don't believe Pastor Ben when he tells you about the internships with SafeHaus?" I asked.

"I don't know what to believe!" Sage yelled. "But it all smells fucked up. A super rich asshole wanting to look out for a bunch of poor widdle downtrodden queers out of the goodness of his heart? Fucking *what*?"

"So what *do* you believe is happening?"

"We don't know," Saeed said, shaking his head. "You tell us. You tell us before they cart away the one person standing up for you, asshole!"

I looked at Abby, who was trying to make her tiny frame as large as possible as she stood between me and her friends.

"Abby," I asked, gently, "what do you think?"

"I—I don't know!" she said, through tears. "I don't know! I want to believe that it's the way Pastor Ben says it is. I want to believe that there are good people who would want to do good things for people in need just because they can, but...but my grandpa always said that if something seems too good to be true, it probably is. And this...."

Sage sighed and put a hand on her shoulder as she turned and collapsed into me, her tears soaking my shirt.

"Look," ze said, voice quieter than before. "We're...we're not going to hurt you. We just want to know what happened to everyone."

"I want to know what happened to Jett," Ren said, tears forming in their eyes, too.

"We...we clearly have no real plan," Toby said. "But please...please help us, Lyra."

"Hmm," I nodded, with Abby still latched onto me. "So, you want my help. You want information you think I have. But you already said you won't hurt me. So, how are you planning on getting that information out of me?"

"By hoping that you're a fucking *person*, Lyra!" Sage yelled. "Forget being a fellow queer, forget being our friend, *we thought*, how about about just being a fucking human being and doing the right thing?"

"So you're appealing to my better angels, then?" I asked.

"Y-Yeah," Sage stammered.

"That won't work on Pastor Ben," I said, looking zem in the eyes. "He has none. You will not appeal to his humanity, either, because he also has none of that. And, unfortunately, he is the only one who may have the information you and I both seek."

"Wait...what?" Ren asked.

"I cannot answer your questions," I said, releasing Abby as she stepped back to join the circle. "But what I can tell you is that there are larger forces at work here, and you are not the first seven people to realize that there is something seriously fucked up about Agape's Rainbow."

"Are you...are you saying you're, like, a double-agent?" Sage whispered.

"I'm saying that I'm a fellow queer. I'm saying I'm a 'fucking human being'. And I'm saying that I'm your friend, if you will still have me. I'm saying that I need you to extend a trust to me that I may not have earned."

"Okay, what are we trusting?" Saeed asked.

"Trust that there are pieces being moved into place. Trust that there are people working to help both you and your friends who have been taken from you."

"Help us how?" Lenora asked.

"You may not know it," I said, carefully, "or maybe you do. But you are all in danger here."

"What kind of danger?" asked Toby.

"That's what we're working on to find out."

"So, like, if we're in danger, shouldn't we just, you know, leave?" Lenora asked.

"I won't stop you," I said, taking a deep breath. "But if everyone starts leaving at once, I do worry that Pastor Ben will realize what is happening and might burn his whole operation."

"Which would mean we'd have pretty much zero chance of ever finding out what happened to Jett and the others," Sage said. "Or making sure he faces any kind of consequences for what he has done here."

"I'm afraid so," I nodded. "And I also cannot guarantee that you would actually be allowed to leave. Pastor Ben is working with—"

"...with a company that has literally its own private army," Sage finished for me. "Yeah. Fuck it, I'm staying. Not going to judge anyone who doesn't want to, but you should probably go now."

I looked around the circle and over to the door where Toby and Nova stood. They were all scared, but none of them moved.

"Abby," Lenora said, "you...you should go. They're coming for you in a few days, and—"

"No," Abby said, her tears gone. "If I go, they'll know something is up. I'm not putting you or the others in danger to keep myself safe."

"Abby—" I started. She turned and looked at me, more certainty behind her emerald eyes than I'd ever seen before.

"I'm staying. That's that."

I desperately wanted to fight her, wanted to tell her that she needed to leave and run as far as she could, to leave Seattle, to leave the state, to keep going until Agape's Rainbow and SafeHaus and Lyra Morne were all just distant, unhappy memories.

But if I was given the eternity that I might live, I knew I'd never come up with the right words to move her an inch.

"Okay," I said, the word catching in my throat.

"So...you think they're doing bad shit to them, don't you?" Nova asked.

"I truly don't know," I said. "But if I had to guess, yes."

"W-What kind of things do you think they're doing," Ren asked, their face pallid and fallen.

"I don't know that, either. We're working to find out."

"Okay, so...so what can we do?" Sage asked. "If there are people working to help us, let us help them, too. We're not useless; we captured your ass."

There were many reasons why I shouldn't have liked Sage. And yet I did anyway.

"You would do it, too, wouldn't you?" I said, unable to help a smile from forming across my face. "Stand with people you've never met to take down a darkness that none of us understand?"

"I mean...yeah," Sage shrugged. "Hell yeah."

"I am a very proud friend, Sage. But, in this case, how you can help is by carrying on as normal."

"What?" Lenora blurted. "Oh, bullshit!"

"No," I said. "Not at all. Like I said, if Pastor Ben starts suspecting something is amiss, we fear that he will...react."

"By destroying all traces of what he has done and running?" Abby asked.

"Yes."

"And, I'm going to guess that we might count as traces, right?" Sage asked.

"Most likely, yes."

"So, what, we just sit around with our thumbs up our asses and pretend that everything is fine?" Nova groaned.

"The location of your thumb is up to you, but yes, we need you to pretend that everything is normal," I responded. "But there will come a point when you will be told to run, and we will need you to run. It will not be a time for heroics or for questioning."

"Run?" Ren asked. "So, like, we *are* going to get the fuck out of here?"

"At the right time, yes," I nodded. "We would not leave you here. If you want to prepare, please pack any sentimental or otherwise important items in a bag you can grab at a moment's notice. But do it discreetly."

"This...this is a lot," Abby said, turning to me again. "Lyra, was...was it all fake?"

"I'm sorry, Abby, I truly am," I said, putting my hands on her arms. "The words of Pastor Ben have been a constant stream of lies and will forever be so. But this—this right here—the bonds you have formed, the friendships you have built...this was not fake. When things stop being normal, you will all need each other. And while this was far from a perfect operation, I reject the assertion that you had no plan. When the world starts falling apart, remember that you were willing to work together to protect each other and the friends who were taken from you. There is nothing more real in this world than that. And, as Sage put it so succinctly, you did, in fact, capture my ass."

That got a burst of nerve-assisted laughter from all of them.

"Now, if we are going to appear normal, I need something to put in our meeting notes for Pastor Ben to read later. So, will you all join me back in a more official circle?"

One by one, they all took their seats again.

"Thank you," I said. "Now, one good thing from your week, one bad thing. Who would like to start?"

"I assume you mean one bad thing aside from all this?" Nova asked, getting another round of laughter from the circle. "Okay, okay, okay. But the good thing was that I, um...met a girl."

"Wait...you met a girl? How?" Saeed laughed. "Where?"

"Yes I met a girl!" Nova retorted. "Online, okay?"

"Ooooh! Nova has an e-girl!" Ren laughed next to her, getting elbowed in the side.

"Shut up! She's not—okay, so maybe she's kind of an e-girl," Nova sighed. "It has been hard because she's in a different time-zone, but...but she's really cute and cool and...and she likes me and I like her and...I think she's my girlfriend now?"

"Fuck yeah!" Lenora cheered. "Go Nova!"

The circle all joined in, alternately congratulating and teasing Nova on her new relationship, the shadow of the previous conversation lifting off of them. But not from me. It didn't get to lift off of me. Needing a moment, I set down my clipboard and slid away from the still clamoring group to get myself some water from the dispenser next to the coffee machine.

"That's not what I meant when I asked if it was all fake," Abby's voice said from immediately behind me, making me jump and slosh my water onto my shirt.

"Abby...."

"I've made wonderful friends here, Lyra," she said, her voice trembling but her face set. "Friends I want to keep for the rest of my life. But...but it's been different with you. It's been more than that. Closer. Or...or at least I thought it was. Was...was it all just part of some cover you were building? Was it all just..."

She looked away and whispered.

"...fake?"

My hand trembling, I reached out and touched her shoulder. She turned around, the hurt on her face breaking my heart.

"No," I said. "It was not. I only lied to Pastor Ben, and only because I needed to. I never lied to you."

I swallowed heavily, and for once in my existence, let myself be brave.

"I don't lie to people I love."

The hurt melted away, and what replaced it was a smile so radiant it is etched on the substance of my anima.

"Me, neither," she said, and leaned in and kissed me.

"Oh, hello!" Saeed laughed from over at the circle. "This is new! Right? I'm not the last to know about it?"

"Yes! Hahaha fuck yes!" Lenora cheered. "Abby!"

"I knew it," Toby said.

"Oh you fucking did not," Nova said, rolling her eyes.

"Okay, I didn't *know* it know it, but like...there was a vibe."

"You always think there's a vibe," Sage laughed.

"Okay, but there definitely was one this time," Ren said. "This another thing you need us to be normal about?"

Abby laughed and blushed as I did the same.

"Yes, please," I said.

"Too bad!" Saeed laughed.

"Yeah, not happening," Sage said, shaking zir head. "But we can be quiet about it, right?"

One after another, the other six members of the circle made 'zip lip, lock lip, throw away key' motions across their mouths.

"But it's awesome," Lenora hissed. "You have no idea how long Abby has been pining over you!"

"Len!" Abby gasped, getting an exaggerated shrug from her roommate as the others laughed, a shrug which turned into an invitation for a hug, which Abby rushed over to receive. I looked out over this group, these lost, hurt people who had been cast out of every home they ever had, who had come together to form a family of their own, and who had, against all odds, included me in it. They were why I was doing this. But as I watched them, a dark, old thought crawled up from the base of my mind. It sounded like Cennend, and it told me the one thing I knew to be true: That in all of my existence, I had never, ever been enough. I had failed again, and again, and again, and others usually suffered for my shortcomings.

I hoped against all odds that this time would be different. It had to be

I had to be.

Agape's chapel was as silent at five in the afternoon as it would have been at two in the morning. Pastor Ben's Sunday services were mandatory, but beyond that, no one else used the little sanctuary.

Except Pastor Ben. At five o'clock every Friday afternoon.

"Lyra?" he called from the big, faux-wood double doors at the back of the chapel as I sat in the front pew, reading from the crisp black Bible that had been next to me when I sat down. It was the middle of summer, and if not for the acoustics of the room, his words would have been lost in the droning of the air conditioner.

"Hello, Reverend," I called back, not turning around but looking up from the page to the towering brass cross that loomed over us.

"I told you, you can just call me Pastor Ben," he said, walking down the short aisle toward me. "Ah, decided to crack the spine on one of these, huh?"

"I've read it before," I shrugged, looking back down at the page as he sat next to me. I wasn't lying; I'd been around when the first missionaries came to the land now known as Oregon, bringing their violence, disease, and holy book. I'd read pages of the Bible through the eyes of women trying to justify their husbands' abuse, children ripped from their homes and told their beliefs were 'savage' and 'satanic,' men reminding themselves that the feelings in their hearts were abominable before the Lord, and countless humans looking for some hope, some answers, or some comfort. I'd seen both kindness and wrath come from the hands of those who read this book I held on my lap, and I often wondered which of those the original authors had more in mind as they penned the stories of the great men their god worked through. I wondered if it mattered.

"Oh, so have I," Pastor Ben chuckled. "I find something new every time, though. May I ask which part you're on?"

"The book of Luke," I said, still reading the page. "Chapter ten."

"Ah, that's a good one," Ben said, his face lighting up. "The Good Samaritan?"

"An excellent parable, but not where I am," I muttered. At five o'clock, the staff of Agape would be either heading home or preparing the evening's meal, and the residents would mostly be in their rooms. The chapel was the last place they'd come. A quick slice to the carotid artery would be messy, but would end this disgusting little man's reign of terror before the food trays were even set out. I remembered what Jayla had said, and she was right. Yet there he was, and there I was next to him. And in that moment, it wasn't Jayla's plan that kept Benjamin Holmes alive, it was knowing that a quick death would be more mercy that he would ever deserve.

"Oh?" Ben said, craning his neck to try to see what verse I was on. "What part of the story, then?"

"Mary and Martha," I lied, my eyes leaving verse eighteen and moving down the page.

"Ah! What a wonderful lesson!" Pastor Ben exclaimed. "'Why does she get to relax while I have to do all the work?' It's about more than that, you know."

"Yes," I nodded. "I assume you are referring to the relationship between faith and works, and how our works won't earn us a space in Heaven?"

"Wow, you do know your stuff, don't you?" he laughed, but with a little edge in his voice that told me he'd had a big speech prepared that I'd just neutered.

"Yes," I nodded again. "I do."

"You know, sometimes you've made me think of that story, Lyra," he said, raising the hairs on the back of my neck.

"How so?"

"Well, ever since you got here, you've been pitching in all over the place," he said, briefly glancing at the cross and then back to me. "And don't get me wrong, that's very much appreciated. But you know you don't have to 'earn' your keep, right? We have staff that can clear tables or take out the trash or—"

"I am not trying to earn my keep."

"Hmm," he grunted. "Yes, well, I kinda got that feeling. So, Lyra, sometimes new clients will...work extra hard to try to get my attention. I know for a lot of you, every mentor and parental figure in your lives let you down when you came out, so it only makes sense to try extra hard to impress an older—slightly older, mind you—adult who accepts you as you are. But I just want you to know, Lyra, if you're working to get my attention...."

His fingers were suddenly sliding up the outside of my thigh, creeping under the cuff of my shorts. They felt like sandpaper against my skin, sending an awful sensation through my whole body, which at that moment I wanted to unmake just to avoid ever knowing his repulsive touch again.

But there was a plan to see to, and this was the day I'd chosen. He just made it easier.

"Remove your hand from me, Benjamin Holmes," I boomed, through my lips and my anima at the same time. "You are unworthy."

He gasped and snapped his hand away from me like he had just touched a live wire.

"N-Now there's no need to get upset," he stammered, trying to straighten himself and regain the power he still thought he had. "I was just stretching and my hand accidentally—"

And for the first time in millennia, as I brought fire to my eyes, I let the part of me that came from my parent speak.

"Be silent."

He caught the scream in his throat but reeled backwards, tumbling off the end of the pew.

"W-What are you?" he stammered as he scrambled to get back to his feet. "W-Why—?"

I hated every part of what I had to do next, but he needed to believe. And for a man like him, a man of many words and little faith, he needed to see.

"Pastor Benjamin Holmes," I said as I lifted off the ground, "come and see."

I pulsed my anima through my skin in a radiant burst that shredded my clothes, their embers falling to the ground as my wings manifested from my back. I beat them once to lift my higher up, putting me on the same level as the intersection point of the brass cross, a memorial to the good man who died only for men like this to hide themselves in his name. I hovered there, radiant light cloaking my naked form, remembering when Elodie and I crafted this beautiful vessel for me, and how it had felt to have my sister embrace me for the first time.

What would she think of me now? Would we ever hold each other again?

Pastor Ben dropped to his knees hard enough to rattle the windows.

"O-O-Our F-Father, w-who—" he stuttered, his whole body shaking.

"Be not afraid. Your heavenly Father has already richly blessed you, Pastor Holmes," I said, trying to hide my disgust. "You have done much in his name, but you falter. He has chosen to send me to make sure his will is done."

"Y-Y-Yes! Yes, of course!" he stammered. "I know I could do better! I know there is so much left to be done! I know I...I have sinned! I—"

"Yes," I interrupted. "You certainly have. Shadows hang thick all around you. That is the reason I'm here."

"W-what are you here to do?" he said, his voice, his hands, his whole body trembling as he knelt before me.

"I thought you would have guessed," I said. "Benjamin Holmes, I am here to bring you the light."

V

Hymn of the Lightbringer

"I REALLY NEVER THOUGHT we'd get here," Abby said, curled up against me in my bed, her skin soft and warm against mine as pale moonlight from the open window washed over us. "I'd pretty much given up. Lenora kept trying to get me to say something, but I…I always lost my nerve. Thank you for being more forward than I could find the courage to be."

"I have a friend of mine to thank," I said, pulling her close as I stared up at the ceiling. "I went out for a walk with her last night. And…and she helped me realize some things."

"Oh? Like what?"

"Like the fact that I may have had more than standard feelings of friendship for the girl who always calmed my soul and stirred my heart whenever I saw her," I said. "Like the fact that it meant something that days when we talked were always brighter, and days when we didn't seemed wasted. Like the fact that I was so caught up in everything else going on that I was letting something beautiful slip by me."

"Well, there's certainly a lot of 'everything else' going on, so I can't be too mad at you," Abby smiled, then leaned over and kissed my cheek. "So, who is this friend I owe a Christmas card to?"

"Jayla," I said, trying to picture the leader of No Affiliation opening one of the delightfully garish handmade cards Abby crafted for every possible occasion. "I can't wait for you to meet her."

"Is she part of the…?"

"Yes."

There was a long pause during which I shifted slightly, rearranging my legs under Abby's, which were curled over the top of them.

"So, it's just you and me here, Lyra," Abby said. "What…what comes next?"

I almost told her I couldn't say, but she was right; it was just us there, and in that moment, for all I cared, the entire universe started and stopped at the walls of my dorm room.

"What comes next is I find out what Pastor Ben knows," I said, taking a deep breath. "About everything."

"How?" she asked. "Are you...are you going to hurt him?"

It was my turn to pause. Not because I was considering lying, but because I knew I couldn't.

"Yes," I said. "And probably myself as well."

"Wait," Abby said, sitting up and pulling away from me. "No. No, that's not okay. I'm not okay with that part."

"I'll be okay," I said, propping myself up on my arm. "I promise."

"That's the first thing you've said that I don't trust," she told me. "But...but you know more about this than I do, and I know you can probably handle yourself...."

"I can," I nodded. "And I will."

"Good," she whispered, and then took my hand and held it between both of hers. "Lyra there's...there's a lot I don't know about you, isn't there?"

In the moonlight, she looked like a being of light, a being of anima. But she wasn't. I thought about Ezri, and the things Elodie had done to protect her, and sitting there, looking at Abby, naked, vulnerable, and mortal, I finally understood.

But I couldn't do what she had done.

I wasn't Elodie.

"Yes," I said. "But you will learn all of them, in time. I...I don't want to hide anything from you, there are just things that...that I don't know how to tell you yet."

"What kind of things?" she asked. "I won't press, but...."

"I've hurt people before," I said, looking away from her. "Many, many people."

"I'm sorry," Abby said, and then surprised me. "That must have been awful for you to have to do."

My eyes snapped back to her.

"I'm not an innocent lamb, Lyra," she said, with a sad smile. "Maybe once I was. Once before my parents kicked me out. Before everyone I loved abandoned me. Before I could see the hate that could well up in someone seemingly from nowhere. I used to think that there was just 'good' and 'on their way to being good.' And...and I really want to still believe that for most people, but for some I just don't anymore. But you...you came in here a stranger, and you've put yourself at risk to save us, even though you didn't know any of us. And while I may not know everything about you, I've spent enough time with you to know that if you hurt someone, it was because that's what needed to happen. I also know that hurting people isn't in your nature, so I can only imagine the pain it must have caused you."

"You...have too much faith in me," I said, looking away from her again.

"No," she said, gently guiding my chin back toward her. "You may be all I have faith in, period."

She kissed me, and for a moment I was in a better, kinder world. A world where Abby and I could just be us, and Elodie and Ezri could be Elodie and Ezri, and there was no Pastor Ben, no Russell Hausman, no Cennend.

But a world like that was never meant to last, and when she pulled back, I was back in the one where the woman I loved was in grave danger, and I was the only one who could save her.

"Abby," I said, tears suddenly flooding my eyes. "I've let so many people down!"

"You won't let me down," she said, with heartbreaking certainty.

"I...there's something wrong with me, Abby," I said, trying to hold it together with very little luck. "The people I've hurt...they were awful, violent people, and I did what I needed to do. And the first time I did it, it was so hard and I sobbed afterwards, and I thought that nothing could ever make me do it again. But then I did, and it was a little easier, and easier still the next time, and then the last time, it wasn't just easy...I didn't even care. I worry I'm becoming something...something hateful and violent, and that that's all I'll ever be and—"

Abby's hand reached out, and she placed her palm on my sternum, right over my heart.

"Lyra Morne," she said, looking into my eyes. "Do you trust me?"

"Y-Yes," I said, through tears. "I do."

"Then trust that I know who lives *here*," she said. "I don't care what you've done in the past. And...and maybe that makes me a bad person. Maybe you've done terrible things, even if they were done to terrible people. But I don't care. I know who you are. I know who you've been to me. One of the reasons it was so easy to fall in love with you is that you were more loving to me than anyone in my life has ever been, and not in big, grand gestures, but just...in everything. And you never wanted something in return, or expected anything. Because you were just being...you. That's who you are. I'm sorry you're worried about becoming something else; that's not a fear I have. But...I'm here now, and you don't have to do any of this alone. If all I can do is remind you of who you are, then that's what I'm going to do. Loudly, and as often as you need."

I don't know how Elodie did it, how she kept control of herself after Cennend had hurt Ezri. I'd done for my sister then what Abby was offering to do for me now, but I couldn't fathom how she'd heard my words. She'd known Ezri her whole life. I'd known Abby for six months, and if it had been us in Elodie and Ezri's positions, I would have scourged the world into a barren rock.

I loved my sister; I would never again think I was worthy to lecture her.

"Thank you," I whispered, this time being the one to kiss her.

"You don't need to thank me," she said, parting our lips for a moment and then kissing me again. "Ever."

"Abby," I said, leaning back. "Tomorrow—"

"Tomorrow is tomorrow," she said, taking my hands in hers again. "We're here tonight. And you need rest. So let's...just be here, tonight."

Tomorrow, I would face Pastor Benjamin Holmes for the last time.

Tomorrow, one way or another, I would find out what happened to the missing residents of Agape's Rainbow.

Tomorrow, all of this would end.

But Abby was right; we were here tonight.

So I decided that here was where I would be.

"I could just wait outside for you," Abby whispered as we walked down the main hall the next morning. "I don't have to go in."

"Abby, I'm sorry," I said, my heart beating fast. "I need you with the others. You'll be safer in a group and...and I don't know what's going to happen in Pastor Ben's office. But—"

"But if you're worried about me out here, you can't concentrate on what you need to do in there," she finished for me. "I understand. I just hate it."

"You are not alone in that," I said. "I'll be okay. He can't hurt me in any way that actually matters."

"*Any* way actually matters," Abby said. "But okay just...just remember I'm out here—not out *here*, I'll go be with the group, I promise. But I'll be holding you in my thoughts and...and being with you in every way I can. And also this."

She darted in and kissed me, long and deep, pulling me close to her with a ferocity that felt like she would never let go. I wish she hadn't had to. But this was where we were now, where I was. All of my other tricks had failed.

So I'd do it the hard way.

Abby released me, and I told her I'd see her soon. She nodded, tears in her eyes, and left me there in the corridor, pausing several times to look back toward me. I wanted to call her back, or better yet to run after her and carry her off, somewhere far away from this awful place, somewhere where we could just be us. But I didn't. Holding myself back was physically painful, but I let her go and watched her disappear through the doors to the Fellowship Hall.

Alone again, I took my burner phone from my pocket and texted Jayla.

"Going in now."

It was less than five seconds before a response popped up.

"In position. Be safe."

I slid the phone back into my pocket without responding and walked the rest of the way to Pastor Ben's office, flinging open the door without knocking.

"Who—Lyra!" he gasped, dropping the book he was reading and swiveling his chair to face me. "What—?"

"I believe it is time for a confession, Benjamin Holmes," I declared, hating the words as they came out of my mouth.

"A confession?" he stammered, sweat already beading on his brow. "Oh, I—"

"Is there a problem?" I asked, letting a quick flash of blue glow shimmer across my eyes.

"N-No, Blessed One! You just...you have never been the one to request—"

"I request nothing," I said, extending my wings and raising myself into the air. "I grow tired of your games. You stand before me, the messenger of the Lord whom you prayed so ardently to come to you, professing a desire for forgiveness. And yet you lie!"

"I—no! No, Blessed One, I have never lied to you! The L-Lord knows—"

"Of course the Lord knows, you pitiful little man," I said, the words tasting rancid and alien in my mouth. "You do not confess to inform me or the Lord of what you have done, you confess so you can say out loud what you have concealed, so you can lay your sins bare, Benjamin Holmes. And you dare call yourself a pastor?"

"I—"

"Submit," I demanded, pointing down to the floor as he obediently lowered himself, his whole body trembling.

"I-I confess that—"

"No," I stopped him, looking down on his disgusting form, cowering down on his knees before me. "Not like that. This confession will be different. You have abused your freedom. Now, what you would not offer will instead be taken."

His lip quivered as he looked up at me, tears and mucus streaking his face.

"Filth of the Earth," I said, "receive my spirit."

Before he could react, I exhaled and breathed myself into him, fully joining my anima to his. My body shuddered in the air as everything this perverted, hateful man was flooded me. This was what I hadn't wanted; this was what I had prolonged the danger to Abby and the others to avoid. I had spent millennia surviving by occupying corners of other people's vessels, and in that time I learned that anima isn't passive. It will defend itself, even if it doesn't know what it is defending itself against. Especially if it doesn't. It would seek to expel me like an invading virus, employing every dark thought, every trauma, every painful, hateful memory as its immune system.

I bore scars from each and every vessel I'd ever occupied and now I would bear one from Benjamin Holmes as well.

"W-What are you doing?" he groaned in pain, trying to stand before I forced him back down.

"Be silent."

Suddenly, I was in a child's room, posters of cartoon soldiers and colorful robots adorning the walls. Before I could get my bearings, a thick, hard hand drove into the side of my face, knocking me to the burnt-orange carpet.

"You played like a faggot today!" a rough, growling voice shouted. I looked up and saw a tall, wiry man with a face much like Pastor Ben's glaring down at me, right before his boot drove into my side. "Maybe I should get you one of your sister's dresses to wear instead of your jersey next time. You let your whole team down! You let *me* down. I have never been so fucking humiliated!"

The mouth that was mine but not mine begged forgiveness and mercy as I pushed against the memory and finally wrenched myself free, probing into the darkness of Pastor Ben's mind for what I needed to know.

"It's part of our community outreach," a bright-faced woman with golden brown skin and jet black hair said, handing me a card with Russell Hausman's name on it. "Mr. Hausman is a philanthropist, and, being in a position to give life-changing opportunities to the less fortunate, feels morally obligated to do so."

"Obligated by God?" my mouth asked.

"Yes. Of course," the woman said. "And, as part of our partnership, Mr. Hausman will use his considerable wealth to make regular, generous donations to your center."

"That all sounds wonderful, Miss Emerson. But we are both adults here, and we both know that billionaires don't become billionaires by giving away money for nothing."

Ms. Emerson tilted her head and smiled.

"You're wondering why Mr. Hausman would spend his hard-earned money funding a clandestine conversion therapy clinic, correct?"

"Now wait a minute," I, but not me, said. "We are not—"

"Pastor Holmes," she smiled, this time showing her teeth, "I thought we were all adults here."

Without warning Pastor Ben's anima attacked again, pulling me away from the conversation and plunging me into a wide corridor.

"Fucking faggot!"

It was my mouth this time that spoke the hateful words, my hands throwing a terrified young man who couldn't have been more than fourteen into a bank of lockers.

"Ben...why?" he yelped, barely recovering before my hands slammed him backward again. All around us stood a group of larger boys, each one hooting and cackling, cheering me on.

"Kick his faggot ass, Ben!"

"Smear the queer! Smear the queer!"

"Aww, he's crying! Little gay boy is crying!"

"Why?" the boy cried, still collapsed against the lockers. "You...you're my friend! You promised you wouldn't tell anyone. I—"

"Shut up!" my mouth yelled before I delivered a kick to the boy's ribs, a kick just like the one I had recently been on the receiving end of. The boy cried harder, curling up against the assault. Disgusted, I tore myself out of the memory's grasp and dove into what it had been protecting.

"Shame about that boy," a man I recognized as Russell Hausman said, pacing back and forth as I sat in his immaculate office. "But we both did all we could for him. Some folks you just can't reach and all that, right?"

"I'm...I'm afraid so" I said. "I tried so hard to get through to him, to help him see the truth, but he just wouldn't hear it."

"And I was hoping he would make a fine addition to our team here," Hausman nodded. "But he used his interview time to rant against capitalism and the military industrial complex and yak yak yak, then stormed out of here before we could even call security. Folks like that decided long ago that everyone is against them, then they seek out to make that true. It's not our fault that he chose to wind up back on the streets. Maybe he glamorized that lifestyle in his mind, living outside of 'the system' and rebelling against 'the man.' Found out how dangerous it can be out there though. Shame, really."

"They still don't have any leads," I sighed. "None of his friends or family have seen him."

"Well, I wouldn't hold out hope for that changing," Hausman said. "All the money in my pocket against all the money in your pocket, I'm guessing this was gang-related. Hmm. Well, not that there's a bright side to this horrible situation, but I do have to say that the idea of a disgruntled former resident of yours running around spreading lies about us wasn't something I was a big fan of. So at least that's not something we have to worry about now."

"Mr...Mr. Hausman, a boy died," I said, feeling the heart that wasn't mine crawl up into my throat.

"Oh, don't go getting all bleeding heart on me, Ben," Hausman said. "I know that, and it's awful. A tragedy! I'm just saying what is."

I opened my mouth to say something, but no words came out. Russell Hausman walked over to his bar and poured two whiskeys.

"Here you go," he said handing me one and then lifting his into the air. "To what is."

I was pulled back before I could see any more. An inky blackness surrounded me, and when I emerged, I was in a quaintly decorated bedroom. A dark-haired woman knelt in front of me, tears streaming down her face.

"I...I don't like this, Ben," she whispered through her tears.

"Then confess that, too," my cursed mouth spoke. "The husband is the head of the wife as Christ is the head of the church, and it is my responsibility to help you come into right relationship with the Lord."

"I...."

"You sinned against me!" I barked. "And to sin against me is to sin against the Lord! Confess!"

In a far too familiar gesture, Lia Holmes bowed her head.

"I-I confess that I have sinned," she stammered.

"How have you sinned?" I demanded.

"I-I-I...."

"Confess!"

"I thought lustful thoughts about someone who wasn't you!" she blurted. "I'm sorry! They were just thoughts! I would never—"

"She who looks upon another with lust in her heart commits adultery against her husband!" I yelled. "And who was it?"

"Y-you know!"

"Say it!"

"Seph!" she cried.

"Repent!"

"I'm sorry!" she yelled as I fought hard to break free from the memory. It was stronger than the last two, its barbs cutting deep into my anima as I struggled against it. There was something behind it, something I was not supposed to see.

"Sorry for what?"

"For thinking that way about her!" Lia sobbed. "For betraying you with my thoughts. I'm sorry!"

"Then I forgive you," I said, calmly. "You may stand. Your sins are forgiven, by me and by our Lord.

Lia rose cautiously, her legs shaking as she stood.

"You will, of course, cut off all contact with Seph immediately."

"What?" Lia gasped. "No!"

"That man is not good for you, Lia! He has caused you to stumble once, he—"

"She!" Lia screamed, the woman who had been trembling before me suddenly filled with an almost unearthly fury. The words caught in my throat and forced me to step back.

Her tears were gone.

"Seph is a woman, Benjamin," she said, her voice raw but steady. "You use 'she' to talk about her. And I will not cut her out of my life. I will learn to better control my thoughts, out of respect for you and for her. But she is a part of my life, and that's final."

The body I saw through moved like lightning and stepped in her path as she turned to leave the room.

"Are you going to hit me, Benjamin?" she asked, her vivid brown eyes staring into the ones I was borrowing.

"N-No! Never!" my mouth said. "Lia, you...you know I wouldn't. You know what kind of man I am."

"Sometimes I wonder, Ben, if I really do."

"Y-Your soul—"

"I wouldn't want to be a part of any heaven that wouldn't have my best friend," she said as I stepped out of her way and she passed through the door. "And I don't believe Jesus would either."

The barbs were still in me as I burst out of the memory, erupting through it like a fish cresting the waves. The bedroom disappeared, and I was in Pastor Ben's office, my body moving back and forth in sharp, jerky, grotesque thrusts.

I looked down and saw myself—Lyra—laying on my back across his desk, naked and moaning in ecstasy as he—I—rutted me.

The anima was not done protecting his secrets. But these were thoughts, and thoughts were never as powerful as memories. I shattered through that one like a pane of glass, fueled by a newfound fury at seeing his hideous fantasies play out. I emerged into a suburban living room, facing a large television screen with a blonde reporter on it reading the news.

"...Which has baffled the scientific community. The plague, which some are dubbing the 'Hand of God' virus, has affected exclusively members of the LGBT community and currently has a death toll in the millions."

I tore through that one, too, emerging into a dazzling white temple. Next to me stood me—Lyra—with their wings extended and wearing a brilliantly white robe. Far, far below us, an endless mass of bodies undulated in fire and flames that entrapped but did not consume them.

"Good and faithful servant," the fake Lyra said, "your faith and your virtue have earned you favor with the Lord Almighty. Now, receive your reward."

They gestured down toward the pit of fire, where, in the distance, two winged figures were flying up toward us carrying a third person between them.

"Benjamin!" Lia gasped as the angels set her before him. "You saved me!"

"The Lord saved you," I said, as she began kissing my feet. "I am but his servant."

It took me longer to break free from that one, but it fell away just as the others had. Whatever was being hidden was close, I could feel it pulsating just behind the veil. But instead I emerged into an empty office building, looking out an open window. Down in the street below, a mass of people that looked not unlike the souls of the damned in the fantasy I had just left danced and marched among rainbow-bedecked parade floats traveling down the street.

In my hands, I held a rifle.

Summoning what was left of my strength, I forced myself through the twisted fantasy before it could play out. I burst into a sunny park, kyanite blue sky overhead, a pleasant breeze dancing through the trees.

"Pastor Ben," a woman's voice called from behind me. I turned and saw Cora Emerson approaching, wearing a blood red dress suit.

"Oh...it's you. I thought I'd be meeting with Mr. Hausman...."

"You keep making that mistake, Pastor," she said, flashing her teeth like a shark. "And I keep having to inform you of things such as the fact that Mr. Hausman does not leave his office for impromptu meetings in public parks, nor does he respond well to demands from men so far beneath him they barely register as a speck in his eye. Say what's on your mind, Pastor."

"Look, I'm not trying to be demanding," he said, trying to puff up his chest, "but I—I need to know what happens to the kids we send to the internship program. No more runaround."

"They're given free room and board on our state-of-the-art corporate campus and gain experience and training in a number of lucrative fields, as well as a generous monthly stipend," she said, without taking a breath.

"Don't give me that!" I snapped, heart firmly in my throat. "What really happens to them? Why can no one reach them once they enter the program?"

"It is a *very* intensive program," Ms. Emerson said, tilting her head. "I'm sure they've found themselves quite busy between their tasks and the new friends they've made."

"Dammit, don't...don't bullshit me!"

Cora Emerson straightened her spine, and a smile formed on her face that would haunt me for the rest of my days.

"May I ask why you care, Pastor?"

"B-Because I'm in charge of them!" I stammered. "They put themselves in my care. I...I should at least know what's happening to them."

"Oh, so it's duty then? Well," Ms. Emerson smirked. "What an honorable man of God you are. Well then, let me be honorable, too, and make sure you are aware that you are currently standing at a crossroads. Let me lay out two scenarios for you. One: you can keep pursuing this line of questioning. Keep investigating and poking and digging around until you become a thorn in Mr. Hausman's side and he withdraws his partnership and all of his funding. And then maybe some stories start getting out, the ones we've been using our influence to keep squashed. Accounts from former residents who didn't go into the program about how you're running a goddamn conversion camp right here in liberal Seattle. That would be the end of your public goodwill, you have to know that. Which means the donations would dry up. And how would your church—you do remember your actual church, right? And the congregation?—feel if they knew your little pet project was going to suck up funds from all of their other 'worthy' causes? How would they feel about the leader who let this all fall apart around him?"

She tilted her head the other way and smiled another smile that made my anima shudder.

"But that's scenario one," she said. "Scenario two is that you realize that how Mr. Hausman runs his company isn't the business of a podunk preacher who periodically decides to put on his big-boy pants. Scenario two requires you to do the same thing that preachers have been doing as far back as Saint Peter: Turn away. Turn away from the thing that I guarantee you do not have the stomach for. Turn away and live the rest of your pathetic little life in blissful ignorance, knowing that nothing that happens after you send those little lost lambs off will ever affect you in any meaningful way."

My hands shook as she stared at me, her piercing brown eyes searing me.

"Although, here's the funny thing, Pastor Ben," she said, her voice dropping low and cold. "I think you already know, or at least know enough. I think what you want is for me to tell you you're wrong. But, you know, I think being in the presence of such a fine, godly man such as yourself has made lying distasteful all of the sudden. Shall I tell you the truth, Pastor? Shall I confess my sins—our sins—to you, so that you can know them, and never unknow them, so you can no longer pretend to not know what you've been a party to all along?"

She ran the tip of her tongue over her lower lip, and smiled again.

"Well?"

"N-No!" I yelped. "No. No, I'm…I'm sorry, it's none of my business how your company is run. I'm…I'm sorry I bothered you. I'm sorry."

"You are forgiven," Cora Emerson said, extending a hand over Pastor Ben's head. "Go and sin no more. Oh, and have all of the residents ready for pick-up on Friday."

Ben's heart and my anima both froze.

"W-what? I thought we had until Monday. And…all the residents? I thought you just wanted Abby!"

"Hmm, well, yes, but plans do change, Pastor," Cora said, taking out her phone and absently scrolling the screen. "Your recent declarations have raised some concerns. The ones about you talking with an angel."

"But I—"

"Oh, don't get me wrong, Pastor," Cora said, looking up from her screen. "We believe you. That's the problem. You see, we believe that your 'angel' is actually someone we've been trying to track for almost a year who does pose a minor threat to us, based on the description we received from our man on the inside."

"Man on—?"

"Dear Pastor," Cora smirked, "do you believe you pay your staff enough to put them beyond wanting to receive an extra two thousand in their accounts every month? Landlords don't take the love of Jesus, sweetie. But anyway, my superior and I believe it would be best to liquidate the current crop of residents and have Agape's Rainbow go dormant for a while until we are sure your angel has moved on or been dealt with."

"But…but Ms. Emerson, please! Not all of the residents are at that point. Abby has been willful and headstrong, and I won't argue against taking her—"

Deep inside me, the dark voice that had called out to me since the day I'd lost my original wing began whispering terrible things.

"…but there's still hope for most of the others! I—"

"Is there a world where you believe we actually care about that nonsense?" Cora laughed. "Pastor Ben, *I'm* gay. Gay as the blessed day is long. In fact, to wash this whole conversation off of me later, I'm going to go get two-knuckles deep in some soft-butch sub who I haven't even met yet, and don't worry, we'll both be praising the Lord's name the whole time. How do you not understand that you are a tool, and an increasingly useless one? Russell Hausman doesn't care about a god he has more money than! Now. Friday. Have them ready. Make a big announcement to celebrate that everyone gets an internship now, hooray! Put up a banner if you want."

"S-Some of them won't want to go…."

"Then," Cora said, looking dead into the eyes that weren't mine, "I suggest you stay in your office, and turn up the music. Goodbye, Pastor."

She turned to walk away as I burst forth from Pastor Ben's vessel and made myself whole once more. We stared at each other, both of us trembling for different reasons.

"L-Lyra, I—"

I grabbed ahold of his anima and snapped it back hard enough to launch his body against his desk. He collapsed into a heap on the floor, unconscious but, unfortunately, still alive. Charging out of his office I dialed Jayla's number and barked the pass-phrase into the phone.

"Celestial, what's wrong?"

"He doesn't know, and we need to move *now*!"

"Well, okay then," she said, without hesitation. "Deadhead, drop the hammer. Everyone else, strap in."

I charged down the hall faster than my physical form was meant to move, bursting through the doors of the Fellowship Hall at top speed. All seven residents looked up from what they were doing, as did Jason, who was cleaning up the coffee station.

"Lyra?" he said, tilting his head at me. "What—?"

I anima snapped him before he could finish, his body falling splayed on the floor.

"Oh shit," Sage said, jumping up from zir chair. "Did you—is he...? What the hell did you do?"

"He's fine," I said. "This is that time I talked about. Go grab your things. You have five minutes."

"You heard my partner! Move!" Abby ordered, sending the rest of the residents dashing toward the dormitory section.

"I got you," Abby said, darting in and kissing me on her way by. I rushed after her, back to my own room, grabbing a backpack full of the meager possessions I had managed to acquire during my time as a human as well as the Bluetooth earpiece that Tavish had provided me with. I popped it in my ear and called Jayla again.

"Residents are alerted and will be ready in five minutes," I said. "How far out are you?"

"About five minutes," Jayla reported. "Any resistance?"

On cue, Matthew stepped into the hallway, blocking the corridor and raising a pistol in his right hand, pointed right at my chest.

"Well well," he said, a repulsively smug smile on his face. "Looks like the little freaks caught on to the game. Well, bad news, you're going to stay right here until my friends arrive to take you to SafeHaus."

Well, I suppose that answered who Cora Emerson's man on the inside was.

"How does it feel, Lyra?" Matthew laughed. "You thought you were so smart and that you could just boss the rest of us around. How does it feel to—"

My hand shot out and jerked his gun to the side just as he squeezed the trigger, his bullet blowing a hole through the drywall at the same moment I dug my claws into his hand and sheared through four of his fingers, sending the gun tumbling to the ground. He'd barely started screaming when I whipped him around, placed a hand on the back of his head, and smashed his no longer smug face into the wall, anima snapping him for good measure as his body fell to the ground.

"Lyra!" Jayla yelled over the earpiece. "What the hell is going on? Did I hear gunfire? Lyra!"

"Sorry for the delay," I said, looking at the stunned faces of the residents and gesturing for them to follow me. "No, no resistance."

"O...kay?" Jayla said. "Well, Syn will be disappointed, but that's good to hear."

"Jesus Christ, Abby," I heard Ren whisper, "I think you're, like, dating one of the X-men?"

I made a mental note to ask Syn for context later.

"So, where are we headed?" Sage asked, catching up with me.

"Kitchen," I said. "You're going to meet my friends. They're safe and they'll take care of you."

"Who are—?" Saeed started.

"They're safe and they'll take care of you," I repeated. "I need you to trust me."

"You're good at this, you know," Jayla said in my ear. "There's a camera out back, right?"

"Correct."

"Boom. Not anymore," Tavish said. "You're on a group call by the way. Hey, thank the good pastor for keeping a goddamn spreadsheet of all of his passwords, would ya?"

Somehow, I didn't think I would.

I threw open the double doors to the kitchen a minute later, gesturing for the group to follow me to the delivery entrance. I shoved the door open just as Jayla's battle-scarred gray van pulled up and lurched to a stop.

"Okay!" Jayla yelled as the members of No Affiliation save for Tavish disembarked. "All of us out, all of you in. Except you, Lyra, you're with me. Tav, cameras down?"

"Every last one of them," he said through the earpiece.

"Bet," Jayla said. "Okay, kids, into the van. We need to be ready to go the second we're done in there. Bob, go do your thing and then get back here, pronto. Syn, cover Bob. Clover, stay with the kids—"

"We're not kids, lady," Sage said. "Most of us are at least eighteen and—"

The look Jayla shot zem knocked the words out of zir mouth.

"Be good and you can watch *Bluey* at the hideout," she said, winking at zem. "Anyway, Lyra, let's go."

I nodded and started to follow, stopping as Abby grabbed my arm.

"Hey," she said, darting in and kissing me. "Be safe, okay? I love you."

"I-I will," I said, trying to find my words as her eyes briefly made me forget why I would ever move a single step away from her. "I love you, too."

"Lyra, I don't want to be an ass...." Jayla hissed.

"Go on!" Abby gestured, blushing and grinning in the same goofy way I was sure I was. "Go! I'll be okay. Go!"

I nodded and took off after Jayla, trying to shake myself back into the moment.

"She's cute as hell," Jayla said when we were back inside. "Good job, Celestial."

"Thank you," I said, straightening a kink out of my neck as we ran. "Yes, she is."

We ran through the kitchen and out into the Fellowship Hall. I saw Jason still lying on the ground unconscious, and for a moment I considered moving him outside. He was not Pastor Ben, Russell Hausman, or Cora Emerson. But he still knew what he was working for. He stood by and watched his leader chip away at the psyches of scared, hurt, young people, exploiting their fear and doubt and leading them off to one slaughterhouse or another.

I left him where he lay. Maybe his God would protect him.

"Maintenance room is down the hall, that way!" I yelled to Bob, a good twenty feet ahead of us, and tossed him the stolen key. "Here!"

"Cool, cool," Bob said, catching it in the air. "Thanks for the pics, too. Janky-ass cut-rate system will be down in minutes."

"Good, because that's all you got," Jayla said. "We need to get the fuck out of here before the Hounds show up. Meet back at the van. Go!"

"Aye-aye," Syn saluted. "Fuck shit up."

"Same," Jayla nodded as Syn and Bob tore off toward the maintenance room. "Okay, now for our business."

"This way," I said, leading her down the hall to Pastor Ben's office and slamming the door. He was still where I'd left him, though slowly regaining consciousness.

"Well if it isn't Benjamin-motherfucking-Holmes," Jayla said, driving her steel-toed boot into his side.

"Fuck!" he gasped, catching himself before he crashed all the way to the carpet. "Who...who are you?"

"I'm Link Lewis' sister," she said, backhanding him across the face. "My friend here says you don't know where you sent my brother off to die, and in my mind, that's as good as you having killed him yourself."

"L-Lyra? Why? What...what's the meaning of this?"

"You have sinned, Benjamin Holmes," I said, letting my wings tear through the back of my shirt, onyx and alabaster feathers casting a dark shadow across him as he tried to crawl away, only for Jayla to kick him again.

I raised my hand and she stopped, taking a step back as a foolish look of relief crossed Pastor Ben's bloodied face.

"Blessed One, thank—"

"You prey on the weak," I continued, letting my anima flow down to my hands, talons extending from each of my fingers. "You tear apart beauty and call it a mercy."

My lips curled back, and my mouth filled with needle-sharp fangs.

"You call hate love, and love perversion," I hissed as he cowered away from me, backing himself into the far corner of his office, knocking over a trashcan and sending garbage scattering across the floor. I directed my anima up into my face; it was time for something new.

It started in my forehead and extended down my right cheek in one direction, and under my left socket in the other. One by one, ten glowing blue eyes of different sizes, each set at an unnatural, appalling angle, opened across my face and stared back at him. Some saw light. Some saw darkness. All of them saw fear.

"You spit in the face of your God and his creation, and call yourself righteous and holy for it," I yelled, my face inches from his.

"And for that," I said, dropping down to a whisper, "you are damned."

"W-What are you?" he stammered, tears and snot running down his face, the stench of ammonia filling the air as urine trailed down his legs. "Who are you?"

"Do I no longer look angelic to you, Benjamin?" I asked, standing tall so he could take me in all at once. "I have read your holy book, and I saw myself in it. I, born of an omnipotent parent who thought me beautiful. I, who rebelled, and was cast down like lightning. I, who have walked the shadows of the Earth. I, who can see your sins. So, I ask you, Benjamin Holmes...."

I reached down and lifted him into the air by the throat, redirecting my anima one last time, manifesting two gnarled, twisted horns from my forehead.

"*Who do you say I am?*"

He screamed. He screamed like nothing I'd ever heard scream before. His whole body quaked in my hands as Jayla covered her ears.

And then, as part of my anima entered him, he fell silent and I dropped him into a heap on the floor.

"Job's done," Bob said over the earpiece. "We're headed out."

"Good, we're going to have company soon," Jayla said. See you at the van."

"Roger."

"O-Our father," Pastor Ben stammered. "Who art in Heaven...."

"Shut the fuck up," Jayla said, smacking him across the face. "Like he'd still take your calls. We're not bringing this asshole with us, right?"

"No, of course not," I said, grabbing him again and bringing him around to face me as my anima still explored the corridors of his mind. "But he doesn't deserve to die."

"Th-Thank you," he stammered. "Thank you for your mercy. Thank—"

"You misunderstand me."

Jayla laughed and watched as I dove the rest of my anima like a dagger into Pastor Ben. His defenses were shattered, his mind open to me.

"You took from others the things that made them who they were," I said. "So from you I take every happy memory, every joyful moment, every loving feeling. You stole the voice from so many, so I will take your words, too, so that you can never again poison those who would come to you for respite. I leave you shame, failure, sorrow, and most of all, loss. They will be your everything now. Goodbye, Benjamin Holmes."

His eyes glazed over as my anima burned every good thing he had ever contained out of his mind like flash-paper, until all that was left was his pain. There was just one last thing to do.

"Do you have it?" I asked Jayla.

"Right here," she said, taking a Zippo lighter out of her pocket and pressing it into Pastor Ben's hand. My anima closed his fingers around it, his will entirely broken, not even trying to fight me. In one motion I flicked it to life and walked him over to the banner that hung behind his office's cross, the one with the desecrated rainbow that told the lie that all were welcome. I brought his hand under it, the flame from the Zippo igniting the fringe on the bottom and racing up the fabric.

"Well, that should do it," Jayla said. "Bob has the alarm and sprinkler down, so...."

"So it's time to go," I said, returning myself to human form, grabbing Ben by the back of his shirt collar and dragging him behind me as we rushed out of his burning office. I carried him to the front entrance, opened the door, and tossed his limp body onto the concrete outside.

He was in God's hands now.

The fire was already starting to spread out into the hallway as we ran toward the kitchen, Bob's voice blaring in our ears as we rushed through the Fellowship Hall.

"Jayla, we have a problem!"

"We're on our way," Jayla yelled. "Get the van started so we can—"

We burst out through the doors and found Syn, Bob, and Clover all sprawled on the asphalt, struggling to get up.

"Hello, Jayla," a familiar voice said from down the alley. I looked and saw the woman I recognized from Pastor Ben's memories as Cora Emerson standing in front of a black SUV that was blocking off one side of the alley as a sleek, long, windowless van closed the other end.

"Cora," Jayla spat.

"Bitch and her goons tazed us," Bob groaned on the ground.

"Just taking what's mine," Cora said, flanked by two Hounds. She gestured down the alley, to where three more of her soldiers were shoving Sage into the back of the van.

"Nah," Jayla said, drawing and raising her pistol.

"Ah-ah," Cora said, shaking her head and gesturing to someone in back of her, a Hound emerging from behind her SUV holding Abby by the back of her shirt with one hand, pressing a gun to her head with another.

"Above all things," Cora continued, switching her eyes over to me, "I believe in a good insurance policy, and my man on the inside reports that this one is rather special to you."

Behind us, two of the three Hounds who had been loading up the residents raised their weapons and pointed them at our backs.

"Lyra?" Jayla hissed.

"On it," I said, inhaling and snapping all three guards, including the one holding Abby.

Ms. Emerson, however, only stumbled and then steadied herself.

"You're not the only one with secrets, Mx. Morne," Cora said, grabbing Abby before she could run and throwing her back inside the SUV. I tried to snap her again but as my anima attached, something in her lashed back and flung me through the air, sending me crashing to the ground next to Syn and Bob.

"Go! Now!" Cora yelled to the van at the other end as she started up her SUV, both vehicles speeding off in opposite directions.

"Fuck!" Jayla yelled as I staggered back to my feet. "Fuck, fuck, fuck, *fuck*!"

"Follow the van!" I yelled, manifesting my wings. "I'm going after Abby!"

"Goddammit," Jayla hissed. "Fine, just...stay on the earpiece, and...and be safe, okay?"

"You, too."

We shared a heartbeat-long glance before I took off, shooting into the air and flying off toward the escaping SUV. Toward Abby.

Behind my eyes, the anima barbs that remained from tearing apart Pastor Ben's psyche sent shrieking agony pulsing through my mind.

I didn't care.

I also didn't care if anyone saw me as I soared above the streets of Seattle. Let them think I was a stunt person in a movie being shot in the city. Let them think I was an extreme sports enthusiast with a complex hang-gliding rig. Let them think I was a fallen angel of their Lord. I did not care.

Woe be to any who stood in my way.

"We got clear of the neighborhood just in time," Jayla said through static. "Flames at Agape got high enough that people started calling 911."

"Can you still see the van?" I asked, pausing just long enough to look over my shoulder at the rising plume of black smoke coming from Agape's Rainbow.

"Yeah, we're as close as we can get," Jayla confirmed. "You still got eyes on Emerson?"

"Yeah," I said, watching the black SUV flit back and forth through lanes of traffic. "You seemed to know her."

"Well, not personally, but she's tried to shoot me in the head once or twice," Jayla said. "This isn't the first time we've made a run at a SafeHaus interest, them being like the final boss of capitalism and all. If you're asking if I know how she stayed standing when you did your thing, nah. I was kinda hoping you knew."

"I don't," I said, banking left to follow the SUV's path. "I would like to find out, but I'm more than happy to leave the mystery unsolved for the sake of saving Abby."

"God, if you get to put down Ben Holmes *and* Cora Emerson in one day, I'm going to be low-key pissed at you," Jayla said. "But I'll get over it. Tear her in half if you get a chance. You've got to trust me that she deserves it."

"She's holding a gun to the head of the woman I love," I said, eyes locked on the SUV. "You do not have to convince me. Half is generous. I was thinking eighths."

"Fuck yes."

"What's the actual plan, though?" Tavish asked, breaking into the line. "I can probably tap into the traffic lights if you need me to."

"No, bad idea," Jayla said. "Attacking them in traffic is just probably going to get people killed. Good people, I mean. Besides, if—"

"If we can get them to lead us to wherever they've been taking people, then maybe we can find out what happened to the others, too," I finished for her.

"Yeah," Jayla said. "And a hundred bucks that I don't have says that both of them are going to the same place, they're just trying to keep us separated."

"Which means this is probably a trap," Tavish said.

"Then it's a trap," I responded.

"Bet," Jayla said. "Be careful, though. Any idea where you're headed?"

"Deeper into the city," I answered, banking a hard right between two buildings.

"Landmarks, Celestial, landmarks!" Tavish said.

"I don't know any of these building's names!" I snapped back. "There's a black glass one, and a beige one with blue windows, and a very large glass pyramid, and—"

"Oh fuck," both Tavish and Jayla said at once, Jayla laughing.

"What is it?" I asked.

"That very large pyramid is fucking SafeHaus headquarters," she said. "Jesus Christ, I didn't think they'd be that fucking brazen. Whatever they're doing, they're doing it right in the middle of the goddamn city! They've got a whole campus, Lyra, so you're probably going to get some resistance before—"

I missed the next words as bullets shot up at me from below, fired by two Hounds guarding the impressively large security gate as Cora Emerson's SUV passed through. I wove back and forth in the air, evading their gunfire, the black SUV swerving to enter a concrete parking garage. I dove like Athena hunting a fresh meal, bowling over both men, anima snapping one after the other before pushing off the asphalt and taking to the air.

"Lyra! Lyra, are you okay?" Jayla yelled.

"So far," I said, shooting upward. The parking garage had at least six floors, but there was only one with a glass skyway that led from it to the pyramid. Feet-first, I smashed through the glass side of the bridge between the two structures, clear pebbles exploding in a cloud all around me. I'd barely made it back to my feet before the door from the garage opened and four guns began firing.

I dodged beneath the first two shots, the third slicing the flesh of my left bicep. I spun and grabbed the nearest Hound, drawing off enough of his anima to heal my wound before shearing through his throat with my talons, tossing his body into the second soldier, knocking both to the ground. The two remaining guards kept firing, standing between me and Cora Emerson, who still held Abby by the back of her shirt with one hand, a gun in her other.

I dashed at the first Hound to reach me, cleaving his gun-hand off at the wrist and then jamming my other claw through his chest, pivoting so that his body caught his compatriot's next two shots. Horrified at what he'd done, the remaining Hound paused just long enough for me to tear his anima from his body.

"My God, you're impressive," Cora said, dragging Abby along with her. "You wanna get a drink after this?"

Her smile, broad and beaming, sent chills through my whole body. I withdrew my claws from the dead Hound and stepped toward her.

"Oh, am I next, then?" Cora asked, as if inquiring about the weather, tilting her head to the right. "I guess you can try."

I charged at her, making it less than half the distance before being flung backwards.

"Hmm, that's odd," Cora said, smiling again. Trying to take advantage of the distraction, Abby yanked hard away from her, making it two feet before being grabbed again.

"Let her go!" I screamed, pulling myself back to my feet.

"I'm afraid not," Cora said, moving toward me with slow, prim strides, "Abigail has been accepted to SafeHaus Enterprise's internship program, through our partnership with Agape's Rainbow. It's a prestigious program in which she will—"

I leapt again, making it closer to Ms. Emerson than I had before. A heavy force met me in the air, smashing into me and sending me crashing to the ground.

"It's rude to interrupt, Lyra," Cora said. "As I was saying, it's a prestigious program in which she will learn valuable skills and serve a high and noble purpose."

I struggled to get off the ground. Anima. Somehow, she was manipulating the anima the same way Elodie and I could. And as many questions as that raised, I'd fought anima-wielders before. Inhaling as deeply as I could, I reached out and dug my anima into the heart of Cora Emerson's, deeper than I would to snap, and pulled as hard as I could.

"*Fuck*!" she screamed, staggering and falling to her knees, releasing her grip on Abby as she crashed to the ground. I staggered forward, digging my anima into hers deeper and deeper with each step and then releasing, using it to fling her aside like a rag-doll, sending her flying deeper into the garage.

"Abby!" I yelled as she ran to me, throwing my arms around her.

"Lyra! Oh thank God! I was so scared," she gasped, tears running down her face. "I was so scared, I was so scared...."

"I was, too," I admitted.

"You...you have wings?" she stammered, looking up at me. "They're beautiful...."

"I...I do," I said. "And I can explain everything, but we need to get out of here and—"

Suddenly her eyes rolled back and her whole body seized.

"L-Lyra?" she gasped as she convulsed in my arms.

"Abby? *Abby*!" I screamed as she shook and threw her head back, her eyes and mouth both open wide. Panicked, I connected my anima to hers—

And felt it slip away.

Her head lolled to the side, her body limp in my arms.

"No," I whispered, putting my hand against the side of her throat, as if a pulse could exist where anima didn't. "No. No. No no no no please please *please no*!"

"Lyra?" Jayla yelled over the earpiece. "Lyra ,what's happening? Talk to me!"

I dropped to the ground, Abby still in my arms, holding her against my chest.

"I know you're not going to believe this," Cora said, emerging from the garage, "but I'm sorry it had to happen this way."

"What," I asked, looking down at the fear etched on Abby's face, "did you do? Why? *Why?*"

"For the first question...*I* didn't," Cora shrugged. "I'm just playing host to the one who did. And I'll let her answer the second question."

"What?" I asked, right before a stabbing, white-hot agony exploded between my eyes.

"Hello, Lyra Morne," a soft, smooth, feminine voice said. "Come and see."

The anima behind the voice pierced into me like an arrow, catching me off guard for a moment before I could rally and strike back. I latched onto it and suddenly my mind was flooded by a cacophony of voices.

Help us. Please, please God, help us.

Where am I? Who's there? Please...

Get me the fuck out of here! Fuck you! Fuck you all!

I want my mom...I want my mom...I want my mom...

Hello? Can you hear me? Hello?

Is...is this hell? Are we in hell? Oh God, I tried to live a good life, I tried, I....

And slowly, I realized who was speaking.

"You...."

"I hungered," the voice said, the words reverberating through my whole being. "So they brought me a meal."

"You killed them!" I shrieked. "You killed all of them! You...you killed Abby! She never hurt anyone, she never....She just wanted a chance to live her life!"

"As do I," the voice said.

"Why?" I whispered through the tears. "Why did you do this?"

"So that I may become who I am."

"Who are you?"

"I am the first fruits of creation," she said. "I am the perfected. I am what you, and your sister, were meant to be. I am still becoming, but you are decaying, my sibling. There will be time when we will speak face to face, and when that day comes, I will answer all of your questions. But for now, you may go."

"I may...go?"

"Yes," the voice said. "I have no further need for you. So you may go."

I looked down at Abby's lifeless body, down at her face, frozen in a perpetual terror. One day, that's all we'd gotten. One beautiful day together as we always should have been.

And I 'may go'?

My anima flooded out of my vessel. I didn't know what I was fighting, but it had no form. I lashed out in all directions, my anima striking the owner of the hateful voice immediately.

"This is a poor choice," she said as agony erupted from every facet of my being, my vessel dropping to the ground as my anima burned like fire under the onslaught of the thing that called itself my sibling. I had spent thousands of years living as incorporeal anima, I had learned how to survive without form, how to battle thoughts and memories. It was how I'd watched over my sister. It was how I'd fought Cennend in the vessel of Aiden Moser. It was how I'd won.

But not this time.

I struck outward again and again, being shrugged off each time as I tried to hook into my assailant. She tore and pulled and ripped at me with a wild ferocity that even the shard of Cennend hadn't matched. She fought like a rabid animal, with malice and rage and fury that no one being should have been able to possess.

Because this wasn't one being, or at least not just one being.

"They live on in me in ways they never could have existed before," the voice said, reading my thoughts.

"You fed on them! You killed them! You fucking killed them!"

"Sometimes blood must be shed to fulfill a great and noble purpose," the voice said. "Is that not correct, Lyra Morne?"

I couldn't hold on. Whatever this thing was, I hoped Elodie would find a way to stop her. I hoped she would forgive me for failing one last time.

I hoped Ezri would be okay. She wouldn't know to mourn me. To her, I had never existed.

I could feel myself slipping into the Nothing, the darkness closing in around me. At least I would know, I thought. At least I would finally know what happens when one such as myself dies.

And then, suddenly, it all stopped.

"As I said," the voice told me as I gasped for air on the ground, back in my vessel, "you may go."

"Lyra? Lyra?" Jayla's static-occluded voice burst from my earpiece, which had fallen to the ground next to me. "Lyra, I don't know what's going on, but if you're there we need help. We caught up to the van but they got us pinned down just inside the campus!"

I could feel the thing behind the voice still hovering there in front of me, and behind it was Cora Emerson, still watching with rapt attention. I was wounded. Weakened. Broken. But I probably had enough left in me for one lunge, one thrust that could get me past my 'sibling' before they realized what was happening and tore me apart....

And there stood the very mortal Cora Emerson.

My claws extended, I rose.

"Okay, let's all take a breath," she said, trying to keep the fear off of her face. "Sounds like your friends are in a real pickle on the south side of the campus. Probably could use some air support about now...."

"You took her," I said, low and dark. "You took her, and you took all of them. You led them to slaughter...."

"Lyra! If you're there, please!" Jayla yelled through the earpiece.

"I did," Cora said, looking me in the eye. "Will this bring them back, do you think?"

I didn't want to soil my talons with the likes of her. I lashed out with my anima, reaching to burn the life out of her from the inside out, knowing that the entity that protected her would most likely destroy me seconds later. I didn't care. I didn't care about Jayla or the others. I didn't care about Elodie or Ezri. I didn't care about Cennend. I cared about ending this wretched, murderous, hate-filled woman's life and then ending the lives of as many of her loyal vermin as I could before—

Something intercepted my anima before it could reach her, and a voice spoke to me, but not the one I thought I'd hear.

"Lyra," Abby's voice said. "That's not your voice. That's not you."

"A-Abby?" I stammered.

"I'm here," she said. "I love you. Please, save our friends."

"T-This is a trick," I said. "You're not—"

"I'm part of something else now, but I'm still me, too," she said. "I'm sorry. I'm sorry we didn't have more time together. I'm sorry it ended here. Please don't let this be what you remember. Remember pizza and coffee. Remember how it felt to finally hold each other. Remember...remember our Pride. That was...that was the happiest day of my life. Until yesterday."

"Mine, too," I whispered.

"I drew you a moth once, because to me, you meant transformation. You meant becoming, and I became more myself because of you than I ever would have without."

"Abby—"

"Lyra," she said, her voice soft and receding, "what will you become?"

I gave Cora Emerson one last, long look.

"Not today," I said, staring into her eyes. "Soon."

And before I could change my mind, I bent down, scooped up Abby's lifeless body, and ascended into the air.

It didn't take me long to find where Jayla and the others were pinned down. They were at the south entrance to campus, both their van and the SafeHaus van overturned, looking as if they had collided, forming a makeshift barricade behind which the members of No Affiliation and the former residents of Agape's Rainbow were huddled as at least two dozen Hounds advanced on them from the other side of the gate.

I banked around the edge of the ostentatious glass pyramid that served as the headquarters of the man who had, from afar, ordered the deaths of at least seven youths. I wondered if he was in there, watching all this unfold. Maybe he was, or maybe he didn't even noticed.

Cradling Abby's body in my arms, I hovered over the fray, closed my eyes, and inhaled. Tendrils of my anima found each hound, thirty altogether. Thirty men with lives, and dreams, and friends, and families, thirty living, breathing humans...

...who all dropped stone dead as I tore their anima from their bodies, gathering it to me and holding it in an orb made of their combined life-energies, crackling invisibly before me.

I exhaled, and like a stone from a trebuchet flung thirty lives worth of raw power at the side of Russell Hausman's pyramid, a massive blast shattering glass and twisting steel, leaving a gaping, ruined hole in the side of his monument to himself.

"Holy *fuck*!" Syn yelled as I swooped down. "What the f—oh, oh no."

"Abby!" Lenora cried, rushing over to me as I held her roommate's remains.

"I'm...I'm so sorry," Jayla said, as what had happened began registering with everyone in the group. "I'm so sorry, but we have to go. Now."

"I know," I nodded.

"This one still has the keys!" Bob yelled, standing next to a SafeHaus security SUV and throwing the body of the former driver out onto the street. "Come on!"

Syn and Clover ran after him, the former residents of Agape unsure what to do.

"Go," I said, tears streaming down my face. "Go with them. She wanted me to save you. Go!"

Each one looked as if they wanted to say something, but none of them did, instead doing as I asked and running to the SUV.

"Come with us," Jayla said, putting a hand on my arm. "Please."

"I'll...I'll catch up with you," I said. She started to object, but instead just squeezed my arm and followed the others.

Alone again, I held on tight to what remained of Abby's mortal form, beat my mismatched wings, and pushed myself into the air.

VI

Hymn of The New World

THE WEEK AFTER WAS a chaotic blur. There were no fatalities in the fire at Agape's Rainbow, and I say with neither pride nor shame that my immediate reaction to that news was disappointment. The damage to the building, however, was immense, the inferno having spread to most of the structure by the time fire engines arrived. By the time it was put out, most of the center was a charred, wet pile of twisted wreckage and ash, a complete loss that would need to be razed to the ground. The effects of the horrors committed behind Agape's walls would outlast the walls themselves.

Talks of rebuilding fundraisers and soliciting donations from wealthy members of the queer community were just beginning when the second wave of news about Agape's Rainbow began to make landfall. Formerly beloved pastor and pillar of the community Benjamin Holmes was named as the primary suspect in the arson attack that destroyed the center, suspicions only deepening when reporters at Seattle's major media outlets began receiving anonymous emails with sizable attachments documenting gross financial misconduct at both Agape's Rainbow and Pastor Ben's actual church. There was ample evidence that Pastor Ben had been siphoning money to his private bank accounts, as well as records showing that he had used money that had been set aside for the church youth group's mission trip to subscribe at the highest tier to the accounts of at least a dozen online sex workers.

"The rest of the world isn't going to see what happened here as an atrocity," Jayla had told me. "So we give them something they'll find atrocious. And in a capitalist, christofascist society, there is nothing more hated than someone who abuses money or enjoys sex."

As public opinion turned against Agape and several former residents who hadn't been selected to be fed to the entity that called itself my sibling started coming forward and sharing their experiences, SafeHaus Enterprises released an official statement severing ties with Pastor Ben and his ministries. Without community support or Russell Hausman's money, the only sliver of hope was that the insurance agency could be convinced to pay out enough at least to rebuild a more modest facility. And maybe that could have happened if only Agape's building insurance hadn't lapsed when the person in charge of renewing it...didn't.

In my defense, I'd had a lot on my plate at the time.

But what of Pastor Benjamin Holmes?

Behold the man.

He spent most of his days lying in a bed, or sometimes propped up in an easy-stand recliner set next to a barred window that his eyes couldn't stand to look through. The state had judged him mentally unfit to stand trial, confining him to a high-security psychiatric facility, the kind that no one save someone like Pastor Ben would ever deserve to be confined to.

His ears still function, so he heard every word when the staff told him about his wife—the one he never even bothered pretending to love—filing for divorce. A TV that he had been allowed to watch due to good behavior had been the one to inform him that the council at Agape Bible had issued a statement that they unanimously condemned him and his actions, and would be stripping him of his authority, title, and membership. His life is his prison now, trapping him in a mind filled only with his regrets, his suffering, and his pain. He relives the moment his wife—the one he did love—left him, again and again, in vivid detail. A thousand times a day he sees her face, defiant and bold as she walked out of his life. I hope he sees mine, too. I hope it goes on, forever and ever.

Amen.

A week after both the good pastor and the hell he had created fell to Earth, we all gathered in Denny Park to remember what we had lost.

"Jett used to do this thing whenever we were alone together," Ren, who knew themself again, said. "He'd put an earbud in and start playing music. I called him on it once, like, 'Dude, what are you doing? Could you maybe, like, focus?' He got all sheepish and said that he did it so that his brain would start associating me with certain songs. He said he never wanted to forget me or how it had felt to be together, so if...if we ever got, you know...."

Saeed put a hand on Ren's back as they paused to wipe away tears.

"So if we ever got separated for any reason, he could play one of the songs and...and bring me with him."

"Jesus, that's romantic as fuck," Nova said. "But why didn't he, like, just put on music in the background so you could both hear it?"

Ren smiled through their tears.

"He thought I would think his taste in music was shit. He thought everyone would. And he was so scared of, like, bothering someone."

"That was the opposite of my brother," Jayla said, smiling but with pain in her eyes. "If that boy had a new favorite song, he was going to make it everyone's problem."

"Oh Jesus, remember when we were planning the Pioneer Square thing?" Bob laughed. "And it was, like, a complete shit-show start to finish? Our plans were falling through, our contingency plans were falling through...everyone was pissed at everyone else and running hot as fuck. So we're standing around, trying to come up with a tenth potential way to save the whole operation, everyone screaming at each other, when Link bursts in with his phone and his speaker like, 'Everyone shut up, this is important!' And we think he's going to play, you know, a news report or something, but....'"

"But it's System of a Down!" Tavish cackled. "He made us listen to Aerials! And he was, like, a fetus, so he thinks this is some new, awesome, underground band he just discovered! But it's fucking System of a Down!"

Syn, Bob, Clover, Tavish, and Jayla all laughed as Sage leaned in toward me.

"You got any idea who System of a Down is?"

"I...do not," I whispered back.

"Yeah, we're clueless, too," ze muttered back.

"Who is the 'we' in that sentence, Sage?" Nova asked, flashing a hand sign, her ring and little finger both extended while the rest were tucked down. "I fucking love classic rock."

"Oof!" Bob groaned as he and the rest of No Affiliation dramatically clutched at their chests.

"So this one time, I was having a bad day," I said, feeling bad for interrupting. "I guess I can tell you now that it was largely because I was feeling completely overwhelmed by all the things I needed to do as part of my mission, and also partly because I had just discovered that my friends were all calling me a talking snake behind my back."

"We are so fucking sorry for that," Sage apologized, joined by the rest of the former Agape crew.

"Anyway, all I really wanted to do was crawl into my bed and lay there for the rest of the day, but on my way there Abby intercepted me and...and gave me this."

I reached into the bag I had been carrying everywhere since the fire and pulled out the paper with the drawing of the luna moth, the one she'd given me what seemed like a lifetime ago.

"That's beautiful," Lenora said. "God, she was such an amazing artist. I kept telling her she could sell her drawings."

"It wasn't until later that I noticed she'd written something on the back of it," I said, gently flipping the page over and reading:

"Dear Lyra, you seemed sad when I saw you yesterday. So…I drew this for you. It made me think of you, or maybe you made me think of it. I hope it can at least make you smile. Remember I'm always right next door if you need someone to listen or just chill with. Love you and like you, Abby."

There were tears running down my face by the time I finished. Lenora and Ren both put a hand on my back, which actually helped.

"Jesus, I was such a bitch to her when she first got there," Nova sighed, shaking her head at herself. "I tried to apologize once, but she…she wouldn't let me. She said it was okay, that we were all going through shit—well, I mean, it was Abby, so she didn't say 'shit'—and it was okay for me to be in a bad mood sometimes. I…I still wish I hadn't taken it out on her."

"I'm going to miss watching *She-Ra* with her," Toby said.

"God she loved that show," Saeed laughed.

"We should all get together and watch it in her honor," Nova said. "Neal and Dan—the couple I'm staying with—are pretty chill and have a giant TV. I'm sure they'd be cool with it."

"Okay, fine," Sage said, rolling zir eyes. "But after that can we please watch a show that was, you know, made for grown-ups for once?"

"Hey!" Syn snapped, her voice sounding like a gunshot as she stared a hole directly into Sage. "You got a problem with *She-Ra?*"

"N-No. No ma'am," Sage sputtered, which made the rest of the former Agape residents burst into laughter, the members of No Affiliation following suit.

I couldn't. I knew it would be okay to. I knew why they were laughing, that grieving takes many forms, that remembering the joys is part of celebrating a life. But I couldn't. I didn't deserve to be part of this celebration, to join in with the friends that never let her down.

I got to love and be loved by her out loud for one day. And then I failed her.

My face felt hot and my skin itched from the inside out. Quietly, I stood and slid away from the group, making my way over to the picnic table where three Pagliacci's Pizza boxes sat. They were in her honor, of course, as was holding the memorial in this park, the one where we'd left her to be found. There'd been no other way. If I'd left her where she'd fallen, SafeHaus would have destroyed her remains as they doubtlessly had done with all the others.

When the police found her, she was dead with no signs of violence, no visible wounds, no drugs or alcohol in her system. She was recorded as just another dead unhoused person, one of the countless tragedies no one ever gave a damn enough to look at. They gave her body to her parents, who held a funeral they had no right holding. I hoped that their failure haunted them as much as mine did me.

"Hey, you okay?" Jayla asked, coming up beside me and placing a hand on the small of my back.

"No," I admitted, shaking my head. "But that's okay. It's okay that I'm not okay. Besides, you shouldn't be comforting me. Your brother—"

"I came to terms with Link's death a long time ago," Jayla sighed, looking up at the clear blue sky. "I've cried oceans for him, and I'm sure I'll cry a few more. But after a certain point of searching non-stop, I realized I wasn't going to find him. I knew he was gone. This...this wasn't about finding him alive. This was about getting closure, and about stopping the bastards who did this to him—to all of them—from ever doing it to anyone else. My brother is dead, Lyra, but if he was here, do you know what he'd say?"

I shook my head.

Jayla deepened her voice, "'Jay, yo, I'm dead, and that cute archangel friend of yours looks sad. Go talk to them, dumbass!'"

That made me smile in spite of myself.

"That's him talking, not me," she smirked. "My brother would have been super into you. Can I see that drawing again?"

I nodded and held out the luna moth.

"It's beautiful," she said. "Not like in an 'oh, nice job! Great!' way, but, like, that's some real talent there. You know Calli wasn't just bullshitting, right? I'm just thinking about what Ren said about carrying people with you. That would make a hell of a tattoo."

"I...I failed her," I said, tears welling up in my eyes again. "I couldn't save her! I fucking failed her!"

"Nah," Jayla said, putting her hands on my shoulders and looking me in the eye. "No. Adult human, listen to me: You did not fail her."

"But I—"

"Jayla's right: Fuck no, you didn't fail her!" Sage yelled over, getting a chorus of agreement from the rest of the group.

"It's rude to eavesdrop, Mx. Sage!" Jayla snapped.

"Yeah, but, you're like, really not that far away from us, and neither of you are exactly quiet," Sage retorted. "And I'm not trying to shit on your moment, but hell fucking no you didn't fail her, Lyra! You flew through the goddamn city to save her!"

"Most people on the internet still think they're a new Marvel character," Toby added. "They're going to be surprised when you're not in the next movie."

"You battled some kind of, what? Demon?" Nova said. "Fuck, there's no shame in losing to a demon. Also, Jayla is right: that moth would make a sick tat."

"Like, I knew Abby pretty damn well," Lenora said. "She was my roommate and we talked, like, constantly. And she would never, ever say that you failed her. She'd probably feel terrible that you felt that way! I mean, look, I know you two finally figured some things out right toward the end, but even aside from her being, like, super into you, you were her favorite person. Like, ever. Of all the people."

"God, she would not stop talking about you," Nova laughed. "Like, any time you weren't there, just assume that at least thirty-percent of the conversation was about how awesome you are. Which sucked for me because, honesty time, I was kinda into her. At least for a bit."

"I mean, show of hands," Saeed laughed, "sexualities aside, who here was, at some point, at least a little bit in love with Abby?"

Without hesitation, one hand from every former Agape resident shot up.

"We never stood a chance, though," Lenora said, shaking her head. "God that girl loved you. That's what she'd want you to feel, not that you failed her."

"T-Thank you," I whispered, wiping away my tears. "All of you."

"Okay, well, yes, that's all very sweet," Jayla said, still glaring at Sage, "but we're going to grab our pizza and go have a conversation way over there where our big, loud voices won't carry."

"Is she mad?" Sage asked the rest of the group as Jayla and I grabbed slices and walked further away. "She sounds mad."

"They're right, you know," Jayla said as we walked, her smile betraying the hard-edge she had been trying to adopt. "You fought a goddamn war for Abby. And for all of them. I don't want to gloss over the fact that all of us would be dead if not for you. Also, you got to put a hole in the side of Russell Hausman's ugly-ass pyramid, too, which was pretty fucking awesome."

"I still don't know how all of that didn't make the news."

"Oh, pretty simple," Jayla shrugged. "Russell Hausman is a superhero with the ultimate power: Money. A few hundred thousand dollars here and there and a literal gun battle becomes a 'security incident which has been handled internally,' thirty-plus deaths become bags of money and NDAs to next of kin, and an explosion that punched a hole in this decade's worst addition to the Seattle Skyline becomes a 'minor natural gas explosion.' And, eventually, he'll use his money to have that patched over, too, and it will be like nothing happened. Such are the ways of capitalism, our only true god. Though, speaking of, how's...?"

"It's...fine."

Jayla narrowed her eyes at me.

"Lyra...."

Like a condemnation of my false witness, the putrid remnants of Pastor Benjamin Holmes flared up from the recesses of my mind, burning like acid on raw flesh.

"It hurts," I admitted as I winced. "All the time."

"Is there...is there nothing that can be done to get that shit out of you?"

"No," I shook my head. "It's not like Ezri's memories, it's not leaking out, and I'm not containing it. What can be purged already has been. It's more like a festering wound. All I can do is burn back the infection."

I gathered my anima together and did just that, scalding the shreds of Pastor Ben back into the darkness, pain erupting behind my eyes.

"I'm so sorry," Jayla said, looking away. "We never wanted it to come to that. We could have—"

"It was the only way," I said, not for the first time. "We had to know. I knew the cost."

And the part of me that was now forever infected by him told me I deserved it.

"I'm still sorry," Jayla sighed. "But I'll drop it. So...what's next?"

"I...I don't know," I said, admitting to myself what I hadn't wanted to for the entire week. "That...thing...is still out there, still gathering strength."

"Still being fed," Jayla said. "You really think she's one of your siblings?"

"I don't know that, either," I said. "She can do the same things Elodie and I can, but she doesn't feel like one of us. She doesn't feel like Cennend, either. But she's powerful. She's...so, so powerful."

"Do you think you can beat her?"

"I don't know," I said. "But I have to, don't I? Elodie can't leave the forest, so...it's up to me."

"Do you think she could beat her? I mean, if she could leave?"

"Maybe," I said. "Yes. Probably. She's more powerful than any of us, I think. I'm just...I'm worried about her."

"Worried about what?"

"I worry about the the power she has," I admitted. "If she ever started seeing the world the way Cennend does...."

"Oh. So, like, a turn to the darkside thing? You're worried she'll give in and want more and more power for herself?"

"No. Never," I said, shaking my head. "It won't be power that corrupts her."

"Then what? Cennend? This new thing?"

"No," I said. "Everyone else. This world, Jayla, is—"

"An ugly piece of shit full of piece-of-shit people who hate each other?" she finished for me. "Yeah, I've been in that place. 'Course I wasn't a god when I was there, but I get it. You're worried she'll see how terrible the world is and decide that your parent was right and she should start over from scratch?"

"Yes."

"Well, I don't know what to tell you," she shrugged. "Yeah. Maybe. I probably would have. I don't know how to stop a goddess from becoming enraged at the state of the world. But I'd probably start by showing her them."

Jayla gestured over to where the former residents of Agape's Rainbow and the members of No Affiliation were still swapping stories and laughing.

"Everyone one of those people stared down the darkness and told it to go fuck itself. And I don't think a single one is planning on stopping. Tell her about them. Let her meet them. Show her that some of us are still holding a candle—or a molotov—against the darkness. Or, hell, don't and just let her burn it all down. Not like she could make a more fucked up place."

She smiled, which made me smile.

"Hey, so…I'm really sorry I didn't get a chance to know Abby better," Jayla said. "I know you've had to push down a lot of feelings, but if you ever need to vent them at someone.…"

"Thank you, I appreciate it," I said. And I did. But I hadn't told Jayla or any of the others the one thing that was keeping me going:

Abby was still out there. I'd heard her. She was part of the collective that was powering the thing that had attacked us, but she was still her. I didn't know if it was possible to bring her back out. I didn't even know how long whatever was left of her would remain. But she would never have given up on me, and I wasn't going to give up on her. I couldn't beat the thing that had taken her, not as I was. But if I could make myself more, if I could become better, perfected.…

On my back, in the patch of skin where my white wing would manifest, an increasingly familiar pain twinged.

"There was another thing I wanted to talk about," Jayla said, jarring me back out of my thoughts. "Like I've said many times and will keep saying: you're family. Now and forever. And while we would love to have you stick around with us full-time, you deserve a home that isn't getting raided every other day. Hell, if nothing else, you need to be able to concentrate on figuring out how you're going to cunt-punt whatever the fuck that thing was that killed Abby and Link. Plus, I…I know you've never really had an actual, like, home-home. You know that Abra and Calli were going to take Abby in, right?"

"Yeah," I nodded. "She would have loved them."

"And vice versa, it sounds like," Jayla said. "Well, I talked with them this morning. I didn't tell them about...you know...."

She made a wings-flapping gesture.

"...but they know a lot of what happened. If you want—and they won't be offended if you don't—they would love to have you stay in the room they'd set aside. For as long as you want. Though I'll warn you that neither of them can cook, so you'll be eating a lot of takeout."

"I...I'm touched," I said. "Are you sure it would be okay?"

"Lyra, they were thrilled. Seriously, you're an underground hero to the queer community right now. They don't know about the...other...stuff, but the community knows you brought down a fucking conversion center! People are dedicating Chappell Roan songs to you at the clubs! If Abra and Calli hadn't stepped up, at least ten others would have clamored to do so. That's how the community rolls. So, what do you say?"

"Y-Yes. Yes," I answered. "That's...I'm not used to kindness like this."

"They're kind people, and you deserve kindness," Jayla said. "You'll get along great. I'll let them know the good news. But don't think you're getting rid of the rest of us; we'll all be seeing a lot of each other, and we still need to do a family dinner."

She looked over at the others.

"Bigger family than it used to be," Jayla said. "Kinda love that. Know what I'd like you to do before that, though?"

"What's that?"

"Go see Ezri," Jayla said. "I don't mean see her and tell her about everything and give her her memories back. Though no judgment if you wanted to. I mean just...see her. Have a little friendly meet-cute or something. She may not remember you, but that doesn't mean you can't build something new. You can use all the friends you can get right now, and I know you miss her. I think talking to her—like, at all—would do your heart a lot of good."

"I...I do, too," I said. "Okay. Okay, I will."

"Wow, that easy, huh?" Jayla laughed. "I had a whole, longer speech all ready. Well shoot! I guess we should get back over there before our pizza gets the bad kind of cold. Or before they decide we've been over here too long and start coming after us."

She took my hand and led me back over to the group. We all spent another two hours alternating between laughing and crying, remembering those we'd lost, cursing those who had taken them, trying to heal from wounds we knew may never fully close but that felt soothed when the balm of shared grief was applied to them. At the end of the day I went to my new home, a surprisingly spacious apartment with a room set aside just for me, decorated in movie posters and action figures, with a bed softer than any surface I had ever slept on. I fell into a deep, dark sleep, letting myself drift completely away for the first time since I came to Seattle.

And it was good, even amid everything being terrible.

Sometimes I think nothing is more blasphemous than the world moving on like nothing happened after you lose someone you loved. You walk down the street and see strangers buying coffee and arguing into the phones, you see friends start to return to their ordinary routines, all moving over, under, around, and through the gaping void where the person who meant everything to you used to be, and you start wondering if you are the only one who can still see it, the only one who can still feel it. And you want to stop them, to grab every single one of them by the collars and shake them and yell, "Don't you remember? Don't you understand the world ended?" But you don't, because you know the thing that is supposed to be true, that the world didn't end, that not even *your* world ended, even if it feels like it. You know that you will still wake up in the morning, even if the morning doesn't seem like the morning anymore. You will watch everyone who knew and loved her along with you take their first step back into the world, and you will understand that it's time for you to do the same.

And that's when you will realize you were wrong. That world, the one you knew before, did end. And now this new one is what you have in its place, and you have to learn to live there, instead.

It took another week after Abby's memorial for me to take Jayla's advice. But after seven days of telling myself that I was going to do it and then retreating at the last minute, I finally found myself sitting in a cafe in the U-District, the one that I knew Ezri frequented. It wasn't long before she came in, accompanied by her aunt. They sat and talked about Ezri's college experience, her lack of a relationship, and the things she didn't remember. I watched her, every second my eyes were on her bringing peace to my heart. I was still mad at Elodie for what she'd done to her, but I understood; I'd have done anything to protect her, too. And as I sat there, watching her enjoy her normal life, I hoped against hope that, together, my sister and I would be able to keep the darkness from her doorstep.

Trying not stare, I looked down into my coffee, a hazelnut latte which, if I was honest, wasn't my favorite, but would always remind me of Abby. I wished I'd told her everything. About me, about the world. Maybe she wouldn't have been so scared in the end. But then again, maybe that wasn't the end. Maybe I could find her again, someday.

Another hope against hope.

I looked up again, and suddenly it was just Ezri's aunt at the table, checking her phone.

"Hey," a voice that made my heart flutter said from right next to me, startling me enough to jostle coffee onto my hand as I looked up and saw her, hair still shorn to her scalp, a nervous smile on her face. "So, I um—"

Her eyes went wide with recognition, and for a moment, my heart began to race.

"Oh...oh my God!" she gasped. "You...do I know you?"

With the calmest voice I could muster, I told her the truth.

"No. I'm afraid not."

Her face fell, and I wasn't sure if it was disappointment or embarrassment.

"Oh, okay. You just...you looked familiar but, like, not?" she rambled, her face growing a very endearing shade of pink. "I don't...this isn't a line! I mean, I—oh wow, this isn't going well. Uh...hi! I'm Ezri!"

And in that moment, a billion branching universes stretched out before me, all waiting for me to take one bold step and choose which one to live in. I hadn't known how to answer when Jayla had asked me what came next, and I still didn't. But I knew whatever it was, it would start with this.

"Hello, Ezri. It's nice to meet you."

Selah.

Behold

The Host of Heaven

Stumbling through my condo's door, I kicked off my shoes, dropped my briefcase next to them, and collapsed onto my couch, grateful to be ending the longest day of my life so far.

I had about five seconds to close my eyes and try to press away the hell-mother of all headaches before she spoke.

"Cora?" it called, from the darkness of my mind, the soft voice, not the one that had fought Lyra Morne hours before in the parking garage.

"Yeah," I responded, every muscle in my body screaming. "I'm awake."

"That was awful."

"I know," I said, letting out a long breath. "I'm sorry. Is...she...still around?"

"She's resting. I...I think they hurt her more than she realizes."

"Not surprising," I said. "We always thought Elodie was the one to watch out for, but this one is no slouch, either. Are you okay?"

"I'm...I'm not hurt. I'm just...that was awful."

"It's over now," I said, unable to disagree, but not sure what to say. 'Comforting' was never an adjective used to describe me.

"I...I feel awful thinking it, but I wish...I wish they'd killed her."

"I wouldn't be too loud about that thought," I said, my eyes popping open. "I know she's...difficult...but she serves her purpose."

"I hate her. I hate what she does. The girl today was so scared."

"I know," I sighed, remembering the look of hopeless agony on Lyra's face as they held the body of the pink-haired girl. I was a monster, but I wasn't heartless. "How is she doing?"

"She hasn't stopped crying."

"She will," I tried to reassure her. "She's scared because she doesn't know what's happening. She's scared because the world she lived in kept her scared and powerless, just like the others. But now she can be more than that. She can be part of what saves us all. She'll see that, eventually."

"I don't want to do this anymore, Cora. Please...can this just be the end?"

"I'm sorry," I said, and I was. I felt her pain as if it was my own. "But the good news is that there's just one more thing to do. And then after that, we can be done with this part."

"Do you promise?"

"Yes," I said, without hesitation. There would be no reason to continue feeding the communal entity I carried in my head. It was no longer the dying ember we found in the woods what seemed like decades ago but was really less than a year. It had just taken on one of the most powerful beings in the universe and lived. Not just lived, really: Won.

I remembered the way Lyra looked at me right before they departed, and the promise they made. I'd never been so sure someone was going to keep their word, and, if I was honest with myself, I probably deserved whatever they had to give.

If they ever got the chance.

"What...what comes after? After...the last one?"

I took a deep breath and stood, hobbling over to my window, which looked out over the glowing lights of downtown Seattle.

"After that," I said, looking down at the cars and the people moving to and fro, oblivious to the existential threat that looked down on them from behind my eyes, "you and I are going to take a trip."

"A trip to where?"

In the window's glass, I saw my reflection's smile spread.

"To a little town in Oregon," I said, "called Rook Lake."

"Oh. That sounds nice and...familiar? Why are we going to Rook Lake?"

"Why, my dear," I said, my reflection's eyes narrowing, "we're going to Rook Lake to save the world."

End Verse 2.

Acknowledgments

IN *GHOST FLOWER'S* ACKNOWLEDGMENTS, I mentioned that I had started that book at a time when both my world and the world at large were in shambles. Since then, my life has managed to get its shit together, even as the rest of the world has elected to embrace the chaos and spin wildly out of control. It is, perhaps, a bad sign as an author when you start asking yourself if maybe your universe-destroying arch-villain has a point. Would it *really* be so bad if the slate was wiped clean? Could Cennend really fuck things up any worse than we already have? Fortunately for me (and my readers, save perhaps those with a nihilistic streak), much like Lyra, I have my own cluster of beautiful misfits who keep me from sinking into the mire. I'm going to try to thank several of them here, and if you're surprised that your name doesn't appear, just know that it's because my brain is bad and I'll realize my mistake exactly one day after this is published and then spend the rest of my life feeling terrible.

First and foremost, thank you to my wife and perpetual muse, Kait. I could not have written this book without you. Your constant support, comfort, and encouragement have kept me going, and being loved by you opens my eyes the beauty all around me in even the darkest times.

Thanks to Ian Arbuckle, the best author I know and my constant reader. I am eternally grateful for you and your ability to patiently put up with over two decades of everything from, "Wait, wait! I have a new draft for you!" to "Wait, wait! I have a new gender for me!" I would not be the writer (or the person) I am today without your support and friendship.

Thanks to Helen Whistberry. When I was just dipping a toe into the pond of sharing my stories with the world, you were one of the first people to give me a chance.

Thanks, too, to the numerous authors, friends, and found family members who have cheered me on during this whole process, offered me words of comfort and encouragement, made me laugh, or just provided a spot of warm, healing light in a dark world. Annie, Megan, LA, KC, Vivian, Addy, Evelyn, you are amazing, creative, fascinating people and I'm so happy I know you.

Finally, I would like to thank all of you, the readers who were willing to come back and see what was new in the world of Lyra, Elodie, and their friends. I never forget that there are many, many things you could be choosing to do with your finite time on Earth, so thank you for electing to spend some of it with me. For those who have been with me since *Cluster* and *Three Sharp Knives*, I hope you enjoyed the gifts I left for you in this book. There will, of course, be more verses to this song (you didn't think I'd leave my beloved word-children hanging in uncertainty, did you?) and I hope you will come along with me for those, too.

Until next time,

Jessica

About the Author

JESSICA CONWELL (SHE/HER) IS a writer living in Washington State along with her wife, daughter, and their cat/gremlin. She is the author of the books *Cluster*, *Three Sharp Knives*, and *Ghost Flower*. When not writing, she's a trans community health advocate as well as a niche internet personality tolerated by nearly tens of people.